KISSING THE CHEF

Daphne didn't think she could concentrate with Tyne so near, but soon she was absorbed in the novel she was reading, and every time she shuffled a little impatiently, he brought her another glass of wine or a cup of tea. After a couple of hours, he carried a chocolate pavlova to the coffee table. He topped it with a layer of whipped cream and sliced strawberries.

It tasted like she was eating something too airy to contain calories. She used a finger to swipe up the last bit on her plate and looked at him. "You know how to treat a woman."

"I try." He reached for her teacup to refill it at the same time she did. Their fingers touched, and electricity shot through Daphne's body. Their gazes locked, and all she could think about was how much she wanted him.

She slid onto the sofa next to him and slowly bent to kiss him. Sleeping Beauty in reverse. She hoped she woke up something inside him. His kiss started slow, friendly, but when she ran her tongue over his lips, he grew more passionate. Finally, he leaned forward to be more thorough. She scooted closer, pressing her body against his. He pulled back and stared.

"Are you sure you want this? It will change things . . ."

"I want it."

"We're friends. This could make things awkward."

"I'm tired of lukewarm. I want to try spicy."

Books by Judi Lynn

COOKING UP TROUBLE

OPPOSITES DISTRACT

LOVE ON TAP

SPICING THINGS UP

Published by Kensington Publishing Corporation

Spicing Things Up

A Mill Pond Romance

Judi Lynn

LYRICAL SHINE
Kensington Publishing Corp.
www.kensingtonbooks.com

LYRICAL SHINE BOOKS are published by

Kensington Publishing Corp.
119 West 40th Street
New York, NY 10018

All Kensington titles, imprints, and distributed lines are available at special quantity discounts for bulk purchases for sales promotion, premiums, fund-raising, educational, or institutional use.

Special book excerpts or customized printings can also be created to fit specific needs. For details, write or phone the office of the Kensington Sales Manager: Kensington Publishing Corp., 119 West 40th Street, New York, NY 10018. Attn. Sales Department. Phone: 1-800-221-2647.

Lyrical Shine and Lyrical Shine logo Reg. U.S. Pat. & TM Off.

First Electronic Edition: March 2017
eISBN-13: 978-1-5161-0135-1
eISBN-10: 1-5161-0135-9

First Print Edition: March 2017
ISBN-13: 978-1-5161-0136-8
ISBN-10: 1-5161-0136-7

Printed in the United States of America

Chapter 1

The alarm buzzed. Tyne Newsome rolled over and ignored it. Five minutes later, it buzzed again. He pulled the pillow over his head and then thought better of it. Might as well get up. He usually beat the alarm, but he'd stayed up later than usual last night. Silly, since he worked early shifts on Mondays, but he and Harley went for a long motorcycle ride after Tyne got off work yesterday. Tyne glanced out the window of his upstairs apartment. A blaze of leaves glowed in the streetlights. Those leaves were what got him in trouble.

He and Harley hadn't meant to stay out as long as they did, but Harley's wife, Kathy, had told them to do whatever felt good. She was going to work on the winery's bookkeeping all day to catch up. The crisp air and glory of autumn had pulled them deeper and deeper into the national forest south of Mill Pond. They hadn't returned to the vineyard until close to sunset, and then Kathy had insisted Tyne stay for supper. By the time he got back to his apartment over Daphne's stained-glass shop it was late, and then he'd stayed up reading an hour more to relax.

Oh, well, the lack of sleep had been worth it. He hustled into the bathroom, took a quick shower, and tugged on his chef's pants and coat. Ian's resort was too swanky for line cooks. He had to look the part, even though he usually wore his worn jeans into work for supper shifts and changed before guests hit the dining room.

He zipped down the inside staircase and stopped to glance at Daphne's shop in the dim light. Most people didn't move at four thirty in the morning, for good reason. When he returned later this afternoon, would the shop be decorated with dangling crepe paper and balloons? The professor she'd been seeing was supposed to be a free man today. All he had to do was sign his divorce papers. Patrick

could finally ask Daphne to marry him. Nothing Tyne would celebrate. The man was as exciting as porridge, but Daphne thought
she'd be happy with him.

On his way out the door to his Jeep, he inhaled the crisp, clean fall
air. It perked him up, cleared his head. Driving down Main Street
with its brick buildings, striped awnings, and old-fashioned street
lamps, he saw Maxwell step out of his bakery to snag the morning
paper by his door. Another early riser. When Maxwell saw Tyne's
orange Jeep, he raised a middle finger and grinned. Tyne laughed and
returned the gesture. As usual, Maxwell's Chihuahua, Chester, was
close to his heels. Tyne had never met a man so attached to his dog.

Tyne passed Ralph's diner and saw lights on in the kitchen. Garth's
gas station was still dark with only a security light shining on its four
pumps. Once outside town, Tyne passed the farms that lined both
sides of the street until he came to the drive for Lakeview Stables,
Ian's resort. He glanced past the tennis courts to the lake at the back
of the property. The water lay still as a mirror.

He drove around to the back of the building—a three-story, lime-
stone center with a wing off each side—and entered the kitchen
through the back door. Monday breakfasts weren't as rushed to prepare. He'd made the potato and sausage strata ahead of time and left
them in the refrigerator to soak up the custard filling. All he had to do
was put them in the oven. Steph, the morning sous chef, walked
through the back door while Tyne was sliding the sausages and
bacon into the second oven. She started putting ramekins in a stainless steel pan for them to start the eggs *en cocotte* with smoked
salmon.

"Have a good weekend?" Tyne asked as they lined each ramekin
with the salmon.

"We spent the weekend at Ben's parents' place on the lake. Had a
great time, played lots of cards, and ate too much food."

Tyne grinned. "The scenery's gorgeous right now. Bet the lake
was beautiful."

Steph started breaking an egg into each ramekin. "It's hard to beat
Mill Pond when the leaves change."

"It's hard to beat Mill Pond in lots of things." He slid her a sideways glance. "You happy you stayed on as the early shift sous chef?"

Paula, his fellow chef, had trained Steph and expected her to go to
culinary school, but Steph had decided to stay in Mill Pond, near her

high-school sweetheart. She slid the eggs into the oven and filled the steel pans with hot water to create a water bath. "What's not to like?"

Tyne couldn't think of anything. The area farmers had worked together to up their standards so that specialty goods were easy to find. The area had become a foodie's delight, one of the reasons the inn was so popular. That, and all the things Ian had to offer—a golf course, tennis courts, horseback riding, and lake activities. Things always slowed down once kids had to return to school, but the inn still did all right. Couples used it as a romantic getaway. This week, enough couples had doubled up to rent the cabins by the lake that sixty people came for meals each day. And Ian had decided to add special weekend offerings for holidays. Every room was booked for Halloween in a couple of weeks.

Steph began slicing oranges for a fresh fruit salad. "Have you and Paula decided what to serve for the long Halloween weekend yet?"

"We just talked about it. Ian wants us to go for fun instead of fancy. We're leaning toward a barbecue of some kind with gory desserts."

"Gory?" Steph raised an eyebrow.

"Dirt cakes with jelly worms and gravestones, eyeball popcorn balls . . ."

"Good idea." She glanced out the windows at the long shoreline. "It's not like kids can trick or treat here, though. How's Ian going to keep them busy?"

The owner himself walked through the kitchen door before she finished the question. "I'm doing a movie night—fun stuff earlier in the evenings for kids, like *Hocus Pocus*, and horror movies later for the adults. I have hay rides and scavenger hunts planned, pumpkin carving and bobbing for apples. The Kruses are building a corn maze." Their boss still held his five-week-old baby boy, Drew. The baby had lots of black hair like his dad and hazel eyes like his mom. Steph loved babies and would have hurried to grab him, but everyone knew you had to use a crowbar to pry the baby away from Ian.

"Hey, Big Daddy!" Tyne called, teasing him. "You gonna wear a pouch and teach the kid how to work the dishwasher later this morning?" Ian would stall as long as he could before he handed Drew over to Paula's mom, who lived in an apartment in the inn's east wing and babysat for the employees here.

"Tessa would hurt me. My wife has the temperament that goes with coppery, wild hair."

Tyne glanced at the clock—close to nine—and he and Steph carried food out to the long buffet tables, then watched over things for the next hour until the last guest left. Betty flew in at ten to help with cleanup.

She looked Tyne up and down. "Lookin' good, Hot Stuff. Heard you had a full weekend."

Ian, who'd settled into work mode, turned to hear his answer.

"Harley and I spent Sunday riding through the national park, enjoying the fall colors."

Ian nodded. "Another reason we have so many guests now. The park's good for business."

They had the kitchen and dining room clean in no time, and Tyne and Steph got busy on lunch. Tyne settled on two international soups—classic posole from Mexico and lemon chicken soup from Greece. He didn't want to push his luck, though, so went for traditional sandwiches—BLTs and chicken salad. Lunch went smoothly, and before long, he and Steph even finished his contribution for the supper menu. He provided the international dish each night, and Paula did the traditional.

Their jobs done, Steph took off her apron. "I'm out of here. See you tomorrow."

"Not for long." Tyne worked the supper shifts for the rest of the week. Paula did the early hours with Steph. On Mondays, she dropped Aiden and Bailey at her mom's apartment before she zipped into the kitchen.

Paula rushed in, glanced at the menu, and then frowned at his scruffy chin. She tsk-tsked. "What? You didn't have time to trim your whiskers this morning?"

She always gave him grief about his chin strap. He returned the favor. "What? You didn't have time to do your hair?" Her thick, black tresses were pulled up in their usual clip, spiking at the back of her head.

She laughed. "What have you got for me tonight?"

"Thai curry with pork and eggplant over rice." Tyne had lived and cooked in Thailand for a year before he returned to the United States. He loved its food and flavors. That, and Vietnamese cuisine were two of his favorites.

Since he loved it spicy, she asked, "You toned it down a little, right?"

He grinned. "For you, Miss Wimpy? Of course. I wouldn't want to send you home too hot for Chase to handle."

She smirked. "Like that could happen."

She had him there. Chase could handle most anything. He'd been tamed by his little Goth mama, though, and Tyne had never seen him happier.

Paula came over to taste a spoonful of his dish. "Oh, this is good."

Tyne untied his apron and hung it on the peg by the door. "You should talk Aiden and Bailey into trying it."

Paula snorted. "It has too many vegetables. They might accidentally get healthy."

Kids. They resisted what was good for them. Come to think of it, though, so had he. Tyne gave her a quick wave and headed to his Jeep. He was going to take it easy tonight, make himself something simple for supper, and chill out.

He drove past Daphne's shop to turn at the corner and pull into the alley that ran behind the buildings. He glanced at the stained-glass pieces displayed in her front window. Was the shop dark? He frowned at the CLOSED sign hanging in the door. What was up? Tourists crowded the sidewalks. They'd come to see the leaves and stopped at Mill Pond to shop and eat. Had she closed up early to run off with Patrick?

Nope, Daphne's SUV was parked in the back lot next to his spot. No matter. They probably took Patrick's car, but when he stepped through the back door to head upstairs, Daphne sat behind the cash register, her head in her hands, her shoulders shaking. *Oh no.* He'd never trusted the professor. Tyne went to her. "Hey, you okay?" Dumb question. Who sits there and sobs when life's good?

She turned away from him. He bent to wrap his arms around her. "He dumped you?" Did the asshole have another girl on the stringer in some other town?

No one but Daphne's parents had been impressed with Patrick. The professor was so self-absorbed, Tyne wondered how he could relate to his students. He probably didn't. Chase had been interested in Daphne before he met Paula. Chase didn't think much of Patrick either. He'd made Tyne promise to be there for Daphne if the misery came. Not a hard promise to keep. Tyne liked her. He'd never make a move on her—she was a for-keeps type of girl—but Tyne didn't just rent his apartment from her; they were friends. Or at least friendly to each other, good neighbors.

She turned and pressed her face against his chest. Tears and snot soaked his T-shirt. Gross, but what were friends for? He patted her head. Love sucked. Sometimes, it worked—like it did for Ian and Tessa, Chase and Paula. But usually? It wasn't worth the bother, the pain. That's why Tyne had promised himself he'd never fall for someone until he reached forty. Maybe not even then, but he might be ready for the crush of romance once he was older and his friends were more tied down. Maybe then he'd be bored enough that a relationship would look good.

Chapter 2

Daphne clutched Tyne's T-shirt and buried her face against his hard chest. So different from Patrick's that it made her cry more. Not that Patrick would appreciate it if she sobbed into one of his expensive tailored shirts. He took pride in his looks, how thin he stayed for his early forties. He cultivated his professor look with baggy trousers and button-down shirts and cashmere sweaters. He took pride in wearing wire-rimmed glasses. He loved the status of academia.

"I should have seen this coming." *Had* seen it coming, but she didn't want to believe Patrick would leave her to return to his wife. The wife he swore was cold and bitter, the wife he couldn't please no matter what he did. The wife that was too much like him. He swore she drained him of any creative energy, that he'd only stayed with her to raise their two kids. "I'd have never, ever dated a married man except that he and his wife had separated, and his wife lived in their house in Bloomington, and he moved to an apartment in Mill Pond. They'd been separated for five months and the papers had been filed." She swallowed hard. The divorce took an ugly turn, and Patrick's wife would receive much more money than Patrick had anticipated. His income would be severely limited. She choked on a sob. "Patrick likes money. So does his wife. Neither of them enjoys pinching pennies, so they reunited. I got cast aside as a budget cut."

Tyne shrugged. "Doesn't surprise me. The man's priorities didn't add up."

"I met his wife once. I could see why Patrick had been attracted to her. She carries herself regally, gives off the essence of money." Patrick, deep down, believed he should be treated like aristocracy, believed he should have more attention and privilege than he did as a professor. He wrote poetry and he'd published it in journals and chapbooks, but once his kids left the nest, he'd decided it was time for him to write a book, his ode to a man who'd bedded many women before he turned to more cerebral pursuits.

Daphne knotted her hands into fists. "Patrick was full of himself." Shame on her. She'd fallen for his drivel because she'd turned thirty-six and decided it was now or never. "We had a lot of common interests—books, music, plays. I hoped that would be enough."

She was a damn coward, and she knew it. Patrick wouldn't demand too much from her except constant support and occasional worship. And even that hadn't been enough.

Bugger! The stinking idiot dumped her. Her tears were as much for her own stupidity as for losing him.

Tyne patted her back. He pulled away to bring her a Kleenex. She grimaced at his T-shirt, probably ruined with smudged makeup and gunk. The man was a luscious length of temptation who didn't seem to think about his looks. Maybe when you were that sexy, you took it for granted. He handed her one tissue and dabbed at her eyes with another. "Hey, people break up all the time and live through it. It's going to hurt for a while, but you'll move on and find someone else."

She snorted. Unladylike. "Bullshit. I've heard that all my life."

He stared, but his brown eyes sparkled. "I've never heard you cuss."

"Neither have my parents. It's my own private pleasure, but the words hardly ever leave my lips."

His handsome face lit up, curious. "What other naughty things do you think about?"

"Like I'd tell you!" She rubbed at her eyes, smearing her mascara she was sure. She probably looked like a puffy-eyed raccoon. But what did it matter? Even when she'd decided to settle for less, the professor had kicked her to the curb.

Tyne tried again. "You have a right to be angry. Anger's good, but you can do better. Just wait and see. You'll meet someone . . ."

She didn't let him finish. "That's a load of crap. I'm not buying it. I bought Patrick's stupid lies for months, and I'm sick of it. Don't you lie to me."

His lips curled at the edges. "So why did you buy into his massive ego? The man was nothing but a spoiled snob."

She winced. Tyne never minced words. She'd forgotten that. He wasn't the best person to spar with verbally. He'd have eaten Patrick alive. She frowned. "You make me sound stupid. No one's talked to me like that. Ever."

"Then it's time they did. Own up. What the hell were you thinking?"

"I'm tired of dating. I'm tired of looking for Mr. Right, and I'm not getting any younger."

"So what? I'd rather be by myself and enjoy my own company than be stuck with a jerk."

She sighed. No one else would say that to her either. But Tyne wasn't like anyone else. He was his own person. Yes, the man was gorgeous with his dirty-blond hair and scruffy whiskers, his body that rippled with muscles, and pheromones that permeated a room, but that's not what she liked about him. She liked his keen wit, his quick mind, and his outspokenness. At least, she *used* to like his out-spokenness.

Her shoulders sagged, the fight seeping out of her. Defending herself took too much energy. Tyne would be too demanding day in and day out. He'd make her tired. "Look, you're the type who goes for it. You've traveled all over the world. You wanted to be a chef, so you became one. I never dreamed that big. I'm happy here in Mill Pond, love working with stained glass. I just wanted a *little* more. That's all."

He circled the counter to get a better look at her. "Maybe you didn't dream big enough."

"Not all of us can get everything we want." She went for another Kleenex and turned her back to blow her nose. She took another Kleenex to wipe under her eyes. The sheet came away covered in black.

Tyne leaned his hip against the counter. "I'm glad you won't be smothered by Mr. Brain Drain."

That was a new one. "Brain Drain?"

"He loved to hear himself talk, but never said anything of impor-tance."

Hmm, she'd never thought about Patrick's rambling lectures that way. "I enjoyed hearing his point of view."

"He did go on and on, though."

"I thought he wrote good poetry."

Tyne crossed his arms over his chest. "Boring."

She blinked, surprised. "You don't like any of those things?"

"Sure I do, but what else did he have to offer?"

"There's more?"

Tyne gave her a look, and she could feel her hackles rise. How could this man annoy her more than anyone else ever had? And still, if she needed something done—furniture moved in her sewing room at home or new shelves put up in the shop—he could make it fun. He knew how to make her laugh. And suddenly, she realized that if she spent too much time with him, he could ruin her equilibrium. So she took a deep breath and smiled. "I'm fine now. The worst is over. I knew I was expecting too much. I'll go back to my work and my sewing. I'll get through this."

His face scrunched. He obviously didn't like her answer. "Oh, for Pete's sake. Get your sweater. Let's get out of here. The leaves are gorgeous. The air smells like energy. Let's go for a hike."

She shook her head. "I can't." She withdrew into herself. She felt it happening. He was going to mock her now.

He looked her up and down. "What? When your heart broke, did your legs break, too? Do your feet still work?"

"I never hike."

He stared. "Why not? You live on the edge of the national park, and you never hike it?"

"I look at it. I enjoy its beauty."

He let out a long breath. "I'm gonna love this, I know, but why just look when you can experience it?"

She pressed her lips together, gathering her thoughts. "My parents weren't happy I moved there. They said it wasn't safe for a woman to hike alone on the trails. I was too far from town. There could be snakes. People have fallen on some of the steep trails and broken their ankles."

He threw back his head and laughed, and she cringed, but he didn't stop there. He grabbed her elbow and pulled her to her feet. "You won't be alone. If we see a snake, I'll lift you on my shoulders so it can't reach you. And if you start to fall, I'll grab you. Enough already. Let's go."

He tugged her along with him, and she wasn't sure she had a choice. "I look horrible. My makeup's a mess. I'm ugly when I cry."

He put a finger on her lips. "You could never be ugly. You don't need makeup. You're one of loveliest women I've ever met. So hush up and move it."

Lovely. He'd called her lovely. But then he yanked again, and she had no choice but to follow. She stalled when he opened the door to his orange Jeep—a deathtrap on wheels. But he gave her a small push, and she slid onto the passenger seat. He slammed the door and went to slide behind the steering wheel.

"Have you ever been in a Jeep before?"

"No." And she was sure that was a good thing.

He grinned. "Then you're in for a treat."

Treats weren't healthy for you, were they? The Jeep jerked forward, and she braced her feet. If she could survive being cast aside, she could survive this.

Chapter 3

Tyne drove to his favorite trail. It wound around the back of a clearing where he'd spot deer if he came early enough in the mornings, then it passed behind Daphne's house. It never hurt if he saw her, too. He'd called her lovely, and he'd chosen the word carefully. Beauty could be sterile, brittle. Lovely implied warmth and character, at least to him. He parked at the small gravel lot by the asphalt-paved path. He loved nature, loved to hike.

When he'd traveled, he'd walk for miles on his days off, climbing mountain trails, trekking along small paths through dense foliage, and wandering through cemeteries. He wanted to breathe in a place, to see it in its natural state. And then he met as many people as he could, drinking in their spirit, their approach to life and food. It seemed that the way a person approached food was often a clue to how they approached everything else.

He circled his Jeep to open the passenger door for Daphne. She hesitantly stepped out of the vehicle, squinting at the trail and all of the foliage on either side of it. He grinned. "I hike this trail a lot, and I'm still alive. Come on, sissy."

She huffed and stayed close. Even with him next to her, she watched for every root or leaf that intruded on the path. "Is that poison ivy?" She pointed at a vine at the edge of the trail.

"Nope, just a creeping vine. Are you allergic? Have you had a bad case of it before?"

"No, but I've never touched it, have I?"

He shook his head. If she didn't know what it looked like, she wouldn't know if she'd touched it, would she? Her backyard bumped up against the park. She could easily have poison ivy on her trees or in her flower beds. "I'm guessing it doesn't bother you."

She didn't believe him, he could tell. She stopped to stare at a hole a few feet from an incline. "Is that a snake's hole?"

A chipmunk ran and dashed inside it. Tyne stepped in front of her to protect her. "You're in danger now. He might think you're a nut."

She gave him a flinty look. Good, she had a little more spine than he thought she did. He liked Daphne, enjoyed her company when she'd invited him for a coffee after she saw him on the trail, but he'd never met anyone so self-contained before. Those types didn't go into the restaurant business. Chase had been attracted to her ethereal quality before he fell for Paula, but Tyne found most mousy people too tepid for his taste. He liked passion, but he suspected there was plenty of that hidden somewhere in Daphne. She just kept it under lock and key.

He motioned to their surroundings. "Have you ever seen so much color?"

It was time to focus on the beauty, not the imaginary dangers. Oak leaves added coppers and bronzes to the mix of vibrant yellows, bright reds, and vivid oranges. He bent to gather a bouquet of leaves for her. "I press them in books to look at in winter."

She smiled. "I iron them between wax paper and string them along a wall in my sewing room."

He picked up acorns and walnuts and filled his hoodie's pockets with them. "They look pretty in a glass jar." Then he snapped off some fountain grasses for her.

She gaped. "You're not supposed to pick anything here."

Tyne shrugged. "I didn't. I took the tops. Besides, I know the park ranger. She gave me permission."

"Would any woman deny you anything?"

He slanted a glance her way. "I don't know. Would you?"

She turned bright scarlet, brighter than the red leaves in her hand, and he couldn't help but laugh. She pressed her lips in a tight line, irritated with him.

She got braver and braver the longer they walked. She stayed behind to gaze at a log covered with fungi. She craned her head to see a downy woodpecker better. The farther they went, the slower she walked. He smiled. She was mesmerized, and then Tyne realized she'd probably never walked this far. She was getting tired. He looked at the sun and said, "It's low enough that it must be near suppertime. Let's go to my place, and I'll fix us something to eat."

She looked surprised. "You cook on your days off?"

He gave a wicked grin. He knew it was wicked, because she looked wary again. "Days off are when I do what I want, complete freedom."

"Is your food spicy?"

"Why?"

She looked flustered, tried to dodge the question. "Never mind. I'll be fine. You've spent enough time with me. I'm sure you have something better to do, someone else to see."

She was trying to get rid of him. How cool! Most women wanted him to stay. She meant to retreat back into her shelter, though, and he had no inclination to let her. "I haven't made any plans. Let's go to the store and grab whatever we want for tonight." He couldn't help himself. He asked, "Want some whiskey? Wine? If you'd like to get plastered, I'll keep an eye on you."

She looked horrified, and he chuckled. She glared. "I usually eat dinner at my parents' house."

"Then you've seen enough of them. Tell them you can't make it tonight. Let's go shopping. I'm hungry for Thai food, my favorite."

"With curry? It's hot, isn't it?"

"It's according to how much you add." Another wicked grin. "How spicy do you want it tonight?"

She actually backed away from him, which amused him even more. "I think I'll just grab a burger at Ralph's."

"Like hell you will. Do you know how many women beg me to cook for them? This is a rare privilege. I'll keep it tame. You'd better enjoy it."

Enjoy it? She looked like he'd offered to take her to the dentist's office for a root canal. He decided to take it easy on her and smiled. "I'm teasing you. Come on. You might like Thai."

She sighed. He ignored it, tucked her into his Jeep, and headed to Art's grocery on Main Street.

Chapter 4

He dragged her into the store with him. "I usually run to Tessa's barn for fresh produce, but I'm in a hurry tonight."

"Is it open this late?" Daphne glanced at her watch. "I thought she closed at five."

"She does, but she leaves a basket on the shelves, and you can just throw in cash for whatever produce you take. Have you shopped there before?"

Daphne gave him a look. Dumb question. He wasn't sure she knew how to turn on her stove. "We'll start with the fresh ingredients. Tell me what you like." Taking her hand, he led her to the produce aisle. "Cilantro?"

She wrinkled her nose. "Not for me."

"Fair enough." He added two limes to their cart, bok choy, and red peppers.

She stared. "I only cook with vegetables out of cans. They're soft."

And easy. If Daphne ever made a salad from scratch, instead of out of a bag, he'd be surprised. "What do you order when you go to restaurants?"

She thought about that and nodded. "I like steamed vegetables or sautéed."

"Then we're good." He took her to the meat case. "Chicken? Pork? What's your favorite?"

"Chicken."

He added that to the cart. Then he went to the international food aisle and chose two cans of coconut milk, jasmine rice, and fish sauce. He had everything else at home in his cupboards. He usually had these, but he'd run out.

"Fish sauce?" She grimaced.

"It gives dishes a salty flavor."

"Then why not use salt?"

"Not the same." By the time they finished shopping, she was worried about their meal, he could tell. "I won't poison you. I cook Thai food at the restaurant. Guests love it."

"But foodies come to the inn. They want something different, unusual."

"Because once they try it, they like it. You will, too."

She looked doubtful. "I have cereal at home."

Good God! He rolled his eyes. "So if you can't eat my food, you won't starve?"

She blushed. He held off telling her she looked pretty with her cheeks bright pink.

He paid for their items and drove her back to her shop, but this time they climbed the inside steps to his apartment.

She turned around to take it all in. He'd hung colorful scarves on the white walls.

"I got those in South America." He carried the grocery bags to the galley kitchen. Its work counter looked out over the sitting room and sleek, wooden table. "Teak," he said when she ran a hand over its smooth surface. Two elaborately carved, wooden panels hung behind his low-slung sofa, and upturned fishing baskets served as side tables. "From Thailand."

"Everything's so neat and uncluttered." She sounded surprised. Tyne had been inside her house often. Her sewing room was organized, but stacks of fabrics lined the shelves on one wall. Partially finished quilts and table runners hung over the backs of chairs. Books and magazines were scattered around her living room.

He shrugged. "I move around a lot. I like to travel light."

She looked up and frowned at him. "Are you going to stay in Mill Pond, or are we just another spot on your travels?"

Good question. "I don't know. I came home to open my own restaurant. Mill Pond has all the specialty farms a chef could want. I like the area and the people, but it's too soon to tell."

She nodded, and from her expression he could tell she'd decided he was only temporary, that he'd be gone before she knew it. She glanced at the chin-up bar attached to the door to his bedroom, noticed the workout weights lying on the floor near his bed. Everything portable. And she smiled. Her shoulders relaxed. Her mood lightened.

Intriguing. She thought he'd lose interest in her soon and move on, that he lived in the moment, and that made her feel better. Little did she know that he'd promised Chase and Paula he'd be there for her when Idiot Professor showed his true colors.

"I could use some help," he said and motioned to the ingredients he'd put on two cutting boards. "You can do the veggies, and I'll do the chicken and sauce."

She came around the counter and stared at the chef's knife beside her board. "Don't you have any gadgets to throw these in? Something to chop them up for you?"

Tyne shut his eyes and counted to ten. "Chefs don't need gadgets. We have skills."

She picked up the knife and cut through the bok choy. He held his breath. He'd never seen worse knife skills. She was lucky she still had fingers. "No, no, not like that." He walked behind her and wrapped his arms around her to show her how to do it right. She tensed. *Oh, lord.* "I'm not trying to feel you up. I'm trying to keep you from cutting yourself. Pay attention."

"I can't."

"Why not?"

"I feel smothered in maleness."

"Really?" He grinned, happy with himself, then stepped aside and rested his knife on his own board. "Like this. Do as I do."

He showed her how to chop an onion. She followed his example and smiled, obviously pleased with herself. In a few strokes, all of the bok choy was chopped. He left her to the rest and started cutting the chicken breasts into chunk-sized pieces and started the rice. She came to stand beside him at the stove to watch him cook.

She listened to the chicken sizzle. "I don't cook very often. I burn everything."

"Do you turn the heat too high?"

She pressed her lips together. "No, I usually get distracted and forget I have something on the stove."

He stared. She was a menace. She was lucky she'd never burned down her house. But he tried to be patient. "Okay, new rule. Never leave the kitchen when you have something on the heat."

She shook her head when he turned off the burners.

"Let's eat."

"Already?" She glanced at the clock. "It only took half an hour."

"Most of the meals I cook at home are fast." Soon they were eating chicken curry over rice at the teak table.

"Mmm." She licked her lips and dished up seconds for herself.

He watched her clean her plate and smiled. "Well?"

"It's good." She grabbed her dirty dishes and headed to the kitchen.

"Don't worry about that. I'll clean up. You've had a big day. You okay now?"

She smiled, but she wasn't fooling him. He'd kept her distracted, but once she was alone, in her own house, she'd fall apart. That was all right. At least now, she knew the professor was just a speed bump in life, nothing more. And if she forgot, Tyne would check in on her often. She'd get past this. He'd make sure of it.

Chapter 5

On the drive home, Daphne cranked up the volume of the car's radio. The minute she climbed behind the steering wheel, she felt alone. Her house wouldn't be any better. She wanted that, right? Time to work through the events of the day, to mourn her loss, to cry and get Patrick out of her system. But the thought of facing an empty house didn't thrill her. She'd lost the professor, and she was beginning to think she'd always be single, forever and ever, in her house by the park.

Farmers had already picked soybeans in the acres she passed. Some had even started picking corn. Streetlights ended at the edge of town, and the road stretched before her headlights, a dark ribbon. She kept a careful watch. This time of year, deer moved around more, foraging in the newly harvested fields. She caught a movement out of the corner of her eye and pressed on the brake. A kitten raced across the road, and she swerved a little to miss it. It was gray with a white chin and back paws, blending in with the cement so well, she'd never have seen it if its eyes hadn't reflected the car's headlights.

She squinted at a shadow on the opposite brim—roadkill. The kitten was drawn to it. The poor thing hunkered down. It must be ravenous. She parked and opened her door. The raccoon was so bloated, the kitten circled it, unsure what to do with it. Daphne opened her glove compartment and took out a sealed stick of beef jerky. She unpeeled it and tossed a scrap on the road. "Here, kitty, kitty!"

The kitten crouched and sniffed. It came closer. She tossed another scrap, and it came to investigate. She wasn't sure if it would eat something so processed, but it wolfed it down. She tossed the next piece closer to her car, and it came for it. She dropped the next piece on the passenger seat, and it eyed her suspiciously, but jumped in for the food. She slid behind the steering wheel, closed the door, and started for home.

The kitten cowered in the far corner on the floor. After a few minutes, it disappeared under the front seat and dragged an old French fry out to eat. She talked to it in a soothing voice and slowed down to pinch off more jerky. Before she could throw it down, the kitten leapt on her passenger seat and she fed it there. It must have been around people when it was tiny. Farmers complained about people who drove out here and dumped young cats after they'd outgrown the "cute" stage. Daphne slowly reached to stroke the cat. It might not be a tiny ball of fluff anymore, but it was still adorable.

She'd always wanted a pet, but her mom was allergic to almost every living thing. Patrick hated cats, complained that they were aloof and independent. She grinned. No, he wouldn't like anything that didn't dote on him. No wonder he was a dog person. She liked dogs, too, but cats had a certain allure. She decided, if the cat was willing, she was going to keep him.

When she got home, she parked in the attached garage and closed its door before she let the cat out of the vehicle. It sped to jump out of her yellow SUV. Her dad advised her to get yellow. It was supposed to be safer. Other drivers noticed it more. It was as bright as Tyne's Jeep.

She opened the door that led into the house and went straight to the kitchen. She opened a can of tuna and emptied it into a bowl. The cat streaked inside to eat. She closed the door and proceeded to find a shallow cardboard box. She shredded newspapers to put inside it to use as kitty litter. When the cat finished its food, its tummy bulged. She put it in the box and watched it scratch knowingly. Yup, it had been house trained.

"I'm going to name you Shadow." Not very original, but she didn't care. He was her cat, and she'd name him whatever she wanted to.

While Shadow explored the house, she made herself a cup of tea and settled in front of the TV to relax. Nothing held her interest, and she found herself on the Food Channel watching four chefs compete against each other. They opened boxes of mystery items and had to make something out of them. She sniffed. Tyne would leave these guys in his dust. She switched to a house show after that, and when the cat was tired, he jumped onto her lap and closed his eyes.

Her heart lurched with happiness. She stroked Shadow's smooth fur until he purred. Two brothers were remodeling a house, and she watched them knock down walls to open it up into one, big great room. Her house was pretty open—the front room, dining room, and kitchen all combined. A back hallway led to two bedrooms on one side with a bathroom between them and a master suite and workroom on the other side. The place wasn't too big, but it was big enough.

Recalling Tyne's place, she pursed her lips, studying her own décor. Cozy, right? Warm-toned, hardwood floors with throw rugs here and there. Wheat-colored walls. Two tapestry-covered sofas sitting across from each other with a big ottoman between them. Magazines covered one side of the ottoman. Tyne wouldn't approve of that. Two armchairs at each end of the sofas. Perfect for an intimate gathering. A gate-leg table, in the front window, held a lamp. Two rocking chairs were pulled close to a fireplace at the back of the room. The brothers on TV probably wouldn't approve of her home. They'd consider it out of style, but it was comfortable.

The TV show ended, and Daphne couldn't stop a yawn. It had been a big day. She carried Shadow to her bedroom—the only room with log walls and an oak floor. She climbed into her queen-sized bed and fell promptly asleep.

When sunlight peeked past her blinds and she woke, thoughts of Patrick flooded her, then a rough, pink tongue licked her arm. She smiled at Shadow, stretched out beside her. Patrick wasn't all that affectionate. He wasn't all that attentive either. Come to think of it, the cat might be a lot better at both.

Chapter 6

Tyne worked the supper shift on Tuesdays through Saturdays. Paula did the morning shifts at the inn. He didn't have to get up early for work today, but he'd promised Maxwell, Mill Pond's bread guru, that he'd help him make four kinds of focaccia for a special wine party Harley was giving on Sunday. Harley and his wife, Kathy, were both excited about it. It was to help Mill Pond raise money to build two new piers for the public beach, so that people could boat and dock there to shop and spend time in town. If they raised enough money, they meant to build a pier close to Harley's winery, too.

For this charity event, Tyne was doing double duty. He was helping Maxwell with the focaccia, and he and Paula had promised to make appetizers. They'd planned on fun finger food that wouldn't break the bank, and Ian had signed up to donate crab for a fancy hors d'oeuvre. Ian was always generous, but he was in an especially giving mood since his baby son was born. Tyne wondered how long the afterglow would last before fatigue washed it away.

People in town were looking forward to the party. Harley had hired a jazz band, and Chase had promised to make lots of sliders. Tyne got ready quickly and walked the short distance to Maxwell's. The crisp morning air snapped him awake. He had to work tonight, so he wanted to finish here early and take a break before reporting to the inn. He tried the doorknob at Maxwell's, and it was open, so he let himself in.

"Hey, man, I'm here!" He started toward the kitchen. The ovens were already cranking out heat.

Maxwell was as tall as Tyne, but thinner, with a ropey build. He wore the same uniform every day—striped, drawstring pants and a white, button-down shirt with an apron tied around him. His brown hair was pulled back in a ponytail, like usual. He was kneading a mound of bread on a marble-topped worktable.

He looked up when Tyne entered the room, and Tyne noticed the dark circles under his eyes. "You look like you need a nap."

Maxwell nodded toward the ceiling. He, too, lived above his shop. "The old girl had a bad night last night. Couldn't get to sleep until three in the morning."

Tyne knew that India wasn't in the best of health. Even with her asthma, she couldn't quit smoking. A cigarette always dangled between her fingers. She dragged an oxygen tank with her wherever she went and turned it off to light up. "Was she better this morning?"

"She was asleep when I came down, plum wore out."

Tyne heard Chester barking and glanced at his friend.

"I'd better let him out for a minute. He probably has to take a piss." Maxwell hurried up the stairs to get his Chihuahua. If he had his way, the dog would be in the kitchen with him. Hell, if Maxwell had his way, he and the dog would be inseparable.

Tyne coated a large, ceramic bowl with oil and placed the dough inside it. He draped a damp towel over it to let it rise. Then he started another batch of dough for a second focaccia. When Maxwell returned, Tyne was kneading that batch.

Maxwell shook his head. "Chester's not happy. He knows you're here, and he wanted to see you."

Tyne liked the dog. It yapped a lot, but was smart and friendly. "When we finish up, why don't we take him outside for a minute before we leave? I don't want to wake India or bother her, though."

"Chester will like that." Maxwell started a third type of focaccia, and while he worked, Tyne started a fourth. By the time they finished, the first dough was ready to punch and roll out. They added parmesan and mozzarella cheese to it and pushed it in the oven to bake.

They added balsamic onions to the second batch, black olives and tomatoes to another, and rosemary and pepperoni to the last. When they finished, they boxed them up for Tyne to drive to Harley's. Then Maxwell went upstairs and returned with Chester. Chester whined and jumped on Tyne, begging for attention.

"Stop that. Where are your manners?" Maxwell scolded.

Everyone knew Chester didn't have any. The dog did what he

wanted because Maxwell couldn't bear to discipline him, but Chester was sweet and loving enough, so Tyne didn't care. He bent to pet him. And then both men donned their jackets and took him outside to play in the fenced yard.

While watching the dog, Tyne asked, "Are you done for the day?"

Maxwell shook his head. "Still need to finish a dozen loaves of French bread for a sandwich shop two towns over."

Tyne was curious. "Where did you learn to cook? Did you go to culinary school and specialize in pastries?"

Maxwell snorted. "Hardly. My second foster mother taught me."

Tyne blinked. "Sorry, Max, I didn't know."

"It ain't no secret. I was a bad 'un when I was young, got in all kinds of trouble. Came by it natural. When my dad went to prison, they took me away from my mom." He was silent a moment. "Not sure she noticed, but it got me in the system. My first foster home was a bust. I ran away so many times, they gave me to Mrs. Worth. That's where they sent the incorrigibles." He chuckled. "Thought they'd punished me good and proper, but that woman killed you with kindness. She was so nice, you didn't want to disappoint her."

"She was a good cook?"

"The best. Baked bread every Monday to feed us all. Always had a pot of soup on the stove. Had three others besides me. No pushover, though. She'd box my ears when I went wrong, then praise and cuddle me when I got things right. Loved that woman till the day she died."

That story explained a lot to Tyne. Maxwell wasn't your typical baker.

Chester ran another lap around the yard, so Tyne asked, "How did you meet India?"

"Wasn't any good in school, so I got jobs in restaurants. India was a waitress in the last one I worked at." He grinned. "Not a good waitress, mind you, but she always showed up on time. There was just something about her. When I left to come here, she came with me."

Chester scratched at the back door. The dog had run enough. Maxwell opened it to let him inside, and Tyne went to the bakery to get Harley's focaccia. Maxwell helped him load it onto the Jeep's seats, then Tyne drove it to Harley's winery. On his way back, he stopped to check on Daphne.

The minute he walked in the crowded shop, three women circled him. He'd meant to casually wander around to take his time to enjoy her work. The white outside walls were covered with big displays— framed, stained-glass windows and screens. The brick wall inside held clocks with stained-glass faces. Five-foot trellis walls lined the center of the shop with her stained-glass fans hanging in some sections and window art in others. A long table in the very center displayed the lamps she'd designed. He liked all of her pieces, but he liked the quilts she made at home every bit as much. The women crowded around him when he stopped to study a floor lamp.

He turned to look at the woman pressing the closest. She smiled up at him. He crooked a half-smile in return. "Do you like stained glass?"

She blinked, never taking her eyes off him. "Our friend's at the cash register, buying one of the glass jewelry boxes. We're just waiting for her."

He glanced at the two women who came to stand behind their friend. They looked to be in their late twenties. He hadn't seen them at the resort. "Hi, ladies, are you staying in Mill Pond?"

The blonde pursed her lips in a moue. "No, we have reservations at the park's lodge. We're just passing through. Do you live here?"

He nodded.

"The lodge is only a ten-minute drive from here." The girl looked at her friends. "If you stop by tonight, we'd make it worth it."

These girls were out to have a good time. He'd be lucky if they didn't tie him to their bed. "I'm sure you would, but I work tonight. I'm booked up for a while."

The brunette pressed her lips together, disappointed. She handed him a slip of paper with her number on it. "If you get a few days free and call us, we'll make a special trip for you."

Now they were scaring him. He grinned. "Where are you from?"

"Miami."

They looked like Florida girls, tanned and fit. They probably lived in bikinis every weekend. He slid the paper in his shirt pocket. "Have a good time on your trip."

The blonde locked gazes with him. "If you could get tonight off, we'd have more fun."

He started to say that he couldn't, he was the chef at Lakeview Stables, then thought better of it. If they booked rooms there, he'd have to leave town for a weekend. Instead, he shook his head.

"Can't. The boss needs me." He was relieved when their friend came to get them and they left the shop. He looked up, and only a few customers remained, happily browsing. He went to Daphne.

She raised an eyebrow at him. "I almost came to give you a *No Touching the Merchandise* sign, but I couldn't leave the cash register."

He smirked. "Do you consider me merchandise?"

"No, but those three women did."

Women like that didn't interest him. He studied her. "How are you doing?"

"I'm going to live. My parents are picking me up when I close shop, and we're going out to eat together."

Tyne grimaced. "Don't you have any girlfriends to take you to a bar and get you tipsy?"

Daphne looked horrified. "Girls make bad decisions when they've had too much to drink."

"That's why they go with friends. Their besties won't let them leave with some ax murderer."

Daphne gave an exasperated sigh. "Alcohol doesn't solve problems. It only makes them worse."

Tyne shook his head, but he wasn't going to argue with her. "Look, I don't work Sunday nights, and Harley's giving his wine party. I told him I was bringing you with me."

Daphne got that defensive look on her face again. "You don't have to babysit me. I'm going to work on quilts this weekend to distract myself."

He gave a pretend yawn. "Boring. Everyone else is going as couples. I haven't snagged anyone yet, so you're going with me. Besides, you'll be able to try the appetizers that Paula and I make. Ian's interested in doing special parties at the inn once in a while during the slow season. You can tell us what you think."

She studied him. "You don't like to take no for an answer, do you?"

He grinned, looking cocky again, he knew. "First, it hardly ever happens. And when it does, a *no* is just a speed bump to a *yes*."

"God, you're full of yourself."

He tilted his head, thinking. "No, just honest. And I don't want you sitting around with too much time on your hands. At least, not for a while. So I signed you up."

She sighed. "You think you're being a good friend, don't you?"

"You'd do the same for me."

"Don't count on it."

He laughed. "But you'll go?"

"I'll go." She sounded grumpy, but he ignored it.

"Good, see you then." Actually, she'd see him more than she wanted to, but it was better if she didn't know that. He didn't want her sitting alone on a Sunday night. With a wave, he took off when the next customers entered the shop. She'd be busy all during the day and with her parents tonight. Two days past the poopy prof, and she was holding in there.

On the way to work he had to stop at Garth's station for gas. Leona's cousin, Chantelle, was at one of the pumps. Leona was Garth's main squeeze. She was man-crazy before Garth claimed her, but Chantelle made her look tame. The girl came over to talk to him, invaded his personal space. He sighed. What was it today? Had the heavens unleashed every aggressive female in a one-mile radius? Heavy flirting started, but he pulled away, didn't offer any encouragement. Chantelle was too aggressive. She annoyed him. When she got in her car to leave, she smacked his ass. *Really?* He asked, "Didn't you forget to pay?"

With a careless wave, she called, "It's on Garth."

Sure it was. On the drive to work, he took courage from the fact that the inn was full of couples right now, people who wanted a quiet getaway to spend time with each other—women who were into their partners, who'd leave him alone.

Chapter 7

The minute Tyne opened the kitchen door, the aromas of lemon, garlic, thyme, and bacon surrounded him. Paula and Steph looked up from the dish they were finishing and grinned. *Uh-oh.* Something was up. Paula could always be naughty, but Steph was usually pretty straightforward. Then he caught the excitement that buzzed in the air. Steph practically vibrated, ready to burst with her news.

He reached for his apron and narrowed his eyes at her. "You look way too happy."

She laughed and hurried toward him, her left hand outstretched so that he'd see the ring. "We finally made it official. I told Ben either he set a date or I was leaving for culinary school."

Steph would, too. She didn't put up with any crap. Thin to the point of no shape, with limp blond hair, she gave the impression of being wimpy. Far from the truth. The girl had a steel core. Tyne had been surprised when she'd decided to stay in Mill Pond instead of going to cooking school with the other kids he and Paula had mentored during the summer, but she'd decided Ben was more important. Tyne had met him. He was a decent enough person. He'd started his own business, cutting and trimming trees. In the busy season, he worked part-time with Buck Krieger at his landscaping business. The boy had ambition, but still, Steph had given up a great opportunity to be with him. Tyne wouldn't have done that.

Steph wiggled her ring finger under his nose. "I know you're a guy, the least romantic one I've ever met, but you have to at least look at it."

He focused on the gold band and small diamond. Yup, it was a ring. He wasn't much into jewelry, didn't have a clue what to look for, but smiled. "It's pretty."

Steph laughed. "It's nothing to brag about, but I don't care. I don't need a big diamond or something expensive. It means Ben's set a date. We're getting married January first, a fresh beginning to start our new life together."

"New Year's Day. Symbolic, I like that." He did, too. Every culture used symbolism to add meaning to their lives—it had probably started when people in ancient times celebrated spring solstice—the promise of sun and crops and survival.

Steph stretched onto her tiptoes to kiss his cheek. "You're a good friend. Glad you're happy for me."

"I am." And he meant it. Every person had his own agenda, his own bucket list that brought him happiness.

"Tell him the bad news," Paula said.

Steph grimaced. "I'll probably have to quit working here to find a full-time job. I'd like to make more money."

She worked eight hour days during the busy seasons, but when the number of customers slowed down in winter, her hours got cut. Tyne pressed his lips together in a grim line. He'd hate to lose her. "I'm bummed. You have talent."

"Thanks, you guys have taught me a lot. I appreciate it." Her voice sounded tight. She gave Paula a wave. "Now that I've made him look at my ring, I'm outta here. Are you about done?"

Paula faked a bright smile. "All I have left is to impress Tyne with our magnificent offering." She motioned him over. "Wait till you see it."

Steph grabbed her jacket and was gone. Paula's shoulders sagged, but she squared them again and lifted the foil off two huge baking pans to reveal forty-eight bacon-wrapped trout, one for each guest staying at the inn this week. "I've seared them, so all you have to do is finish them in the oven for twenty-five minutes."

They were beauties. Tyne loved the variety of offerings in Mill Pond, but he doubted these had come from around here.

"We made sweet potato casserole to go with it," Paula said.

"Perfect." Tyne followed her lead. They wouldn't talk about Steph leaving them. They'd force themselves to be happy for her, and they'd concentrate on their food.

Tonight, he was making lamb, olive, and caramelized onion tagine with couscous. Paula's traditional dishes would blend well with that and the other sides he'd planned. He'd cooked the tagine ahead and only had to reheat it. It benefited from resting for a while to let the flavors mingle.

Paula stalled a minute before leaving. "Chase told me the professor went back to his wife. How's Daphne doing?"

Another tricky topic. Chase had been entranced by Daphne before he'd fallen for Paula. Some women would hold that against her. Not Paula. Two women couldn't be more different. Daphne was quiet, cerebral. Paula was a go-getter with tattoos and two kids. But they were both warm and giving. Tyne told her about taking Daphne to Harley's wine party. "I had to practically twist her arm, but I got her to agree to go."

"She didn't want to go with you? Are you losing your touch?"

Tyne rubbed his scruffy chin, thinking. "From what I can tell, Daphne either works, holes up at home, or spends time with her parents. She'd rather curl up with a book or watch a movie with subtitles than mingle and have fun."

Paula nodded sadly. "That girl needs to spread her wings."

"She doesn't trust she can fly. It's going to take her a while, and it will be one small step at a time."

Paula patted him on the shoulder. "Get her in gear, Hot Stuff. If anyone can do it, it's you."

"Hot Stuff? Really? The Goth Girl is going to follow Betty's lead and use her nickname for me?"

Paula spread her hands in innocence. "Hey, you're in the kitchen and you love the heat. Besides, you just called me *Goth Girl*."

He laughed. "Yeah, and I kinda liked it. I might do it again."

She shook her head on the way out the door, and he turned his attention to the food he needed to prepare. He put the lamb stew in the oven to reheat and had started on the slow-roasted tomato, goat cheese, and mint salad when a woman knocked on the back door and walked into the kitchen. A sign clearly said PRIVATE, PERSONNEL ONLY, so his hands went to his hips. What the hell did she think she was doing?

The woman motioned to herself and said, "We've never met, but I'm Miriam Reinhardt, Daphne's best friend. We've known each other since I stole her lunch in second grade."

He scowled. "I can't picture you two together." Miriam was almost as tall as he was, had to be close to six feet, and toothpick thin. Short, dark curls—like corkscrews—framed her narrow face. Vivid blue eyes pinned him in place, and her wide mouth was quirked to one side as she studied him. "Are you an artist, too?"

She barked a laugh. "Nope, we don't have much in common besides books, but I knew I wanted her as a friend the minute we met. She tried to run, but our school only had one of each grade back then, so she couldn't escape me. She finally had to make nice to keep me from driving her nuts."

Interesting. "What drew you to her?" And what could possibly keep them together?

"Her big heart. Quick mind. You'll never meet a more generous friend."

He nodded. That, he knew. He supposed she and Miriam were alike that way.

Miriam looked him up and down. "So what's the deal? Why are you pestering Daphne? Because if you've tagged her for sloppy seconds, I'll tar and feather you and drive you out of town."

A warrior. He grinned. He liked this woman more and more. "What are you, her protector?"

"Yes." She crossed her arms. "The professor hurt her enough. I'm warning you off."

"You've got it wrong. I don't have to chase women. They chase me. I'm pestering Daphne because she's a friend. I think the professor's a dick, and I don't want her to retreat back into her shell since he dumped her."

Miriam's eyes went wide. He doubted too many people surprised her, but he must have. "So, you're playing the Good Samaritan?"

"I don't make a habit of it. And I'm not all that patient, but I thought I'd give it a shot."

He watched Miriam's right eyebrow rise. He knew that look. He was the recipient of it many times. "Are you a teacher?"

"That obvious? High school English. But don't think I hide behind books. I intend to rattle Daphne's cage, too. I don't care if I end up single, living with cats, and talking to myself, but she will. She took a step. I want her to keep going."

"So do I."

Miriam nodded. "Good, then I don't have to threaten you or hire someone to hurt you. You do your thing, and I'll do mine, and hopefully, we'll move Daphne in the right direction."

Holy crap! He loved this woman. Miriam didn't scare him, but he sure wouldn't want to be on her bad side. "Nice meeting you."

She smiled. "A dismissal. I get it. You have to get back to work. Thanks for hearing me out."

He thought about her and Daphne long after she left the kitchen. He'd just met a formidable woman, and he liked that Daphne had her for a friend.

Chapter 8

Daphne's mother reached across the square table and patted her hand. Customers at nearby tables sent Daphne sympathetic looks. Everyone in Mill Pond had heard that the professor had moved back to Bloomington and returned to his wife. At first, Daphne worried they'd consider her a floozy for dating a married man, but they all knew Patrick had filed for divorce and moved to Mill Pond to put distance between him and his almost-ex-wife. That, and everyone wanted her to meet someone so much, they were willing to overlook the small technicality of the divorce not being final. She was that pitiful, she realized. Not a cheerful thought.

Her mother tsk-tsked. "It's hard to find a good man. I hate to say it, but most men these days run from commitment and never intend to stay faithful like your father here. Men like your dad are hard to come by."

Her dad beamed. Her parents had married in their late twenties, but hadn't had her until Mom was almost forty. She was an only child. "So we can smother you with love," Mom used to tell her.

"Smother you is right," Daphne's friend Miriam often complained.

Daphne watched Chase, who owned the bar, carry burgers to the people at a far booth. He was an only child, too, but he'd grown up helping his mom and dad run the business. He was constantly surrounded by people and friends. Her mom was a librarian and her dad, an accountant. They preferred a quiet life and didn't encourage her to have friends over. Daphne always thought that someday, she'd find a man—like her—who'd rather stay home in the evenings to work in the garden or listen to opera and read, but it had never happened—until Patrick. And that hadn't ended well.

When she thought of Patrick lately, anger boiled in her veins. What had she been thinking? And why didn't she drive to Bloomington to slash his car's tires?

That thought shocked her. She wasn't that type of person. But then again, wasn't anger one of the stages of grief? So much anger? She pushed it away.

Chase came to take their order. He gave her one of his dazzling smiles. There was a time, close to when she'd met Patrick, that she'd suspected that Chase might be interested in her, but she must have read that wrong. Why would he be? The man was gorgeous—tall, with streaked, blond hair and a chiseled jaw. What would he see in her? Tonight, he raised an eyebrow at her and asked, "What'll it be?"

Chase was as good-looking as Tyne, but their personalities couldn't be more different. Chase was the laid-back, easy-going type, whereas Tyne could be in your face and intense. Her heart did a tiny, jealous twist, and she was ashamed of herself. Chase sure looked happy now that he was with Paula. He'd found his soul mate. She'd yet to find hers.

"I have a new burger on the menu, if you want to live dangerously," Chase told her and her parents. "Some customers have been asking for something spicy, so I made jalapeño burgers to try out."

Her mom quickly shook her head. "Peppers give me heartburn."

Her dad ordered his usual. "A burger, no bun, no condiments, just plain. No fries. Only carrot sticks on the side. And water."

Her mom was a little more adventurous. "Same for me, but I'll take ketchup."

Daphne squared her shoulders. "Bring me the new one and a glass of wine."

Her mother stared. Neither of her parents believed in drinking, but she and Patrick usually ordered wine with dinner. Daphne liked a good Riesling, and it just so happened Chase served wines from Harley's vineyard. Top quality.

Chase's turquoise eyes sparkled. "We serve the new burger with a southwest mayo to kick it up even more. Want that?"

"Why not?" What was in southwest mayo? Would smoke come out her ears? Would her tongue burn and fall out of her mouth? Daphne licked her lips. She was turning over a new leaf. She was going to be more daring. "And add fries."

Her mother gaped. "Are you sure, dear? At your age, women need to watch their weight."

Daphne shrugged. "What good has staying thin done me? I want something fried."

Chase chuckled and gave a small salute. "Coming right up." He left to turn in their order, and her mother frowned at her.

"Drowning your sorrows with bad habits is only a temporary respite."

Temporary or not, Daphne wanted to enjoy herself tonight. "Tyne cooked Thai curry chicken for me a few nights ago, and I liked it."

Her mother looked horrified. You'd have thought Daphne told her Tyne had offered to smoke pot with her. Or worse. "You ate dinner with a man in his apartment?"

Uh-oh, she hadn't thought this through. "He's a chef. He found me crying in my shop and wanted to be nice to me."

"A respectable man would have taken you to a restaurant."

"He lives above my shop. We bump into each other all the time. For Tyne, cooking food for someone is an act of love." She hurried to add, "Or friendship. It shows he cares."

Her mother sniffed in disgust. "He must not have many social graces."

Daphne couldn't argue that. "He marches to his own drum, that's for sure." Tyne wouldn't give a rat's ass—as Miriam would say—about inviting her to his place. He didn't waste time worrying about what people thought about him.

Chase came with their burgers, and she bit into hers, relieved to end the conversation. Two chews, and she felt heat hit her tongue and clear her sinuses. She would have grabbed for her glass of water, but her mother would know her mouth was in flames and shake her head disapprovingly. She was determined to finish the burger if it killed her, and it might. But the more bites she took, the more she liked it. And before she finished, she even ordered a second glass of wine.

Chase rested a hand on her shoulder. "Tyne would be proud of you. That guy loves the heat."

Why hadn't she guessed? "Did he help you come up with this?" It seemed obvious. It was bold and demanded your attention, just like Tyne did.

"He contributed ideas for it."

Daphne could picture him, playing with different tastes to kick up the old standby recipe. "Tell him he done good. I liked it."

Her mother ignored the humor and sighed at her improper grammar. "What's gotten into you?"

What *had* gotten into her? She wasn't sure.

Chase laughed and said, "Your burger's on me tonight for being a guinea pig. I'll keep it on the menu."

When they left the bar, her parents started to their car and she headed to her bright yellow SUV.

"Have a nice night, dear," her father called to her. Her parents would drive home and change into their pajamas and robes, then settle in to listen to classical music and read. She usually did the same, but tonight she surprised herself again by heading to Miriam's stone cottage on the lake.

As always, when she pulled into its drive, she breathed a sigh of relief. Its Wedgewood-blue trim and doors and its slate roof gave it an English-cottage feel. Its perennial flower beds and many rosebushes added to the effect. Miriam loved anything Agatha Christie, and her house reflected that.

Glancing to the water behind the house, she saw Miriam's rowboat pulled onto the grassy slope. Her friend had already taken in the dock, preparing for colder weather, but she wouldn't stop puttering around the lake until the water froze.

Miriam opened the door and came out to greet Daphne before she wandered down the curved sidewalk. She was dressed in jeans and a faded sweatshirt that hung down over her hips. "Still nice outside, isn't it? We haven't even had a killing frost yet."

Daphne motioned toward her heavy, navy sweater. "I left my jacket at home."

"It gets chilly when the sun goes down. You might want to come inside." Miriam started toward the house.

The walls of the living room and kitchen were painted white. Dark beams lined the ceiling, and oak floorboards creaked underfoot. A stone fireplace stretched floor to ceiling on the far wall of the living room, and Daphne could glance the blue Aga on the back wall of the eat-in kitchen. Miriam's cottage would fit in perfectly in the Cotswolds.

"You hungry?" Miriam asked.

"I just came from Chase's bar. Too much to eat."

Miriam nodded and headed toward the overstuffed chair by the fireplace. Daphne sank into its match, facing her. Daphne sighed. "You've heard, I'm sure."

"The pitiful penis professor left you. Are you all right?"

Daphne considered the question. "I'm angrier than I thought I'd be."

"Good for you!" A cat leapt on Miriam's lap, then another. One rested on one leg, the second on the other. She stroked them both. The orange tabby was a male; the smoky gray cat, a female. Miriam had named them Tommy and Tuppence.

Daphne patted her lap for Tuppence to come over, but the cat ignored her. "I ate a jalapeño burger tonight and fries."

Miriam's jaw fell. "With your parents?"

"Mom didn't approve."

Miriam rolled her eyes. "What *does* she approve of?"

"Don't start." Daphne grinned. With Miriam, she could be herself, warts and all. "I drank two glasses of wine, too."

"You rebel, you." Miriam stared at her friend. "The professor got to you, didn't he?"

"Not so much. I don't miss him. More than anything, I'm mad at myself."

"Really? What for?"

"For telling myself I'd be happy if I settled for less than I wanted, less than I deserved."

Miriam tilted her head, studying her. "Settling's never good. Maybe you should give up on men. We could become a couple, except I have no sexual interest in you at all. And I don't have anywhere for your sewing room."

Daphne laughed. "We'd make horrible lesbians. We'll just have to stay friends."

"Perhaps that's best." Miriam leaned forward, curious. "I met your chef friend, Tyne."

"You did?" Daphne pulled a face. "He loves to push me, dragged me to a hiking trail with him."

Miriam stared, astounded. "Did he piggyback you so that no snakes or poison ivy could harm you? You'll never go with me.

You'd think the national park was Snow White's forest, where the tree branches reach for you. I haven't met any evil spirits in the woods around here."

"Very funny. No, he mostly mocked me into keeping up with him. I have to admit, the scenery was beautiful."

"I mock you, and you ignore me."

"He's harder to ignore."

"Good for him." Miriam leaned back again to stroke her cats. "So what are your plans now? You need to meet another guy."

"Screw that."

Miriam laughed. "You *are* in a mood! But no one wants to screw me. Too long and bony."

Daphne shook her head. "I'm done with men. No more. I'm going to be like you and enjoy being on my own."

"We're not the same. You won't like it. I do."

"I'll learn to."

"Maybe." Miriam glanced out the side windows as the sun lowered over the water, painting it a rosy orange. "Lick your wounds for a while, and then get out there again, find somebody."

Daphne looked at the stacks of papers beside Miriam's chair. "Looks like you have a lot of homework to grade tonight."

Miriam looked at them, too, and sighed. "That's what happens when you assign essay questions."

"You're a damn good teacher." She'd never use the word *damn* around her mother, only with Miriam.

"I know, but teachers are under attack these days. If our country doesn't change, we'll become extinct. Who needs the grief that politicians and hostile parents give us?"

Daphne smiled and stood. "I appreciate you, and so do your students. I'll get out of here. Good luck with those. And thanks for listening to me."

"Anytime, and don't push this Tyne guy away. He's going to be good for you."

Daphne wrinkled her nose. "Who likes something that's good for them?"

This time, Miriam gave a wicked grin. "It's possible he's a pain in the ass you might learn to enjoy."

Daphne shook her head. How did you respond to that?

Chapter 9

It was all hands on deck for Sunday brunch at the inn. After having done it so often, Tyne, Paula, and Steph worked together in synchronized harmony. Steph stood ready to carve the ham at the buffet line. The lemon crepes were filled and on the serving dishes. Paula was on omelet duty. Tyne worked the Belgian waffle station, and Cody—the dishwasher—kept all of the trays filled with bacon, sausages, and bacon, caramelized onions and mushrooms, and the traditional sides of fresh-fruit salad, breads, and muffins. Lox and bagels sat ready, as did the potato pancakes with smoked trout. Guests came and went until the dining room cleared at one thirty.

When brunch was over and the cleanup finished, Tyne and Paula stayed to make the appetizers for Harley's party. They started with stuffed mushrooms, bruschetta, and fancy deviled eggs. They went on to creamy crab-and-bacon endive boats, roast beef and beets in filo cups, chicken satay with peanut sauce, and chocolate-dipped strawberries. Finger foods took a while, but when they finished, Paula drove home to Chase and her kids. Tyne drove the food to Harley's.

A new woman stood behind the bar with Kathy. Harley introduced her. "Tyne, meet Vicki. We've gotten busy enough, we needed to hire someone else. Vicki, Tyne. He's a chef at the resort."

Tyne took a second to measure her up. Probably sixty. Attractive, with pure white hair pulled back in a low ponytail. Gray eyes. She looked intelligent and classy. She'd make a perfect addition here. She gave him a brief smile before helping Kathy line up more wine glasses for the tastings.

Harley helped Tyne unload food, and his dad came to help them set up. When he noticed Vicki, he stopped to stare. "You hired the person we talked about?"

Harley nodded. "She said she'd be happy working part-time when it's slow and full-time when we're busy. That's not easy to find."

Gino thought about that. "Most people need a steady income." He stopped to stare at her for a moment. She felt his gaze and looked up. Their eyes met, and Tyne swore chemistry buzzed between them.

Harley blinked. He'd noticed it, too. He elbowed his dad. "Nice. Mom's been gone a while." Tyne and Harley often visited her grave at the end of their motorcycle rides. "I know she's not here," Harley once told him. "But it makes me feel close to her." Tyne understood. He liked cemeteries.

Gino gave his head a quick shake. "It will be nice to have an extra hand around here. We won't be so pressured." He went to set up more tables and chairs.

Harley worked with Tyne to arrange the food in a few different locations, so there'd be a good flow. When they finished, Tyne drove back to his apartment. After a quick shower, he dressed in khaki pants and a dark-green, button-down shirt. He pulled a tan sweater over it. It was going to be chilly tonight. Then he drove to pick up Daphne.

They couldn't have picked a better night for the event. The air was crisp, but not cold. Autumn leaves glowed when the last of the sunlight hit them. Lights beamed in the windows of Daphne's log cabin with its green-tin roof, sitting snug in its small clearing with the park as its background. Tyne bounced up its front steps to the wide porch and knocked on the front door.

When Daphne opened it, he stared. Her light brown hair curled over her shoulders. She'd lined her hazel eyes with brown liner and applied a bronze shadow. A soft blush highlighted her high cheek-bones. She wore a long, brown skirt with a pumpkin-colored sweater belted at her narrow waist.

Words blurted from his lips. "Hell, if you can't find a guy when you're this damn gorgeous, you're going after men who don't have pulses."

Her cheeks turned an even deeper pink. "Thank you."

"Come on. We're cutting it close." He led her to his Jeep, and they raced to the other side of town. Soft background music was playing when they entered the Spanish-style building that held the tasting room. The relaxed atmosphere encouraged people to mingle as they ate and drank.

Daphne spotted Miriam sitting with a gray-haired man near the dance floor. She and Tyne stood in line for appetizers, grabbed glasses of wine, and went to join her. Miriam looked up, surprised.

"Didn't expect to see you here," she told Daphne. "Have you met our school's principal, Albert Snyder? His wife's playing piano in the jazz quartet."

After introductions, Miriam looked Tyne up and down. "You clean up pretty good."

"Yeah, no apron. I can blend in when I have to."

Daphne frowned at them. "How did you say you two met?"

Tyne enjoyed watching Miriam squirm. He had a feeling it didn't happen very often. "Miriam came to deliver some goods at the inn."

"What kind of goods?"

"Don't ask." Miriam waved it away.

Daphne studied her friend, alarmed, but Tyne laughed it away. He nodded at Miriam's wide, tweed trousers, white blouse, and red sweater. "You're dressed like Kate Hepburn."

"You're too young to know much about her."

"I'm thirty-one. What about you, oh wise one?"

Miriam's eyes glinted when he mocked her. "Thirty-six, like Daphne. But we're film buffs, love old movies. You don't strike me that way."

"I got hooked when I saw Hepburn in *Bringing Up Baby*."

"With Cary Grant? I love that one!"

Tyne shrugged. "Bet you love her with Spencer Tracy more."

Miriam arched an eyebrow at him. "Be cautious, young Skywalker. You're wading into hallowed grounds now."

"Sounds like I'll need my lightsaber to protect myself." He popped a stuffed mushroom into his mouth.

"You might." She raised her chin.

Daphne watched them spar and smiled. She turned to Miriam. "There aren't too many people who can keep up with you. Tyne can."

"He does all right for a snot nose. And he cooks. I love every bite." Miriam reached for more bruschetta.

Albert nodded approval. "The boy makes a mean crab dip."

The boy. Tyne got a kick out of that. The musicians stopped playing, and Albert's wife came to claim him. Harley came over to say hi to Tyne and the women. "We've raised enough money to install both piers and a dock close to the winery. This has been a bigger success than we expected."

"The winery will be even busier," Tyne warned him.

Kathy called for Harley at the tasting bar, and he gave Tyne a light punch on the arm before leaving. "Thanks for all the help."

"No problem."

Daphne gave him an odd look. "You helped Maxwell make the focaccia for the other party, too, didn't you?"

"India was too sick to help in the bakery. That was for a charity Harley was supporting, not as much work."

"But you pitch in where needed?" Miriam asked.

Time to be wary. Miriam sounded too pleasant. "I don't cater private parties."

"But you're a good friend." Miriam motioned toward Daphne. "My girl needs a friend right now."

Daphne glared. *How interesting.* She didn't monitor herself when she was around Miriam. What was she like when she wasn't on her best behavior? Tyne wanted her to have a good time tonight, though, so smiled. "Lucky for her, she has two of us."

Music started up again, this time old-school style. Tyne reached for Daphne's hand. "Come on. Let's dance."

She yanked away from him. "I can't."

"Can't, or won't?"

"I'm not a good dancer."

Tyne took her elbow and heaved her to her feet. "Who cares? We're not the entertainers. We're here to have fun."

"Go for it!" Miriam cried.

When Daphne tried to hold back, he wasn't about to let it happen. He pulled her into his arms and swirled off with her. At first, she went rigid, stumbled, and stepped on his feet, but that wasn't going to save her. He just kept going. Soon, she not only kept up, but she got into the music's rhythm and flow. He loved to dance, and she was a natural. He had her dipping and twirling until a hand tapped on her shoulder. *What the hell? Who cuts in at an event like this?* Daphne turned her head to see who was there.

Chantelle stood ready to take her place. Tyne glowered at her, was about to tell her to take a hike but Daphne, beet red, pushed away from him and headed back to Miriam. *Son of a gun!* He thought about calling her back, but she'd looked too embarrassed. He'd make the best of this, even though he wanted to throttle Little Miss Lust.

She gave him a predatory smile. *So, she thought she'd won, huh? She didn't know him very well.* With arms stiff, he held her a foot away from him and moved in place, putting his weight on one foot and then the next. She stared at him.

"What are you doing? I watched you dance. I love your moves."

"I didn't appreciate your last move at all, so guess what? Keep your distance."

"You'd really rather do this than hold me close? I'm awfully good in tight spots."

"I'll have to take your word for it. This is as close as you get."

When the dance ended, he returned to their table. Miriam tried to keep a straight face. "Were you trying to defend your honor out there? You did a good job."

"That girl should be on a leash." Tyne reached for his glass of wine. "A muzzle might not hurt either."

They sat out the next set, but when the music started for the last one, Tyne reached for Daphne's hand again. She shook her head. "I'm too tired."

He couldn't bully her, he could tell, so he yanked Miriam to her feet instead. "Your turn."

To his surprise, Miriam had moves that could match his own. He'd never danced with a woman who was almost as tall as he was, so their first dip was a little sloppy, but then they found their groove. Miriam was getting into the music and rhythm, but when she tried to lead, he had to put his foot down. "*Nuh-uh*, I'm the guy. You might be my equal, but on the dance floor, you follow *me*, not vice versa."

"You're such a traditionalist." She laughed at him. "Come on, pretty boy, keep up."

They finished out the last dance, then returned to Daphne. She stared at her friend. "I didn't know you could dance like that."

Miriam shrugged. "I took dance aerobics for a few years to stay in shape."

"You did? When?"

"When I asked you to go with me, and you turned me down. No biggie."

The last guests started drifting to the doors. *Time to leave.* Tyne went to say good-bye to Harley and Kathy. Harley's dad was helping Vicki wash wine glasses. Then Tyne came to collect Daphne and drive her home.

Miriam walked to the parking lot with them, and Tyne held her car door for her. "Thanks for the dance, ET," he told her.

Her blue eyes sparkled. "ET?"

"English Teacher."

"Any time, PB."

"I'm not."

"You are, Pretty Boy." With a grin, she rolled up her window and pulled away.

Chuckling, Tyne led Daphne to his Jeep and helped her in. On the drive to her place, he asked, "Did you have fun?" She'd sat out the entire last set. Tonight might have been a mixed bag for her.

"It was wonderful." She leaned back against her seat and hummed the last song.

Good. She'd enjoyed herself. He was curious. "Why don't you go to Chase's on Fridays or Saturdays? He has a band. Lots of guys would dance with you."

The humming stopped. She stared at him. He'd pushed her too far. "They all know me," she said.

"That's a bad thing?"

She sidestepped his question. "I ordered a jalapeño burger at Chase's on Tuesday."

"You?" He couldn't hide his surprise. "I could hardly get you to eat curry."

"I liked it. Chase said you helped him with the recipe."

"It's spicy."

She nodded. "I needed two glasses of wine to cool down my mouth."

He laughed. "You might enjoy lots of things if you try them."

She looked doubtful, retreated again.

He let it slide. They'd taken a step forward. That was enough for tonight. He'd think of more things to push her envelope, and a month from now when she thought of Patrick, she'd yawn.

Chapter 10

Monday morning, the alarm went off, and Daphne woke with a headache. Her muscles ached, too. When was the last time she'd danced, had so much fun? And drunk three glasses of wine?

She stretched her legs under the blankets, and Shadow pounced on one of them. She wiggled her toes, and the cat swatted at them. She moved her fingers under the sheets, and he chased them. Why hadn't she gotten a kitten before? Shadow was wonderful!

She padded to the kitchen to feed him before stepping into the shower. The hot water felt good. It cleared her head, soothed her body. When she toweled off, her stomach rumbled. She was hungrier than usual so tugged on her robe and opened the refrigerator with hope. Obviously, false hope. When was the last time she'd gone to the store? When she went with Tyne? She had a crust of bread, a little milk, no eggs. The cat had a wider selection to choose from than she did.

She opened the cupboard. An empty box of cereal. Why did she put it away empty? And then miracle of miracles! She found one packet of Pop Tarts. She toasted and ate those. She really needed to stop at the store. That, or starve.

Shadow wanted some attention. She sat at the kitchen table and flicked paper clips for him to chase. The cat had a whole condo thing going now. When she'd gone to the pet store, she couldn't resist the three-tiered play area with a cat bed at the very top. She filled his bowl with dry cat food and refreshed his water. She'd bought lots of toys and a kitty litter box that cleaned itself. Mom considered the expenditures a waste of money, but Daphne loved seeing the kitten happy.

She picked up Shadow and nuzzled him. Purrs hummed in her

ears. His soft fur invited her to stroke it. Too bad she couldn't take him to work with her. A kitten in a stained-glass studio? No, maybe not a good idea. What did he do with himself all day? On weekends, afternoons meant nap time. The kitten curled in his new penthouse bed and snoozed for hours. She knew where she'd find him when she came home. He'd be perched on one of the deep window ledges that overlooked her back yard. A blue jay called at the peanut feeder, and Shadow squirmed for her to let him down. He raced to the window ledge to see it. She left to drive to Mill Pond.

No matter how many times she looked at the leaves, she couldn't soak in all of their beauty. The sky was so blue, the puffy clouds looked pasted on it—like a picture kids would make in grade school. Art's grocery store was already open when she passed it, and Grams was pushing a cartload of groceries to her car. She waved at Daphne when she saw her. The aroma of fresh bread wafted to her as she passed Maxwell's bakery, making her mouth water. There was something about the smell of fresh bread. Either that or Pop Tarts were a crappy breakfast.

When she pulled behind her shop, Tyne's Jeep was already gone. He had to work the early shift every Monday. She wondered how he managed to stay up late and get up early, but it didn't seem to faze him.

Business was usually slow on Mondays. She often worked on new projects between customers, but the weather was beautiful and the leaves had reached their full glory. People crowded into her shop, and she sold more stained glass than usual. She even got a specialty order to finish during the slow season. By the time she turned the sign to CLOSED at five thirty, the shop looked a little empty. Her parents were attending a lecture tonight, so they'd eaten earlier than usual, leaving her on her own. She went to the workroom to finish a few small projects she'd started last week.

When she finished the third stained-glass fan to hang in windows, she heard the back door open. Tyne must be home. She looked up to see him standing in the workroom's doorway, grinning at her. "Still here?"

She glanced at the wall clock, surprised to see that it was almost seven. "I sold out of more inventory than usual. I thought I'd try to make a few more."

Tyne looked scruffier than usual today, his hair spiky, his whiskers longer. He wore low jeans and a long-sleeved, thermal T-shirt.

Jeez. They only made him sexier. Not that she cared. She didn't. Her parents had told her often that lust was a sad substitute for love. Tyne glanced around the room. "Have you had anything to eat? I'm going for pizza. Not in the mood to cook tonight. Wanna come to keep me company?"

She doubted he needed that. Some woman would be glad to share his table, to flirt and laugh with him. But maybe he wanted a chaperone, so that he didn't have to bother with that tonight. Her stomach grumbled, and she realized she was hungry. At home, the cupboards were bare. She bit her bottom lip, tempted, but then shook her head. "I can't. I left my cat alone last night. I don't want to neglect him two nights in a row."

Tyne's brown eyes lit up. "You have a cat?"

Oh, nuts! "You like cats?"

"Love 'em."

"He's a stray. I just got him. A kitten."

"A kitten? Even better." Tyne motioned for her to wrap things up. "Come on. I'll stop and get the pizza and bring it to your place."

"My parents don't like the kind I do. Don't worry about it."

"What do you usually order?"

She hesitated. Now he'd know how low-class she really was. "The meat lovers' special."

"Great! We can share. I'll get a chicken club pizza, too. I like both of them."

She stared. "How much pizza do you eat?"

He grinned, and she braced herself. What would come out of his mouth this time? "I have a healthy appetite," he told her.

He would, wouldn't he? She thought of something else. "My refrigerator's empty. No beer. No soda. Only water."

He shook his head. "I need to drag you to the store again. No worries. I'll bring a bottle of wine."

"But . . ."

He waved away her concerns. "Hurry it up. I'm hungry."

She doubted it would make any difference if she argued. She grabbed her jacket and purse and locked up when they left the building.

"See you soon," he said, hopped in his Jeep, and sped away.

It would take a while for them to make the pizzas. She stopped at Art's Groceries to grab some milk, cereal, and bread. On the drive home, she thought about how hard it was to sidestep Tyne. For her entire life, men had considered her unapproachable. She usually withdrew when they advanced, and then they stopped. But Tyne didn't. He just kept coming. Yet he didn't scare her away. How did he do that?

She scurried around inside the cabin to pick up newspapers she'd tossed on the floor and the towel she'd draped over the bathtub, doing a quick job of straightening up. Shadow loved it. Thought it was a game. He raced from room to room with her. By the time Tyne parked in the drive, the house was less cluttered.

She went to hold the door for him. He carried in two boxes of pizzas and a bottle of wine. When Shadow tried to dart past him to get outside, Tyne pushed the wine under his arm and scooped him up. "Are you allowed outside?" he asked.

He handed Shadow to Daphne, who hugged him close and stroked his chin. "My back yard has a picket fence. It's high enough to keep him in right now. I hope by the time he's older, he'll be trained to stay inside it."

Tyne headed to the kitchen and deposited his goodies on the wooden table. "I don't know. Shadow looks like the naughty type to me." He opened one of the boxes and reached for a slice of chicken club pizza. He'd finished it before she found paper plates for them. Then he rummaged in a kitchen drawer until he found the wine opener to remove the cork.

She handed him two water glasses. "Sorry, I don't have any flutes or crystal."

"What does it matter?" He poured them each some red wine, then reached for more pizza. When Shadow dug his claws into his jeans to climb his leg, Tyne offered him a piece of bacon. The kitten wolfed it down.

"You're going to teach him bad habits." But she smiled.

"Who can resist bacon?" Tyne held out a tiny piece of chicken next.

The kitten liked that, too. Daphne shook her head. She opened the meat lovers' box and snorted. "This might make the kitten crazy."

They ate and drank in companionable silence, feeding the kitten whenever he begged. If her mother saw this, she'd die of apoplexy. Daphne was surprised when she took the last slice of the chicken club and refilled her glass with the last of the wine. "I'll share," she said. "Want half?"

"It's yours. I can't eat another bite." Tyne walked into the living room and sprawled out on the wooden floor. He tugged at the string for his hood until he removed it. Then he squiggled it around on the floor for the cat.

Shadow leapt on it and chased it. He crouched, ready to attack again. Tyne wiggled it up the leg of the coffee table, like a caterpillar climbing a stalk, and Shadow leapt onto the table to catch it. Tyne played with the cat for a good twenty minutes, then he gently lifted him and laid him across his long arm. Shadow yawned and stretched.

"I think I've worn him out." Tyne's expression went soft, and Daphne had a hard time dragging her gaze away from him. "He shouldn't pounce on you tonight."

She grew serious. "I can't believe someone tossed him out of a car and left him to cope on his own."

"He wouldn't have survived," Tyne said. "The odds are against him. If the road didn't get him, an owl or coyote would have."

She shivered and reached for Shadow, and Tyne pushed to his feet.

"It's getting late. You have a great cat. Have fun together."

"Thanks for a free supper."

His grin returned. "Food doesn't just fuel us, it inspires us. You need to go to the store more often."

Daphne watched him walk out the door and drive away. She cradled Shadow closer, but suddenly the house felt too quiet. Too empty.

Chapter 11

A tour bus was parked in the overflow lot for Mill Pond's shops. Daphne bit her bottom lip when she drove past it. She glanced down the street to Ralph's diner. Full. So was Bob and Bertha's coffee and donut shop. Nuts, she'd meant to dash in there to grab a cinnamon roll for lunch. The line would be too long. She should have packed a sandwich, but she'd forgotten to buy deli meat at the store, and she was out of peanut butter. It looked like this was going to be another long, busy day.

Once in her shop, she went to her workroom and carried every piece of inventory out to hang. She placed the clocks with their stained-glass faces on the brick wall. She'd had four-foot walls, built out of trellis material, installed up and down as rows on both sides of the shop, leaving a wide center aisle. She hung the fan-shaped pieces and window hangings on those. The bigger pieces hung in the front windows.

Then she turned the sign in her door to OPEN, and people started coming in. She wondered how long the tour would stay in town before it moved on to the national park. Usually, the bus stopped at Mill Pond for breakfast, gave the people a few hours to shop, and then took them to the rustic lodge near the small lake in the forest. People tended to shy away from buying glass pieces to store on the bus, afraid they might break before they got home, so she didn't expect lots of sales, mostly window shoppers.

She thought wrong.

"The brochure told us to bring plenty of Bubble Wrap in case we found something we really loved," one of the women told her. She smiled. "We brought lots of it."

That woman and her friend each bought an eighteen-by-twenty-four-inch window hanging. "That's why we chose this tour," her friend told Daphne. "We've heard about Mill Pond's artisans and came prepared. We're going to the jewelry store next. The brochure said the owner lets you choose your gem and then fixes it in the band of your choice. He makes one-of-a-kind products, like you do."

Daphne wished whoever had printed the brochure had warned her ahead of time. Before the tour bus pulled away, she would worry that she might run out of stock by the end of the year. Business during the peak months had been brisk this year, but she hadn't worried about replenishing items, because the pace of customers usually slowed down once school started. But it hadn't. Fall was staying busy. People were placing more specialty orders than usual, too. She was going to be busy during the slow season. Maybe a good thing. She wouldn't have time to feel sorry for herself.

In winter months, owners typically opened their shops only on Thursdays, Fridays, and Saturdays. Even then, there usually weren't many visitors. So Daphne would spend most of her time in her workroom, producing pieces for the upcoming year, she imagined. At home, Monday through Wednesday, she would work on sewing projects—her quilts and wall hangings.

"You should sell those, too," Tyne often told her. She was beginning to think about it.

"The problem is room," she'd argued once. "I don't have the space to display anything else."

But when she said that, he'd grinned, and she knew he was one step ahead of her. "I've talked to Ian. He'd love to hang them in the inn's lobby, and you could put your name and price on them. Tessa said she'd hang them in her bakery, too."

Not a bad idea. She might take Tyne up on it. If she did, she'd have even more to keep her busy when the weather turned bad.

She thought when the bus left, business would slow down, but customers came and went all day. She only had time to munch on crackers in her workroom during a brief lull. Betty's daughter-in-law, Leesa, who manned the shop on Saturdays so that Daphne could sew, told Daphne she'd been extra busy, too. The town mostly closed down on Sundays. Even Chase's bar shut its doors. Daphne didn't know how Ian did it, staying open seven days a week. She needed the time off.

Most nights, after she was done for the day, she drove to her parents' house for supper, but during the rush that morning, she'd called Mom to tell her she couldn't make it. "I'll need to stay later than usual to rearrange the shop, move things around, so that there aren't so many bare spots."

She'd started on that when Tyne called. "I peeked in today, and you were swamped. Bet you didn't eat. If you come to the inn, I'll feed you in the kitchen."

To the inn? She'd never been inside it. Betty would be gone by now. She wasn't close to anyone else who worked there. She hesitated. "Is that allowed?"

She could picture a security guard escorting her from the kitchen. She'd die of embarrassment.

"No worries," Tyne assured her. "Ian thought if you checked us out, you might find a spot to hang your stuff."

She sighed. Too much pressure. "I can't. I usually eat supper with my parents."

"Usually? Are you eating with them tonight?"

"Well, no, but I don't want them to think I cancelled on them to eat supper with you."

He laughed. "I won't tell, if you don't."

"This is Mill Pond. They'll hear."

"Tell them it was a business dinner. Besides, they see enough of you. I'll dish you up a plate. See you at six."

The phone went dead. He'd done it again. Hung up on her. That didn't mean she had to go. She hadn't said *yes*. But she'd always wondered about the inn. What did it look like? How had Ian converted it? He'd bought two stained-glass windows from her to hang in its dining room. Did they look good there?

She decided to go. What could it hurt? And she'd get free food. She glanced at her watch and moved even faster. By the time she needed to leave, the shop looked presentable again. People might not notice that the inventory was skimpier than usual.

She drove down Main Street to Lake Drive and circled the shoreline to Lakeview Stables. She'd been amazed when Ian installed a golf course and tennis courts on the property. The inn sat back from the road, and she couldn't help but admire its fieldstone facade, red-tin roof, and red double doors. It looked warm and inviting. Enough cars were parked in its lot to let Daphne know that plenty of guests were housed here.

She found an empty parking spot and took a minute to enjoy the view. The water was too cold for swimming, but the lake sprawled at the back of the property, deep blue and serene. Her cabin had the national forest as its backdrop, with nature only a few steps away. She wondered if looking at a lake would be even better, then shrugged. For her, it was pretty much of a toss-up. She walked to the entrance doors and stepped into the lobby.

A high, beamed ceiling soared above. Two antler chandeliers dangled overhead, adding to the inn's rustic charm. Maple floors stretched to the check-in desk, and leather sofas invited guests to linger. A woman with gray hair and glasses looked up at her from the counter. Daphne recognized Gladys, one of her mother's friends. She'd forgotten she manned the desk after Ian went home for the night. Daphne smiled. "I'm looking for the kitchen."

"Tyne told me he invited you for supper. Down the hallway there." Gladys pointed.

Daphne followed the aroma of roast chicken and seared beef to the dining room. Lord, she was hungry. Crackers were a lousy substitute for lunch. She stopped at a metal door with PRIVATE, PERSONNEL ONLY painted on it and a small sign that said KITCHEN.

"Go on in!" Gladys called. "He's expecting you."

She pushed the door open and stepped just inside. People were coming and going at doors that led to the dining room, filling the buffet table. She didn't want to get in their way. When things slowed down, Tyne looked up and noticed her.

"Hey, you made it. Grab a seat. I'll be with you in a minute." He motioned to a long, wooden table. Everything else was stainless steel.

She sat facing the dishwasher and appliances, fascinated with the bustle and efficiency of the cooks and kitchen help. Everything moved smoothly, well-coordinated. When the doors to the dining room opened, she could see guests lining up at the buffet while others found tables and settled at them. Things fell into place, and Tyne came to join her.

"Bet you're hungry. We have two choices for dinner every night. This time, you can have guava-stuffed chicken breasts with caramelized mango or London broil with rum-molasses sauce."

"Does everything here have a sauce or a topping?"

"Not always. You just got lucky tonight."

She frowned. Maybe this food was too fancy for her. "I've never had guava. I'll take the London broil."

He wagged his finger at her. "You don't want to try something new? The chicken's stuffed with a cream-cheese-and-guava paste and fresh spinach."

"I don't like that many foods to touch."

He sat back, stared. "That's what little kids do. They don't want their chicken fingers to touch their mashed potatoes."

Really? He was going to lecture her again? "I'm not a kid. Some people are purists. When they eat chicken, they want to taste chicken."

"You liked my Thai dinner."

She sighed. "Okay, give me the chicken. You made it, didn't you?"

"Maybe." He gave her his lopsided grin and went to get her a plate. It had roasted vegetables on the side.

She studied the chicken breast. It looked pretty, like something you'd see in a magazine.

"It doesn't bite. Try some."

She sliced off a small end, reluctantly put it in her mouth, then moaned. Lord, it was good!

Tyne's face lit with pleasure. "You like it?"

"It tastes sweet, and rich, and savory . . ." She shook her head. "It's delicious."

He looked cocky. "That's what fusion cooking is all about, combining flavors. It's my specialty."

No wonder the inn was always full. With food like this, a gorgeous property, and a plethora of places to visit, it made a perfect getaway. "You cook dinner almost every night, don't you?"

He leaned forward, happy to talk about his job. "I work the night shift Tuesday through Saturday, but before Paula leaves for the day, she makes a traditional dish for me to serve, along with my international dish. Then I do all of the sides. She does suppers on Sunday and Monday, so that I can have two nights off in a row. I take her early shift those days."

She tried to keep it all straight. Couldn't. "That sounds complicated . . . and exhausting. Don't you end up working two shifts back to back somewhere?"

He nodded. "We thought about switching things up when she

married Chase, since he only closes the bar on Sunday, but Chase likes having the kids to himself on Sunday nights while Paula works. And that way, Chase and Paula can sleep in"—he winked—"on Monday mornings."

She blushed at his innuendo. What was she? A nun? If Miriam had said that, she'd have laughed. But there was something about Tyne that made her feel self-conscious. Okay, correct that. Almost *everything* made her self-conscious. She went for another bite of food to distract herself.

He frowned and rose to his feet. "Sorry. I didn't give you anything to drink." He came back with a glass of white wine.

She took a sip and made a face. "What is it?"

"Chardonnay."

Not every new experience was good. She shook her head. "Too dry."

"It's an acquired taste."

"Someone else can acquire it." She took another forkful of food to erase the taste of the wine.

Tyne went for a glass of water and looked at her, amused. "You were dead-out honest about that. You're turning over a new leaf. I've never heard you be so frank."

She blinked. He was right. Mostly, she tried to be diplomatic. She didn't seem to mind being blunt around him, though. Was that a good thing?

He nodded, as though he'd read her mind. "I like it."

Her shoulders relaxed, and she finished her meal. "Thanks for this. It was wonderful."

He glanced at the clock. "I've gotta get back to work, but stop at the store on your way home tonight. I saw inside your refrigerator and cupboards. No wonder you don't have mice at your place. They'd starve."

She flushed. "It's because of the cat."

"Sure it is. Stop at Art's and push a cart around and try to fill it."

She nodded. She deserved the lecture. "Will you get off early tonight?"

"Nah." He motioned to the young boy at the dishwasher. "I promised Cody I'd help him tinker on his truck. It's his first set of wheels. It needs a little work to hold the rust together."

She stared at him, surprised. "You're staying over to help a kid?"

Tyne gave Cody a teasing glance. "He's not too bad for being wet behind the ears."

They liked each other, she could tell. How did Tyne make friends so easily?

She thought about that on her drive home that night. Bags of groceries bumped on her back seat. Tyne had told her to stop at Art's, so she had. Not that she *had* to, but he was right. She did her best to avoid shopping, but sometimes it was necessary.

She passed the turnoff to the high school and thought of Miriam. Would they be friends if Miriam hadn't bullied her into it? Probably not. What was the deal? Was she trying to be a recluse or hermit? No, she'd like to hang out with more people, but whenever she saw someone interesting, she always asked herself why they'd want to spend time with her. What did she have to offer anyone?

She pulled into her double garage and closed the overhead door. When she opened the door to the kitchen, Shadow came running. The cat "helped" her unload the groceries and put them away. Shadow jumped into the empty brown bags and knocked them over. Daphne wadded up papers and tossed them inside the sacks for him to chase. She was enjoying herself so much, everything was put away before she realized it. And then her thoughts returned to Tyne.

He made friends easily. Why wouldn't he? He was good-looking, funny, and smart. When she met people, she became tongue-tied. The right words never came out. She made a horrible first impression. People had to be stuck with her for a while to appreciate her at all.

She changed into her pajamas and sank onto the couch to watch TV. Some people were exciting. She wasn't. And she'd been fine with that. She didn't know why she was feeling so restless lately, like she wanted more. It must be because Patrick dumped her. She felt even more inadequate than she had before. But that was silly. She'd been happy on her own before Patrick, and she'd be happy on her own again. Shadow jumped onto her lap. And this time, she had a cat. She'd be fine.

Chapter 12

The phone rang at four a.m. Tyne scrubbed a hand through his hair. Had something happened to one of his parents? Nah, if it had, they wouldn't call him. They'd call Holden, and eventually, his brother would let him know.

The buzzes stopped, then started again. He punched the button and recognized Maxwell's voice.

"Sorry to bother you, but India's not doing well this morning. I spent most of the night up with her and could use a little help at the bakery to get all the bread done for today."

Tyne inwardly groaned. After working on Cody's truck last night, he'd stayed up later than usual, reading. The last thing he wanted was to leave his bed, but he knew it had cost Maxwell a lot to call him. Max didn't like to ask for favors. "How soon do you need me?"

"A half hour ago."

Tyne grumbled, but stopped himself. Maxwell sounded stressed enough. "Give me fifteen minutes."

He washed his face, brushed his teeth, and yanked on his old jeans and T-shirt. The bakery got too warm for long sleeves. Then he slipped into his hoodie and set off. It was still dark outside. The air nipped.

Maxwell met him at the door. He looked flustered, unusual for him. Maxwell didn't get hot and bothered about much of anything, took life's ups and downs in stride. "Thanks for coming. I can't get everything done on my own. India usually helps."

"No worries. How's India doing? Is she okay?"

"She finally fell asleep. She's breathing better."

Tyne nodded. She must have given Maxwell a good scare. "What do you want me to do?"

"I have a special order for two dozen tea breads. Six different kinds. I have the recipes all laid out over there. If you could do those, I can do the yeast breads."

Tyne nodded. "No biggie." He could manage both, if he had to, but avoided baking when possible. Tea breads were a lot easier than fiddling with yeast.

They settled in to work, and the kitchen got warmer and warmer. Tyne was glad he'd worn short sleeves under his hoodie. He glanced at Maxwell in his usual striped, drawstring pants and button-down shirt. How did the man keep from melting in those long sleeves? Maxwell had turned the radio on, and music blared as Tyne made four apricot-walnut loaves, four blueberry loaves, four banana breads, four pumpkins, four cherry-almond breads, and finally, four zucchini breads. Twenty-four loaves in all, six different kinds. Jeez! When he slid the last loaf pans into the ovens, he wiped his forehead and turned to see how Maxwell was doing.

The man was already removing long, crusty loaves of Italian bread from the ovens that lined his side of the kitchen. Tyne hadn't seen so many huge mixers and ovens in one place except at Tessa's bakery. She specialized in cakes, pies, and cookies, besides making the desserts for Ian's lunch-hour teas, the breakfast muffins, and two desserts to choose from at suppers. Yup, she needed a lot of ovens, too.

Tyne looked at the giant bowls of dough rising on Maxwell's far counter. "You make a lot of bread."

"That, I do." Maxwell slid loaves of challah into an oven. Rye rounds went into another. "Area restaurants keep calling and wanting more. More customers are coming in for individual orders. I'm reaching my limit."

"Are you this buried when India helps you?"

Maxwell grimaced. "I love my woman, but tea breads are about all she can handle. Everyone wants something unique these days. I have orders for Tuscan, pumpernickel, and gluten-free. It's getting to be too much."

"Maybe you should hire some help."

Maxwell didn't argue. "I'd love to, but it's not so easy to find someone who's dependable and learns fast."

Tyne thought about Steph. "Paula's sous chef works part-time at the inn, but needs more hours. She's getting married and wants more cash. Could you hire her full-time?"

"Not right now, but like I said, things are getting busier. Give me her number."

Tyne reached for his cell phone and read it off. "She's a good worker, always shows up on time. Will India mind, having someone else in the kitchen?"

"She'll be relieved. It's been a struggle for her to help as much as she used to. Thinks she ate something that didn't agree with her last night. Had chili for supper. I like it hot—lots of spice. Might have been too much for her. She coughs a lot these days."

They stopped for a coffee break, then got back to work. Tyne was helping with an order of four hundred dinner rolls when Maxwell raised his head and turned down the radio. Only then could Tyne hear the dog barking.

"Chester needs a pit stop."

Tyne stared. "You have to quit to take your dog out to whizz?"

"India isn't up to doing the stairs most days. I can't keep Chester down here with me, so I have to get him. Come with me. Say hi to the old girl. She loves company."

Tyne had never been up to their apartment. He stopped by every once in a while to shoot the breeze with Maxwell, and sometimes, India was in the kitchen with him. Other than that, they didn't socialize, so he was surprised when he climbed the stairs to their apartment and it turned out be a bohemian holdover. Big pillows were scattered on the floor. Huge posters decorated the walls. A bong sat on their low coffee table.

India waved a limp hand when she saw him. She sat on their oversized sofa, propped up with bright-colored pillows. Tyne did a double take when he saw her. She looked bad, was having a hard time breathing.

"Has she been to a doctor?"

India gave a slight smile. Maxwell looked frustrated. "The doc's done with her. Says he can't treat her until she slows down on the cigs and the smoking."

Tyne caught that cigarettes and smoking were two, distinct activities. "I thought pot was good for your health." They grew medicinal marijuana, didn't they?

"My girl might overindulge." Maxwell cast an affectionate glance her way.

India smiled. Part black, part white, and part Hispanic, she was beautiful, but frail. A charming mix. When she pushed to her feet to stand beside Maxwell, she looked tiny. Maxwell hugged her to him. "You just take it easy, luv. We're in good shape downstairs, and I can take care of Chester. Just be nice to yourself." He helped lower her back on the couch.

She looked worn out from the effort.

"You sleep now. We'll be back later." Maxwell picked up the Chihuahua to carry him downstairs. "He'll bark when he wants to come in."

Once Maxwell got the dog settled, they washed their hands and got back to their baking. When they finished the bread orders for the day, Maxwell thanked Tyne. "Don't know what I would have done if you hadn't shown up."

"No problem, but you might want to call Steph, maybe hire her. We might even be able to work out something so that she works part-time for both of us. You have a lot of volume these days."

As Tyne left, though, he wasn't thinking about how much bread Maxwell had to bake. He was thinking about India. Her health was iffy, at best. She was going to be able to help Maxwell less and less.

Chapter 13

Tyne walked into the lodge later than usual for work that night. He usually came early, so that Paula could leave once the bus dropped her kids off after school. The door to Paula's old apartment—located in the east wing and now occupied by her mother and Maya, who helped her with babysitting—flew open. Aiden and his little sister, Bailey, raced across the lobby and attached themselves to his legs.

Tyne grinned at them. "You're here? Your mom hasn't taken you home yet?" Paula's mother watched them until Paula finished her work in the kitchen. Tyne had spent more time with the kids than he'd expected last summer, when they'd hung out at the inn while their mom worked. He wasn't exactly a kid lover, but these two were pretty cool.

Aiden made a face. "Mom and Steph are waiting to hug you. They went on and on about how wonderful you are."

Maxwell must have already called Steph, and she must have liked his offer. "I *am* wonderful. Just ask me."

Bailey tugged on his arm. "We've missed you."

"Who wouldn't?" He scooped up each one of them by an ankle and dangled them, upside-down, in front of him. It was easy with six-year-old Bailey, but Aiden had grown since the last time he did it. He'd turned nine in September. It took more effort. "I haven't seen you two hooligans much since school started. What have you been up to?"

Squealing and giggling, they fought for balance when he returned them to their feet. "You always go to the kitchen too early. We're not home yet," Bailey pouted.

He gave a solemn nod. "That way, I'm safe. Two ruffians don't attack me."

"We might be able to beat you now." Aiden pushed back his shoulders, proud of himself. "We've learned three new karate moves since you practiced with us last time."

Tyne cocked an eyebrow. He'd taken martial arts all during middle school and high school. It came in handy once when he was hiking in South America. A thug should think twice about jumping him on a nature trail. "Really?" He smirked. He knew how to get Aiden wound up. "Bet you're not good at them."

"Are too!" Bailey protested.

"Prove it." Aiden went through the motions and Bailey followed him. Tyne couldn't help but smile. Time to rattle their chains. "I've seen better."

"*Nuh-uh.*" Bailey stuck out her chin.

"Three teddy bears could whoop you. Come on. Let's sneak outside. Your kicks need to be sharper." He let them "practice" on him until he was out of time. "Chase can work with you tonight." He'd taken martial arts, too. "I have to get in the kitchen. Your mom's probably wondering what happened to me. Don't attack her when she comes to take you home."

They gave him quick hugs before they took off. He made his way into the steamy realm of chefs. Pots simmered on the stove, and the ovens cranked out heat. When Paula saw him, a huge smile split her face. "Maxwell offered Steph a job. She can bake with him from four to eight and then come work with me. If he gets busier, Steph can work more hours, and Grams will help us find someone else."

"You're okay with that?"

"Are you kidding?" Paula came to hug him. "This way, Steph can keep up her cooking skills."

Steph hugged the other side of him. "Sandwich time for Hot Stuff. Thanks, friend."

He sighed, smashed between them. What was it about nicknames? They stuck, even when you didn't want them to. "Maxwell's a decent guy. You'll learn a lot about yeast and breads."

Steph gave him one more small squeeze and then headed for the door. "I have to go. You're later than usual tonight. I'm meeting Ben at his parents' cottage. His cousin's coming for supper."

"Have fun!" Paula called and watched her leave. Then she cracked the oven doors so that Tyne could see the long pans inside it. "Osso buco. Steph made mashed potatoes and has them ready for you to re-heat."

"Yum." He loved that combination. "Tell Chase your kids need to work on a few karate moves."

"Did they attack you?"

"Only a little." He went to put on his apron. "But when Aiden turns ten, I won't be able to lift him with one hand anymore. The kid's grown."

"Yeah, kids do that." She glanced at the checkmarks on the chalkboard Tyne used for their friendly competition. Aiden and Bailey chose pretty evenly between his dishes and hers. "I heard you brought Daphne here for supper last night. Her vote doesn't count. You probably charmed her into trying yours."

"Would I do that?" He pulled chicken breasts out of the refrigerator for the Spanish chicken with chorizo and potatoes he was making tonight. He usually wouldn't cook chicken two nights in a row, but they complemented Paula's dishes so well, he'd decided to go for it.

"How *is* Daphne?" Paula asked. "Hanging in there?"

Tyne reached for the salt, pepper, and smoked paprika. "I'm pestering her enough to keep her off balance. She hasn't had time to disappear back into her usual-usual."

Paula thought about that. "Maybe she likes her usual-usual."

"Maybe, but at least she'll have to choose. She'll know what she's giving up."

Paula tilted her head and gave him a saucy look. "You'd better watch out, you know. You're spending time with a woman who's not throwing herself at you. That's how she caught Chase's attention, by being elusive. *Every* woman threw herself at Chase."

"God, that's true. I bet they all went into mourning when he married you. Has anyone stepped up to take his place?"

She snorted. "Who could? Maybe you, if you didn't ignore them all. The thing is, women hang on you, too. Daphne won't. You might like that."

Tyne gave his cocky grin. He knew it was cocky, because it used to drive his brother nuts. "If I wanted a spark from Daphne, I'd get one, but I'm just being a good neighbor."

Paula laughed. "You're so full of yourself! But that's how Ian and Tessa ended up married, because she considered him off limits. Proceed with caution."

They bantered back and forth a while longer. They enjoyed teasing each other. Before she was ready to leave, though, Tyne asked, "Has Ian decided what we're doing for Halloween yet? A sit-down dinner? Finger food? Bobbing for apples?"

"He told me he wants something fun, not fancy. Not exactly a party, but not the usual either."

"What's the time frame?"

"Guests check in on Friday and leave after brunch on Sunday. Ian doesn't want to compete with Harley's Halloween party at the winery, so they agreed to have them on different nights. We need to plan ours out."

They would have by now, if they hadn't been so busy with Harley's last party. That had been worth it, though.

Paula glanced at the wall clock. "I'm going to make you late. I don't want you to have to rush. I'll grab my munchkins and you and your staff can get busy."

He nodded. He'd lost some time tonight. He had to get serious. Paula left, and he hurried to finish his dishes.

Chapter 14

Daphne drove to her parents' house for supper. They lived in the old part of town with big, impressive Tudors, Queen Annes, and Colonial Revivals. She pulled in front of their American Foursquare—"Solid and simple like us," her mom often said—and walked down its brick sidewalk to the front door. She gave a brief knock and went inside.

The front room's furniture was stiff and formal, for guests: A rose-sprigged, Victorian-style sofa. Two wing-back chairs in rose-colored satin. A green velvet settee. Two matching shepherdess lamps with fringed shades. She passed through to the dining room. They always ate at the walnut dining-room table. A modest chandelier hung overhead, its crystals blinking in the slanting rays of the sun. The small kitchen held a tiny table with two chairs where Mom and Dad ate breakfast and lunch, but dinner meant sitting in the dining room.

Water glasses were already filled, waiting by each white plate. Mom carried carved roast chicken to the table on a white platter and her dad followed with a dish of green beans—the same meal Mom made every Wednesday night.

She could tell the day by the meal on the table: Mondays were meatloaf; Tuesdays, spaghetti; Fridays, baked fish; Saturdays, pork chops; and Sundays, roast beef. They usually ate pizzas on Wednesdays and stopped at Chase's bar on Thursdays. Occasionally, they switched it up and changed days, but the choices were the same. She smiled. Mom and Dad were creatures of habit.

When they'd filled their plates, Daphne mentioned that Tyne had invited her to eat at the inn's kitchen, and she'd been surprised how much she loved the stuffed chicken breasts he'd made. Her mom pinched her lips together and shook her head. "A waste of money. Good, simple food is enough. Chicken is delicious as is."

"I love roast chicken," Daphne hurried to say, "but his recipe was fun for a change."

Dad forked a roasted potato and shook his head. "All of a sudden, everyone wants to make Mill Pond into something it isn't. They want it to be a bigger tourist destination. That will only bring more people to our town. The stores and streets are already crowded."

"Isn't that good? I'll sell more if more people come. It's good business."

Mom tsk-tsked. "It will change the fiber of our town. We're a quiet, close-knit community with solid values. Tourists only care about having fun, being entertained. Harley's already throwing more and more wine parties at his vineyard, and Ian's starting to offer special holiday deals. Before you know it, we'll have the same morals as Indy. We'll sink to their level."

"Indy?" Daphne had never thought of it as especially scandalous. When she wanted to splurge and find new things, she was happy to make the hour-and-a-half drive to the bigger city. "I've never felt threatened there. I like visiting it."

"People like New Orleans, too, but would you want to live there with all that jazz and drinking? And then there's the drugs."

Daphne supposed most big cities dealt with drugs, but she didn't comment. Instead, she asked, "Harley's giving a Halloween party. Have you thought about going?"

Her mother wrinkled her nose. "We don't drink. We've never attended his events, even though we do enjoy jazz."

"You *are* going to hand out trick-or-treat candy, though, aren't you? You talked about quitting, but kids love going from house to house. I sure enjoyed it when I was little." It wasn't the same these days. Kids were only allowed to go from house to house for a few hours, most of them when it was still daylight. When she was little, you waited until the sun sank, then raced to every house you could before people went to bed. You came home with a pillowcase brimming with candy, and you tried to eat as much of it as possible without getting sick.

Her dad rose and gathered their dirty plates to take to the kitchen. "Are we ready for dessert?"

"You made one?" Daphne couldn't believe it. She turned to her mom. "That's so sweet. You went all out since we missed a couple of dinners together. Sure, I'd love some."

Mom stood to carry the chicken platter and bowl to the kitchen. When her parents returned, Mom brought three small bowls of sorbet and Dad carried a tray with three cups and a carafe for coffee.

"Decaf," her mom assured her. "It won't keep you up tonight."

They usually only had desserts for special occasions, so Daphne tried not to be disappointed. She loved sorbet. But no cookie? Not even a wafer? But those were empty calories, as her mother often told her.

After her father filled each cup, he said, "We wanted to let you know, dear, that we're not going to be in town for Halloween. We know you've always come here to help us pass out candy, but children don't really need so many sweets."

Daphne stared. "It's Halloween, once a year. It's tradition."

Her mother hurried to explain. "What your father meant to say is that we're leaving for a short vacation soon."

Daphne's hand went to her throat, she was so shocked. Her parents traveled twice a year. They spent a week in Florida every February and a week sightseeing somewhere different every July. "Where are you going?"

Mom and Dad exchanged glances. "We feel so bad about this," her mom said, "but you were with Patrick when my sister invited us to spend two weeks with her in Carolina. We'd have invited you, too, but we thought you'd rather stay in Mill Pond with him."

"Two weeks?" Even if they'd asked, she couldn't leave her shop that long this time of year. Her shop was still too busy.

Her dad said, "Sophia and I both have an abundance of vacation time, so we said yes. Your mom's sister lives close to a historical area that we can explore, and she's close to the ocean . . ."

Her mother added, "We're so sorry about this. We can cancel. We can be here for you since you lost Patrick."

Oh, no! Not that. The gut reaction caught her by surprise, but she hurried to say, "No, please, I want you to go. I want you to have fun. You've earned it."

She meant it. They had. It was time they enjoyed life more. Her father looked relieved. Her mom looked worried.

Daphne smiled. "Don't worry about me." She almost said that

Tyne would keep her busy, but decided that wasn't a good idea. "I've sold out of so much inventory, I need to make more stained-glass items. I can get caught up in the evenings."

Her mom hesitated, still not satisfied. "I could make meals ahead for you, and you could freeze them."

"That's just silly." Maybe Daphne would experiment with cooking for herself. She bit her lip. Her mom wouldn't want to hear that either. "No, I'll go to Ralph's diner and buy frozen dinners to have on hand. Your supper's are better, but I'll survive for two weeks."

Her mom looked hopeful. "Are you sure?"

"Positive. Go! Enjoy. I'll be fine. When do you leave?"

"On Monday morning. We couldn't make up our minds whether we should go or not."

"And miss Carolina? And seeing your sister? I'm happy for you." As much as she loved her parents, a small hope blossomed. She'd never been a child who rebelled, not even during her teen years, but the promise of being on her own, to do as she pleased, suddenly appealed to her. The allure of freedom almost made her giddy. She tried to quash it, but it wouldn't die. Two weeks. Alone. She couldn't wait.

Chapter 15

Before work the next night, Tyne bundled into his black leather jacket and climbed on his motorcycle for one more ride to Harley's winery. Paula had agreed to leave the inn early to meet him there. Yes, the wind had a nip to it. Yes, he was glad he wore gloves. But the roar of the bike and the drone of the tires pulsed in his veins, singing of freedom. Once the snow fell, his bike would be stored for the winter. He meant to enjoy it as long as he could.

He found Paula and Harley in the tasting barn, sitting at one of the square tables. Harley's dad and Vicki were busy behind the bar, and Kathy was in the office, doing paperwork.

Since Paula wasn't in a kitchen, she'd unclipped her black hair and let it fall to her shoulders. Tyne was always surprised how much that changed her look. She was cute with her hair up or down, but she looked softer with it framing her face. That face reminded him of a Kewpie doll with her huge, sapphire-blue eyes, small nose, and round cheeks.

She grinned up at him now. "You have a nice, rosy glow about you. Hope you don't sneeze or those jeans are going to fall right off you, they're so low. Lookin' good, Hot Stuff."

Tyne groaned and turned to Harley. "Don't encourage her. She's enjoying herself too much."

Harley, who was just as tall as Tyne, wore his jeans low, too, so decided to play it safe. "Paula was telling me you guys are going for fun for Halloween at the inn, but you're not doing finger foods. I can do those. Have you thought of anything for Ian?"

"As a matter of fact, I have." Tyne looked at Paula. "What do you think of a hog roast?"

"Perfect!" Her face lit with excitement. "We can do the old-style, backyard get-together—potato skins, baked beans, mac and cheese . . ."

Tyne nodded. "I thought we could do a seven-layer salad, popcorn balls, and dirt cakes with jelly worms, maybe cupcakes decorated like eyeballs."

"I love it! We can have apple cider and mulled wine to drink." Satisfied, she leaned back, looking pleased with the world.

Tyne knew something that would please her even more. He looked at Harley. "You've heard that Steph's going to start working with Maxwell, haven't you?"

Harley narrowed his eyes. He could tell there was more news coming. "Yes?"

"Maxwell has all those ovens. Steph has always wanted to get into catering, so they've agreed to work together on that, too, on the side."

Paula's eyes went wide. "Steph told you and not me?"

"Only because I was free and you were working. She's meeting us today. Thought she'd already be here by now. She volunteered to help with the food Harley needs."

Paula gave a satisfied sigh. "Good, it's time Mill Pond has a caterer. It'll make everything easier."

They heard tires crunch on the gravel drive, and they turned to see Steph stride through the doors to join them. "Tyne told us the good news. Congratulations all around."

"What good news?" his dad called from the bar.

"I'm engaged." Steph waved her ring for all to see. "And I've started working with Maxwell. We're going to bake breads together and start catering on the side."

"Way to go!" Gino gave her a thumbs up, then glanced at Vicki. "Steph works at the inn with Tyne and Paula, but she's expanding."

Vicki sent a smile Steph's way. "I'm happy for you."

Gino's expression almost melted, and Tyne and Harley exchanged smug glances.

Harley lowered his voice. "The old man's got it bad. He's trying to fight it, but I don't think he's winning."

Paula shot him a sympathetic glance. "It's hard. When I lost Alex, I didn't think I'd ever get over it, and then, when I realized that I was happy once in a while, I felt guilty—like I shouldn't. But it's lonely being a widow. It's wonderful to find someone new. I wish him the best."

"Me, too, but it will take him time," Harley said. "It's too soon to talk about it."

He didn't have to tell them to keep the news to themselves. Steph sat across from Tyne and said, "So, what have we decided about Halloween?"

Paula told her about the hog roast, and then they moved on to ideas for Harley.

"I want my party to be fun, too," Harley told them, "but on a smaller scale. What kind of finger foods would work?"

"Mummy dogs," Paula said. "Hot dogs and sausages wrapped in cornbread dough to look like mummies."

"Shrimp with creamy cashew nut sauce," Tyne added. "It has fall colors. And buffalo-chicken bites on crostini. They don't look like Halloween, but they taste good."

"Caramel apples and cookies decorated like ghosts and spiders," Steph said.

Tyne went on. "Korean ribs and coconut curry puffs, shaped like half-moons. I'm all about fun food, but I want something with substance, too."

Harley nodded. "That should be enough, don't you think?"

"Maybe little pumpkin cakes, too." Steph liked to bake.

Paula, who knew the basics for appetizers at parties—how many to make per person to keep the budget intact—put down her pen to scan the list. "Looks like a good mix to me. I think we're set."

Tyne glanced at Paula. She got his message without his having to say it. She needed to take Steph aside and teach her the business side of catering. Maxwell wouldn't know. He'd never done it before. Thinking of Maxwell made Tyne ask, "How's India? Any better?"

Steph shook her head. "She couldn't get out of bed today. I'm glad Maxwell hired me. He had a big order for bread sticks that he couldn't get to. I did those and the braided loaves. He struggled to finish his regular orders."

Harley grew serious. "How old do you think India is?"

"Forty-five," Steph said. "Maxwell told me that she's three years younger than he is."

"She looks older." Tyne realized how bad that sounded and grimaced.

"I've never seen her without a cigarette." Harley glanced at Vicki at the bar. She had pure white hair, but smooth skin. "Smoking ages you."

"Hell, it kills you," Paula said. "I'm glad I quit."

"You smoked?" Tyne realized he shouldn't be surprised. She must have been something in her late teens and early twenties. She had more tattoos than he did.

"Let me guess." Paula rolled her eyes at him. "You kept your body pure?"

He motioned at his muscled torso and grinned. "My body's a temple. I have to be good to it."

She snorted. "Well, this body pushed out two kids, and it shows. But Chase loves it, and I'm going home to him now. He worships it, pudgy or not."

"Not that pudgy anymore. You've lost weight." Steph sounded proud of her.

"Sex is great exercise." When Harley choked with surprise, she laughed. "If Steph here doesn't watch out, she's going to be skin and bones. She's already thin."

Harley gaped at Tyne, but Tyne just shrugged. "You never know what's going to come out of that woman's mouth. I was young and innocent before I started working with her."

Harley threw back his head and laughed. "Sure, you were."

They all stood to leave then, and Tyne teased, "You sure know how to clear a room, Goth Girl."

"Isn't it time you got to work?" she asked him.

He was still chuckling when he started the drive back toward town. He had to make a quick stop at his apartment to change into his chef's clothes, and as he circled the block to the alley that ran behind Daphne's shop, he noticed the professor's car parked at the front curb. What the hell was he doing here? Instead of trotting up the back steps to his apartment, Tyne meandered into the shop. Business was brisk. Tyne spotted the professor lurking around while customers chose items and paid for them. Tyne decided to stall around, too.

Daphne, he noticed, offered stiff smiles to her customers and glanced nervously at the professor between transactions. Why was the guy here? How did Daphne feel about it? If he'd left his wife again, would she take him back? Anger simmered, and Tyne tried to shrug it off. That was Daphne's decision, not his. But the thought still rankled. Surely, Daphne was smarter than that. Besides . . . His thoughts pulled up short, then he forced himself to be honest. He'd been about to admit that he'd miss Daphne if she hooked up with Professor Plum again. The good prof was such a waste; Tyne would like to strangle him in the library with the handy dandy rope.

A woman came to look at a stained-glass piece, and Tyne backed away to give her more room. She stepped to look at the piece where he stood. When he moved again, she followed. Duh! She wasn't interested in the glass; she was invading his personal space. She turned her head and smiled at him. "These are beautiful, aren't they?"

He nodded. "Almost as beautiful as the artist who makes them."

Her expression crumpled. "You two are hooked up?"

"We're seeing each other." It was true, just not in the way she'd interpret it. But that gave him an idea.

She gave him a rueful sigh. "Sorry, can't blame a girl for trying."

"Hey"—he held up his hand—"no ring. I look like fair game."

"No, you look like a good time. If you and your artist break up, give me a call." She reached in her purse and handed him a business card.

He grinned and jammed it in his back pocket. "Enjoy your stay in Mill Pond."

She glanced toward Daphne. "Oh, I will, but not as much as she does." Then she went to her friend, and they left the shop together.

People started clearing out, and Daphne had a minute with no one at the cash register. When the professor started toward her, Tyne hurried to swing behind the counter first. He threw his arm around her shoulder and tugged her close. "I have to leave for work soon, but thought I'd better remind you about our date tonight."

She blinked up at him. "Date?"

"You promised to stop by the kitchen to keep me company, remember? I'll be looking for you." He bent to drop a kiss on her nose. "Nope, you forgot. Thought you would."

The professor stood at the counter, glaring at him.

Tyne smiled and focused on Patrick's empty hands. "Nothing to buy? Sorry. You must want to ask her a question. I'm Tyne, and I'm leaving. She can help you now."

"I'm a friend of Daphne's," Patrick said stiffly.

Tyne narrowed his eyes to size him up. "You're the professor she used to see, aren't you? So happy you and your wife worked things out."

Patrick looked flustered, then affronted. "I came to speak to Daphne. I'd rather do it in private."

"In her shop? During business hours? Go figure." Tyne gave Daphne one more hug, then headed to the stairs. "See you tonight!" he called and jogged up the steps.

Once he was alone in his apartment, he smacked himself on the forehead. That probably wasn't the smartest thing he'd ever done, but the professor left a sour taste in his mouth. How mad had his antics made Daphne? Would she speak to him the next time he saw her? Then he cussed under his breath. What had gotten into him? Hopefully, he'd shown Daphne that she didn't have to settle for old stick-in-the-mud. But Tyne was still irritated. If he had his way, he'd plant his foot on the professor's backside and shove him out the door.

Chapter 16

Daphne started to turn to Patrick, hesitated, and then instead smiled at the last customer as she started toward the counter to make a purchase. "That piece is one of my favorites. I'm glad you like it."

She'd designed a leaf pattern with different shades of gold, red, and orange gleaming between each vein of lead. When the sun hit the beveled glass in the cut sections, the prisms split the light into a myriad of tiny rainbows.

The woman held it like a cherished possession. "Do you make stained-glass patterns for every holiday?"

Daphne nodded. "I design cornucopias for Thanksgiving and wreaths for winter."

"Do you have any in stock now?"

"I might have a cornucopia in the back room. Let me check."

Patrick shifted impatiently, but Daphne left and returned shortly with the last one. She'd have to make more. She'd saved this one, intending to donate it to a raffle Grams ran every Thanksgiving to raise money for Christmas toys for the poor. This year, she'd have to donate a stained-glass wreath. She had some of those in storage at home.

The woman smiled with satisfaction as she paid for her two purchases and left the shop. Then Daphne and Patrick were finally alone. Daphne turned the sign in her shop door to CLOSED and motioned for Patrick to join her in her workroom, where they wouldn't be seen. She wanted to get this over with. Whatever Patrick came to tell her, she'd rather not hear it, and the sooner he left, the better. It still hurt too much to be around him. A sign of failure. Of not being worthy enough.

She closed the workroom door, moved behind its large center table, and looked at him. Was he sorry he'd returned to his wife? Had they realized that sharing a roof and money wasn't worth sustaining a loveless marriage? Did he want her back? *I hope not.* The thought whispered in her mind, tentative, but obstinate.

A smile lifted Patrick's lips. "I've missed you. I hate the idea of not having you in my life. I've allowed myself to hope that you've missed me, too. And then I realized that we could still see each other. I could drive to Mill Pond, to your house, the third Thursday night of each month."

Her back stiffened. Outrage clogged her throat. She stared at him. "Isn't that the night your wife drives to her friend's house to play bridge and spends the night?"

His smile widened. "Exactly."

"You're asking me to be your whore?"

He blinked, surprised. "Of course not. I'm asking you to be my lover."

"Same thing." She didn't recognize her voice. It sounded cold and brittle. It reminded her of his wife's tone.

Patrick's brows furrowed in a disapproving scowl. "Really, Daphne, we enjoyed each other's company so much before, why not keep doing it? I could bring a sumptuous supper and wine. We could listen to classical music together and then make love. Why deprive ourselves?"

"You went back to your wife. You're a married man."

"I was married before."

"You were separated, filed for divorce."

"But married."

"It's different, and you know it. You made a choice. You didn't choose me."

"I'm staying with my wife for practical reasons," he argued. "I'd see you because we're so right together."

She narrowed her eyes. "Do you love me?"

She'd caught him off guard. He glanced at the tools that she used for cutting glass and making designs. They were arranged on a narrow, side table on the far wall. She waited, and finally he said, "Do you love me?"

"I thought I did. Not anymore." She spoke the truth, but it surprised her.

"I see, and does that have anything to do with the man who kissed your nose and has a date with you this evening?" His tone changed. "You certainly didn't waste any time replacing me."

He sounded put out. *Too bad for him.* "Tyne? He's my upstairs neighbor." She was about to say that he felt sorry for her and was trying to keep her occupied, but changed her mind. Instead, she shrugged her shoulders. "The minute you dumped me, he started dropping in more often." Patrick didn't need to know that it was to check on her, nothing more.

Patrick wrinkled his nose. "He smelled like garlic."

"You noticed?" Daphne smiled. "He's a chef. He's traveled most of the world to perfect his cuisine."

Patrick's lips thinned into a tight line. "Then you two have little in common. You won't eat food that's seasoned with anything more exotic than salt and pepper."

"I do now. Tyne's tempted me to try a lot of new things."

"I'm sure he tempts lots of women." Patrick couldn't hide a sneer.

"Probably, but he doesn't talk about himself very much."

Patrick snorted. "I doubt he has much to say. Where has he traveled to? Canada and Mexico?"

Daphne had never realized what a snob Patrick was. And how condescending. She said the countries as she counted them off on her fingers. "Italy, Germany, France, Spain, Portugal, Brazil, Argentina, Thailand . . ."

Patrick interrupted. "It must be nice to have parents who can send you anywhere."

"Did I imply that? His parents are rich, but he didn't use their money. He cooked his way from one place to another. He wanted to learn the local cuisines."

"And now he's in Mill Pond, and he's found a lonely, lovesick woman to entertain himself with. He's a pro at a lot of things, isn't he?"

That stung, but it ticked her off, too. "In case you haven't noticed, women flock to Tyne. He doesn't have to look for one." She motioned to the clock on the wall. "These are my business hours. I have to open the shop again. Your offer doesn't appeal to me, but I wish you the best with your wife."

Shoulders stiff, he left the shop, and Daphne turned the door's sign to OPEN. People who'd passed it by returned. She stayed busy until closing time. Then she locked the door, returned to her workroom, out of sight, and called Tyne.

When he answered, she tried to keep her voice light, but she wasn't that good at hiding what she felt. "I called to thank you for your display in my shop. It was for Patrick's benefit, and it worked."

"Are you all right?" he asked.

"Patrick has a bit of a cruel streak, but I'll be fine. I don't know if you were sincere or not when you invited me for supper, but I'm going to my parents' house tonight. They're leaving Mill Pond for a vacation on Monday, so they won't be happy if I don't show up."

"No parents when they leave on Monday?"

A warning bell alerted her to trouble. There was something about his tone. Had she made a mistake telling him? She hurried to say, "I have lots of orders to work on. I won't have time to miss them."

Tyne laughed. "Life isn't all work, no play, Daphne. I have plans for you."

"Plans?" What did that mean? But then she remembered that she worked days and he worked most nights. Their schedules would keep them apart.

"You're mine on Sunday and Monday nights."

"Harley's Halloween party isn't this Sunday. It's the next one."

"I know, and you're going with me."

"I can't do that." There'd be lots of people, lots of noise.

"It's not good to sit and twiddle your thumbs. I'll think of something for us to do. You'll have to drop in at the inn for supper a few nights, and you like motorcycles, don't you?"

"Motorcycles?" Her voice squeaked. "No, I can't."

Another laugh. "Sure you can. Gotta go." And he hung up. *Again. Drat the man!*

But a tiny voice, somewhere deep inside her, began to hum. A motorcycle would scare her half to death, but time spent with Tyne might be just what she needed right now.

Chapter 17

Tyne stared at his cell phone. What had he been thinking? What the hell was he going to do with Daphne two nights in a row? Relief wriggled through him. From the sound of it, she hadn't gone back to the professor. He should have asked how things went between them. What had that jerk come to talk to her about? He'd do that the next time he saw her.

He turned off the heat for the tarragon butter he'd drizzle over the grilled swordfish, then began to dish up the food. The guests would crowd into the dining room soon. He finished his side of burnt carrots with goat cheese and arugula.

When he remembered Daphne's reaction to a motorcycle ride, he grinned. You'd think he'd invited her to ride bulls with him at a rodeo. Damn, she lived a sheltered life. What was she afraid of? Almost everything. It was time for that to change.

He removed Paula's pan-fried veal chops with lemon, sage, and mascarpone from the oven. Howard, the evening kitchen helper, carried it to the dining room. Tyne had made parslied potatoes as a side to mop up all of the sauce. And he'd added roasted tomatoes with bread crumbs for variety.

Paula and Ian had asked him to be a friend to Daphne, so that she'd have a shoulder to cry on. But he'd taken it a step farther. He'd signed himself up to be her social director, too. He did enjoy spending time with her, though. And he was pretty sure Shadow had to be missing him by now. That was one cute cat! He enjoyed jostling Daphne out of her comfort zone, but his brother, Holden, would say that was due to his perverse nature. It was true. He did love a challenge.

Daphne was beautiful in a classy, understated way with her thick, wavy, light-brown hair, hazel eyes, and willowy figure. Tyne could understand why Chase had a thing for her a while back. Her skin glowed like fine porcelain.

Tyne removed the tossed greens from the refrigerator and added black olives, anchovies, and feta to the other ingredients for his Greek salad. Tonight, he'd added pickled beets for fun.

He frowned, his thoughts returning to Daphne. Maybe Paula was right. Maybe he was spending time with too many happy couples, and it was warping the way he viewed things. Normally, he wouldn't have even noticed Daphne. She was too subtle. But hell, everyone he spent time with in Mill Pond had already said their *I do's*. The only guy who still hung out with his buddies was Jason Baxter, and he was an idiot. He'd gotten Jodi pregnant, and they were living together, but Jason still acted like he was single.

"Maybe when Jodi has her baby, he'll change," Ian had said. "Holding your kid in your arms changes everything."

For Ian, sure. Ian couldn't wait until Drew was born. Ian was an upstanding family man. Tyne doubted fatherhood would affect Jason, but for Jodi's sake, he hoped the baby would make some difference. Tyne remembered when Ian had handed him Drew to hold. He'd tried to finagle a way out of it, but once that baby looked up at him, all serious and concentrating on his features, he'd felt a direct hit to his gut. And the kid wasn't even his.

Was he getting too settled in Mill Pond? Or had he reached a different stage of life? He'd passed thirty, and most people his age were married with kids. He'd focused on his career and traveling. They'd focused on meeting and settling down. He thought about starting a new restaurant. They thought about paying their mortgage and signing up their kids to be in sports.

The doors to the dining room opened and closed. The buffet groaned with food. Guests flooded to the square tables and lined up to fill their plates. Gratefully, Tyne pushed Daphne out of his mind. He needed to concentrate on his job.

But the night flew by, and it ended sooner than usual. When he locked the kitchen doors behind him, he wasn't ready to go home. A good book waited for him there, but he was too restless to concentrate. Someone had mentioned that there was a football game on TV. He couldn't miss that, so he jumped in his Jeep and drove to Chase's bar. Would it be different if he had someone waiting for him at home? Where had that thought come from? Ian couldn't wait to drive home to Tessa and Drew, though. Paula got antsy to see Chase, Aiden, and Bailey. Even Cody, a senior in high school, couldn't wait to hang up his dishtowel and drive to his girlfriend Lexy's house.

Tyne shook his head. Nope, not for him. He still had more mountains to climb, more things to achieve. When he walked into the bar, he started for an empty stool and then realized that Miriam sat, hunched over a drink, a dozen stools down. An aura of *stay the hell away from me* circled her. Well, that wouldn't do. He dropped down next to her.

She glowered at him in a sideways glare—almost eye-level, she was so tall. Her thin, pointy elbows rested on the bar, and her dark, corkscrew curls stood askew. Miriam must have repeatedly raked her hands through them. Her generous mouth turned down at the corners.

He had to give her credit. She had that schoolteacher thing going for her, could look more intimidating than most. Not enough to get rid of him, but it probably worked on the majority of people. He motioned to Chase for his favorite beer and turned to look at her. "Drinking away your sorrows, huh? If you need a ride home, you can count on me."

Another glare. "I know my limits."

"Which gin 'n tonic are you on?"

"Only my second, and I'm sipping." She nodded to Chase when he brought Tyne's beer. "Ask him. I'm not drowning myself in alcohol."

Chase leveled a look her way. "Something's eating at her, but she shooed me away when I offered a shoulder to cry on."

"Is that so?" Tyne got comfortable and settled in. "So what's the deal? Why are you here?"

She locked gazes with him. "If I'd have called Daphne, she'd have come to hold my hand, but she's at her parents' tonight, and I didn't want to bother her. I don't intend to spill my guts to anyone else."

An unsubtle clue for him to get lost. Except he wasn't going to. "Did your longtime, secret lover break up with you?"

She grunted. "You know better."

"We can play a round of twenty questions, or you can tell me. You look like you need a friend."

"You're not my friend."

"Yet. I can feel the bonds forming."

She closed her eyes. Her lips moved as if she were silently counting to ten. "You don't care about boundaries, do you?"

"Nope, you've got me there. I'm a man of few social graces, for sure, and I'm in no hurry. I can wait till you're ready to talk."

The words spilled out in a rush. "One of my students tried to kill herself today." She looked surprised at herself and took another sip of her drink.

He reached for his beer. Damn, that was heavier than he'd expected. "She's just a kid, right? How big can her problems be?"

Miriam rolled her eyes. He probably deserved that. He'd worked with teenagers in different kitchens, and he liked them, but other than that, he didn't know much about them. When he was that age, he'd been a real pill. He was lucky some teacher or adult hadn't murdered him before he reached twenty.

Miriam turned to face him. "*Everything's* blown out of proportion to teenagers. No one's felt pain like they do. No one suffers, laughs, excels like they do. Everything revolves around them, the good and the bad."

He frowned. "And they don't see anything as temporary? They haven't heard the words *This, too, shall pass*?"

Miriam drained the last of her gin and tonic, then motioned to Chase for a beer. "This girl was quiet, held everything in. I knew that, but I didn't see it coming. I didn't see how much she was suffering under the surface. I can usually tell."

Tyne gave a low whistle, impressed. "You must really pay attention to each student."

"I do. I usually see some clue, some change in behavior. Not this time." Her hand went through her curls again, making them stand on end. She could double for Medusa.

"If the girl was quiet and never got in trouble, what could be so bad she couldn't face it?" Teachers had threatened to flunk Tyne, not because he got Fs, but because he "didn't work up to his potential." How many times had he heard that? His parents had threatened to disown him on more than one occasion. But that was their problem, not his. "Was she pregnant?"

"Lord, no! She never fit in, didn't have any friends. The other kids teased her. Self-esteem's fragile at seventeen."

"Her parents should have taught her martial arts."

Miriam shook her head. "Not everyone's a fighter, like you. Someday, the kids who tormented her will read her name in the newspapers for some big achievement or award. She's a brain. Persistent and creative, but no one values that much in high school. She'll grow into herself."

"Since she'll live." Tyne took another draw on his beer. "She will live, right? No permanent damage?"

"She's going to be okay. Hopefully, she'll learn from this, grow stronger. If I have anything to do with it, this will be a wake-up call."

He studied Miriam. "You're one hell of a teacher."

"I like to think so." Her shoulders relaxed. She picked up her beer mug to clink it against Tyne's. "I feel better now. I'm talked out. Thanks."

"That's what friends do."

She snorted. "We're friends now?"

"Why not? What's not to like about me?"

She laughed. "You won't win any modesty contests. You know that, don't you?"

"Modesty's overrated. I don't believe in tooting your horn, but I don't believe in hiding your talents under a rock either."

She gave him a sharp look. "I like you."

"I like you, too. You okay now?"

She nodded. "You can't win 'em all. I do the best I can with what I've got."

They sat there, side by side, and watched the football game while they finished their beers. They made small talk between plays while Miriam drank two glasses of water and Tyne drained a second mug. "Are you safe to drive home?" he asked when Miriam pushed to her feet.

"I'm in good shape. You?"

"Ready to go home." Tyne motioned to Chase and paid for him and Miriam and then walked her to her car. "When are you going to go visit her?"

"Once she gets out of the hospital. She has good parents. She needs to know there are other people who care about her, too."

They parted on that note, and Tyne decided that Daphne had one hell of a good friend in Miriam. She had another one in him.

Chapter 18

Daphne glanced at the clock. Only three more minutes and she'd turn the sign on the door to Closed. It had been a slow day. Gray clouds brooded over Mill Pond since early morning. Cold rain pelted her storefront windows, making customers few and far between. She loved rainy days, loved holing up and losing herself in projects. She'd spent most of her time in the workroom, creating more inventory.

When the minute hand hit the twelve on the clock, she closed up shop. A few moments later, her phone buzzed. She glanced at the I.D. and smiled. "Hey, what's up?" Miriam's stories about her students usually entertained her. Not this time.

Miriam ended with, "Your friend, Tyne, didn't give up on me, didn't walk away. He sat there with me until I'd worked through the worst of it."

"I wish you'd have called me. I'm sorry I wasn't there."

"Your parents would have gotten squirrely. They're leaving soon, and if you'd have stood them up, your mom would have gotten shitty about it. She barely tolerates me, as is. Doesn't like my potty mouth. If I took you away from them, I'd have sunk even lower on her list."

Daphne couldn't argue. "I still wish I'd have been there when you needed me."

"Tyne stood in for you. You're lucky you have him. He doesn't back away."

"Not even when you tell him to." She admired that about him even when it frustrated her at times. "I'm glad he showed up." And she was, but somewhere deep inside it made her feel unsettled. Why?

"He matched up Maxwell and Steph, too, didn't he?"

"Yeah, he came through for both of them." He'd been in Mill Pond for less than a year, and he'd already connected with more people than she had after a lifetime here. What was wrong with her? People liked her, but she wasn't close to most of them. She came through for people when she could, but no one came to her with their problems except Miriam. And Miriam hadn't called last night. She hadn't wanted to displease Mom and Dad.

When Miriam hung up, saying she needed to scrounge for something to make for supper, Daphne sagged onto her work stool and brooded. She always told herself she liked being self-contained, but did she? Another thought niggled in the back of her mind. To Tyne, she was just another friend who needed a boost, but would he grow impatient with her over time? She'd never be as adventurous as he was, as outgoing. She'd bore him sooner rather than later.

She shook her thoughts away and went to grab her raincoat. If she was late picking up her parents, she'd hear about it. They often ate at Chase's on Thursdays, and since her mother was trying to empty the refrigerator before they left on their trip, this was a perfect night for it. There wasn't much food in the house.

"We might have to eat out every night before we leave," Dad said on the short ride to the bar.

Mom gave Daphne a sheepish smile. "I can buy enough to fix suppers for you before we leave, though, dear."

Daphne shook her head. "No need to. We'll eat out and enjoy each other's company before you go. I vote for pizza tomorrow night."

"We'll treat you to dinner at Ralph's diner on Saturday," Dad said.

Daphne got into the spirit of near-vacation time. "What if I cook something and have you come to my place on Sunday?" She could tell by the deafening silence that she'd made a mistake. Her mother didn't like it when she tried to cook. Not that it took much to discourage her. She'd rather do crafts than spend time in the kitchen, but still, she hurried to remedy it. "I'll throw hot dogs on the grill and buy sides at the deli."

Her mother nodded. "Buy the hot dogs with no nitrates and preservatives. The store has them now. And no buns."

And no chili sauce or cheese. What was the use of having a hot dog if it was that damn healthy? Daphne bit her lip. Had she really thought that? She gave a bright smile. "This will be fun. You can meet my cat before you leave Mill Pond."

Her mother stiffened. "I'm allergic. You know that. We'll have to make other plans."

Daphne sighed. "I could lock Shadow in my bedroom."

"There'd still be fur everywhere. It's out of the question." Her mother smiled. "We'll grill. You bring the deli to our house."

Not the same, but Daphne gave in gracefully. She sometimes wondered if her mother was really allergic or if she simply hated pets. Everyone had their quirks, she reminded herself. When they reached the bar, the rain came down harder. Daphne pulled up the hood on her raincoat, and her dad opened his umbrella for him and Mom.

Autumn rain didn't have the joy of its spring counterpoint. It served as a foreboding for worse weather to come. When they walked inside the bar, warmth greeted them. There were more empty tables than usual, and Daphne saw Paula sitting at a table by herself. She waved them over.

Mom tried to hide a grimace. She didn't approve of Paula's small eyebrow ring and the stud in her cheek. She glanced away from her tattoos.

But Paula was all smiles and cheerfulness. "Hi! I hear there's a trip in your near future."

Mom's eyebrows shot up, surprised. "Where did you hear that?"

"Tyne told us. He said you're going to Carolina."

The eyebrows furrowed into a frown. "Really?" She shot a dirty look at Daphne.

Daphne hung her raincoat on a nearby peg and held up her hands in surrender. "He asked me about meeting him for supper next week, and I said I could because you'd be out of town."

Her mother didn't look happy. Her dad looked downright nervous.

Daphne shrugged. "I didn't know your trip was a secret."

"It's not." Mom left it at that.

Paula looked back and forth between them, confused. "What's wrong with having Tyne feed your daughter? He's one hell of a cook."

"We've heard." Mom's tone could form glaciers.

Louise Draper came to take their orders. Paula already had a hamburger, and they each ordered one, too. Of course, Mom and Dad ordered theirs plain, no bun.

When Louise left, Daphne decided it was a good time to change the subject. She turned to Paula. "Tyne's brother is a chef, too, isn't he?"

When Paula's lips twitched, Daphne knew she'd recognized her dodge tactic. But Daphne had to give her credit. She answered quickly, "Holden's won lots of awards. Of course, that's what his parents expected. They always thought Holden would do well. He was a straight-A student and excelled at culinary school. They never expected much out of Tyne."

Daphne could feel heat rush through her veins. "Why not? It's hard to miss his talent." Her voice held more of an edge than she expected. Her mother narrowed her eyes.

Paula glanced at the bar where Chase was taking someone's order. "Tyne does things his own way, like Chase. Neither of them care if they impress anyone or not, and *that* didn't impress Tyne's parents. They're big into status."

Daphne fiddled with the paper napkin on her lap. What was wrong with Tyne's parents? How could they miss how wonderful he was? She'd have never guessed Tyne had any challenges in his life. He seemed so sure of himself, so successful. She'd assumed everyone encouraged him, like her parents encouraged her.

When no one said anything, Paula went on. "Tyne came to Mill Pond to get experience, so that he can open his own restaurant someday."

Mom breathed a sigh of relief. "So he doesn't plan on staying here?"

Louise returned with their drinks—water with lemon for Mom and Dad, wine for Daphne.

Daphne gulped down disappointment. Most people moved to Mill Pond and never left. They fell in love with the area. But Tyne wasn't like most people. Her heart lurched, surprising her. She didn't want Tyne to leave. She realized she'd liked him from the moment they met, when he wanted to rent the apartment above her shop. It was an instant click. She often found herself watching for him on the nature trail that wound behind her cabin. Not because she had a crush on him or anything. He was just fun to be around. He was a good person. A friend.

Paula didn't sound too concerned about losing Tyne. "He plans on staying a year or two, but you know how that goes. Mill Pond is a great place to live. It'll be harder for him to leave us than he thinks."

Mom grimaced, and Paula gave her an odd look. Daphne tried to think of a new topic to change the conversation again when Chase came to sit with them.

Paula looked at him and said, "What's wrong?"

"Steph just called. She can't make it to the inn tomorrow morning. She'll have to make all of the bread for Maxwell. He just rushed India to the emergency room, and the docs are keeping her for some tests."

Paula chewed on her bottom lip. "She hasn't been doing well lately."

"She smokes too much." Daphne's mom sounded judgmental, and everyone stared at her. She shrugged. "What can you expect when you have as many bad habits as she does?"

"Mom!" Daphne couldn't believe her mom didn't have a little sympathy for India. "I still feel sorry for her and Maxwell."

"It's a waste of time." Her mom's lips pinched together before she went on. "People with genetic diseases deserve sympathy. They didn't do anything wrong, and they're being punished anyway. But people who know better and don't care? They brought their problems on themselves."

Daphne blinked. Her mother had always been opinionated, but she was growing less tolerant the older she got. She wondered why. She was more conservative and fearful, too. Daphne sighed. Mom had been more fun when she was less rigid. Was *my way or the highway* part of aging? Then Daphne thought of Grams. Nope, attitude was a life choice, too, just as much as habits.

A group of people walked into the bar and Chase had to leave the table. A man Dad worked with came in with his wife, and Dad waved hello to them. The man smiled as if he'd like Dad to stop by his table and say *hi*, but Dad glanced at Daphne, torn.

"Go on," Daphne said. "You have a minute before our food gets here."

When Mom and Dad left to greet Dad's friend, Daphne studied Paula with a thoughtful expression.

Paula quirked an eyebrow. "Just ask. It's better to be direct."

Daphne built up her courage and blurted, "Was Chase ever interested in me?"

Paula laughed. "He doted on you, had a crush a mile wide. If anyone said anything derogatory about you, Lord help them."

Daphne felt dazed. She shook her head, surprised. "I never realized."

"And I thank you for that." Paula smiled. "When you didn't give him any encouragement—nada, nothing—he turned his attention to me. A man can't live on fantasies."

"I was such an idiot, fawning over Patrick like I did."

"Hey, I thought I wanted Jason Baxter, and I couldn't think of a thing to do to make him notice me."

"That's a good thing. He's stupid and petty." Daphne's eyes grew round and she put a hand over her mouth. "I can't believe I said that."

Paula leaned closer to her. "Why shouldn't you? You're right. If everyone said what they think, there'd be a lot less misunderstandings in the world."

"I don't want to sound like my mom." This time, heat soared up Daphne's throat and face, she was so embarrassed. "I don't know what's gotten into me. Things are just popping out of my mouth."

Paula studied her, amused. "That's what Tyne does."

Daphne nodded. "There's no guessing with him. If he likes you, you know it. If he doesn't, you know that, too. You always know where he stands on things."

"He says what he thinks."

Daphne pursed her lips, trying to sort the conflicting thoughts buzzing in her head. "I don't want to mess up again. How can you tell if you're interested in the right guy?"

Paula thought a minute, then shook her head in defeat. "Damned if I know. Like I said, I set my sights on Jason Baxter."

Louise came with their food, and Daphne's parents returned to the table. Paula glanced at her watch and said, "It's time to pick up my kids. Gotta go." She looked at Daphne. "It was great talking to you."

Daphne smiled. She'd enjoyed it, too.

Her mother's scowl returned, and Daphne asked them about the historical sites they meant to visit in Carolina. The talk turned to general subjects while they enjoyed their supper.

Chapter 19

Friday nights were low-key, and that was a relief. It was one supper that Tyne didn't have to fuss over. He'd gone to visit India at the hospital this afternoon. She was in good spirits, but Maxwell was a mess. Seeing Maxwell's distress had thrown Tyne off. He was glad he didn't have to concentrate tonight.

He took the prime rib and salmon out of the oven. Guests looked forward to them. They didn't care what version of salmon Tyne chose, as long as it was on the buffet. Tonight, he made baked potatoes and red beans and rice as accompaniments. He added a caramelized apple salad with blue cheese and walnuts and a huge tossed salad for variety. Guests could pick and choose.

Cody helped him carry food to the buffet before he started rinsing the pans and bowls used for food prep.

"Your truck sounded rough when you pulled in," Tyne told him.

"My muffler's falling off. I can't afford a new one for a few more weeks."

"We can wire it in place."

Cody scrunched his nose. "I can't. Don't know how."

"If you can stay after work for a while, I can do it for you."

Cody looked relieved. "You already helped me with the spark plugs."

"That's how you learn. You watch someone tinker."

At six sharp, the guests filed into the dining room and things got busy. People lingered over their meals longer than usual since the weather wasn't conducive for leaving the inn. Ian's wife, Tessa, had supplied coconut cakes and chocolate fudge pies with a praline crumble for dessert. When guests finished those, they wandered into the large lobby where urns kept water hot for instant hot chocolate or tea, and bags of microwave popcorn were fanned out for late-evening snacks. Ian did everything possible to make his guests' stay pleasurable when the weather turned bad.

Some people settled in the comfortable seating areas with books or magazines. Others grabbed snacks and headed to their rooms to rent a movie or watch sports on their large screen TVs. Some reached for their partners' hands and obviously had other things in mind.

Tyne and Cody worked with the kitchen crew to finish cleaning up, then headed outside to work on Cody's truck. "Pull it under the portico, out of the rain," Tyne told him.

Ian's brother, Brody, had built a roof for Jason to pull under when he delivered supplies to the inn. The space wasn't heated, but it was dry. Tyne changed into his jeans and a long-sleeved T-shirt before skootching under the vehicle to work on the muffler. The cement felt cool and damp, even with a tarp on the ground that he kept in his Jeep. He got situated, then called, "You can hand me the wire now."

Cody bent to place the heavy wire and a pair of pliers in Tyne's hand and watched as Tyne started securing the muffler in place. He was concentrating on what he was doing, so when someone wrapped a hand around his privates and squeezed, he jerked with surprise. His forehead banged the metal pipe, and it hurt.

"Damn it all to hell, what are you playing at?" He slid out from under the truck, rubbing his head, and blinked at Chantelle.

She wore skintight jeans, a low-cut sweater, and a seductive smile. "Did you hurt yourself? You smeared dirt on your forehead when you rubbed it. Here, let me help you." She bent so low, he thought her boobs might pop out of their moorings, and great boobs they were. She brandished a handkerchief to dab at the dirt.

He wiped at it with his sleeve. "I'll live."

Her gaze lowered to his crotch. "Sorry, I couldn't resist."

Lots of women couldn't, but Tyne had his limits. "I don't walk up and grab your ass or rub your tits," he snapped.

Her smile widened. "You could."

"It'll never happen, so don't do that again."

Cody rolled back and forth from the balls of his feet to his heels. He looked like he'd run if someone lunged for him. "Are you all right?" he asked Tyne.

"I'm gonna have a bruise, that's for sure." Tyne raised an eyebrow at Chantelle. "What are you here for?" He knew better than to say *What do you want?*

She pouted. "You get off work early on Fridays. I thought you could take me to Chase's and we could dance."

"Can't. I promised Cody I'd help him work on his truck."

"I never see you at Chase's." Her dark eyes sparkled with curiosity. "Where do you usually go?"

He almost said *none of your business*, but she was Leona's cousin, and Garth and Leona were together now. He considered Garth a friend, so he decided to keep things polite. "I like to switch things up every week and surprise myself."

A lie. He usually headed to Harley's winery and hung out with him behind the bar. That way, women couldn't bother him. Tyne had a bartending license, so in a pinch, he could even help out with the wine tastings.

"Have you ever gone to Chase's on the weekends?" Chantelle had pulled her long, auburn hair up, so that loose curls fell at random. The girl was all dressed up and ready for action.

"Only once." He'd barely made it out alive. He loved to dance, but when he got on the dance floor, women circled him and mimicked his moves. They didn't let him leave until the band stopped for a break. When Daphne had been his partner at Harley's, though, women had left him alone. There was something classy enough about her, they felt cheap making moves on him when he was with her. All but Chantelle, of course. The girl had no shame.

"When you finish here tonight, where are you going?"

"Haven't decided yet." She gave him a poison look that he returned with one of his smiles. "This is going to take us some time. You might as well take off and have a nice night."

He turned his back on her to talk to Cody. She took the hint and left.

Cody stared at him. "Does that happen to you all the time?"

Tyne laughed. "Not *that*, in particular, but don't fool yourself. Size *does* matter, and Chantelle's been wanting to do that for a long time."

Cody blushed. "My girlfriend doesn't care about things like that."

Tyne snorted. "That just means she's not disappointed."

Cody's gaze drifted downward and Tyne's grin broadened. "I don't disappoint either, but Chantelle's never going to find out."

Chapter 20

The rain had stopped, but it was a gray, gloomy day. Daphne kept glancing out the back windows of her house on Saturday morning. She'd made a fresh pot of coffee and set out clean mugs. She'd put out the toaster and a loaf of raisin bread. Leaves blazed with color. She almost liked the vivid hues better against the moody background, a contrast to the sunny days they'd had for most of the month. Usually, she'd gaze in awe at nature's beauty, but today wasn't one of those moments. Where was he? Had he decided to hike deeper in the forest today? Maybe it was too dreary for him to tramp the trails. But finally, she spotted Tyne on the path that ran behind her property. Just as he approached her yard, she whipped on a sweater and stepped outside, leading Shadow on a leash.

Tyne glanced over and waved, then came to see the kitten. "Well, look at you." He opened the back gate and came to join them, frowning at the leash.

"I'm trying to teach him the yard's boundaries, so I can let him outside and not worry about him jumping the fence when he's bigger."

"And the leash is working?"

A bug flew past them and landed on her picket fence. The cat crouched to spring on it. Shadow leapt, and the leash jerked him back. Then he fussed and howled. Daphne sighed. "Not so well. It's going to be a process." She bent and released the clasp so that Shadow could run off. Right now, he couldn't escape the fence, but she knew that time would come.

When the bug flew away, Shadow scampered back to check out Tyne. Tyne scooped him up and rubbed under his chin. "You've grown since the last time I saw you."

The cat's body went limp and he started purring.

Daphne smiled. How cute was her pet? "It's not safe for him to go into the forest, but he doesn't want to stay in the house. Maybe if I got a privacy fence?"

"That would ruin your view. You couldn't see outside your yard."

"Then I need to train him. There are too many coyotes around here, and I heard an owl last night." Daphne tilted her head, feigning surprise at seeing him. "I thought you'd hike deeper in the forest to see more leaves."

He gestured to the maples that bordered her yard. "Nothing beats the reds and yellows of these."

Shadow squirmed to get down to explore the yard. He pounced on every leaf that blew by. They stood, watching him, while Daphne admired how good Tyne looked in low-riding, shabby jeans and a thermal shirt. He wore an open, lightweight jacket, too.

"I got warm hiking," he explained. "It's cool, but once you start moving, it's comfortable enough."

She shivered. She'd tossed on a cardigan, but she should have worn her heavier sweater. "I made coffee. Want some?"

They walked to the house together. When he stepped inside, he noticed the open door to her sewing room and the new quilt she was working on. "Do you mind?"

She nodded for him to go look. He was still admiring it when she brought him a mug of black coffee. That's how he liked it. No frills. "It's for the community center," she told him.

"A tree." He read the names on each branch that tilted off the trunk—families who lived in the area. Each leaf was a name of one of the family members. "Do you plan on listing every single person who lives in Mill Pond?"

"No, just prominent people." They bumped shoulders as she explained how she tried to match the fabric of each leaf to something about the family it represented. "Milk cans are on the fabric for the Evans family." They made cheeses. Ducks waddled across bright swaths of material for the Danzas' farm. "And boats are on Chase's because he loves being on the lake." There were cupcakes on the bright fabrics for Ian and Tessa's leaves. Grams's had little, steepled churches.

Tyne bent to study some of the leaves she'd cut, but hadn't sewn in place yet. He shook his head. "I'm impressed."

When she glanced up at him, she realized how close they were to each other. Lips barely inches apart. Their gazes locked, and Daphne had never wanted a man to kiss her so badly. She ached with the need. He smelled of fresh air and musk. Of maleness. His gaze went to her lips, lingered there, then he turned away.

No, no, no! What had Paula told her? That a man can't survive without encouragement. But what was she supposed to do? Purse her lips? Smile more? The moment had passed. She settled on, "I was going to make some eggs for myself. Are you hungry?"

His shoulders relaxed. Kitchens and food were his comfort zone. "Starving, I'll take mine over easy."

She stared. She'd never made those before, only scrambled. But how hard could they be? You broke eggs in a pan and turned them over, right?

She led him into the kitchen and poured him another mug of coffee. He fiddled with bread and the toaster while she started the eggs. She broke them into the pan and watched them cook. How dark did you let the edges get? Maybe dark meant they were burned. She got nervous and flipped them. Yolks ran. She gave a disappointed sound.

Tyne came up behind her. He chuckled. "These aren't so easy. Let me show you."

She dumped the eggs onto a paper plate for Shadow, and then Tyne showed her what to do, talked her through it. She was unjustifiably proud of herself when she slid them onto his plate. Then she quickly made her own.

"I'll have to fix eggs for you sometime," he said. "You won't believe how good they are with truffle butter."

She frowned. "Eggs and chocolate?"

His crooked grin told her he was amused. "There *are* chocolate truffles, but I'm talking about the fungus variety. You can buy butter with truffles blended into it."

They sat at the small kitchen table to eat their late breakfast. Tyne was easy to talk to—asked questions and seemed interested in her answers. She found herself jabbering about the different stained-glass and quilt patterns she designed for each season. She finally bit her bottom lip and said, "I haven't shut up. You haven't had a chance to talk."

"I've enjoyed listening to you. You're usually so private."

She frowned. "Am I?"

"You can be."

"Well, enough about me. So you're interested in owning your own restaurant someday. Do you have anything particular in mind?"

He told her about his travels, the countries he'd visited, the cuisines he'd tried. "You know I like to do a lot of fusion cooking, combine the elements of the best of each place. Ian's letting me experiment at the inn. I have a lot of freedom there."

She was surprised, later, when she glanced at the clock: Two hours had sped by. He seemed surprised, too.

"I've got to go. I want to finish my hike before my shift starts. Your parents are still here tomorrow, right?"

She nodded. Why hadn't they left a day sooner? That way, she'd have Tyne to herself after he finished brunch at the inn on Sunday.

I'd rather have supper with Tyne. She scolded herself for the thought. What had gotten into her lately? She wasn't sure, but she'd better figure out a way to distract herself, or she'd moon about Tyne most of the day tomorrow. She decided to call Miriam and spend the day with her. Miriam could distract anyone when she took off on a subject. Any subject would do.

Daphne walked Tyne to the door and waved him good-bye. It was pretty clear how things were between them. She couldn't even compete with a nature trail. He'd rather see colored leaves than spend time with her. She couldn't blame him. She wasn't all that exciting, was she?

Chapter 21

Neither of them could cook their way out of a burlap bag. Kitchens weren't their strong point. Miriam read the directions for the pasta sauce again. "It's supposed to be a white sauce," she said. "Why is ours brown?"

Daphne's stomach growled. "I don't care what color it is. I'm starving."

"How long are we supposed to cook the fettucine?"

Daphne read the instructions on the side of the box. "I think the water's supposed to be boiling by now."

Miriam glanced at the burner under the pot and sighed. "I forgot and turned the heat off."

"What use is having an Aga cooker if you don't know how to use it?"

"I didn't buy it to cook. I bought it because it's pretty. It suits my cabin."

Daphne scooped out strands of firm pasta. They stuck together. "Want to eat some ice cream? I saw some in the freezer. I'll help you clean up later."

"Will that be enough for lunch?" Miriam rummaged in her cupboards and shook her head. "No more pasta anyway."

Daphne shrugged. "I'm eating supper with my parents tonight. I'll buy more deli sides and fill up."

They dug out scoops of Neapolitan, drizzled chocolate sauce over them, and settled in front of the living room's fireplace for their lunch. The white walls and dark beams reminded Daphne of an old English tavern. All she needed was a tankard of ale. When Miriam had scrounged in the cupboards, she found half a bag of stale Oreo cookies she'd hidden so that she'd stop eating them. They dipped those in their ice cream.

"What are you teaching now?" Daphne asked. She knew from experience that Miriam concentrated on different subjects every three or four weeks.

Miriam rolled her eyes. "We're reading *Romeo and Juliet*. It should be against the law to let high school students read Shakespeare out loud. They butcher iambic pentameter."

Daphne laughed. "I'm surprised you still teach that. I thought you'd go for modern literature now to hold the kids' interest."

"What do you suggest? *The Hunger Games*?"

"I wouldn't have a clue. I'm not up on YA novels and authors."

Miriam tipped her bowl to drain the last of its contents. "It doesn't hurt kids to know a few of the classics. I personally think they'd like *Macbeth* with its witches and murder better than romantic agonizing, but no one asked my opinion."

Daphne wrinkled her nose. "Romances are a bunch of sappy lies."

Miriam barked a laugh. "You? Who rereads *Pride and Prejudice* every few years and still has a crush on Mr. Darcy?"

"I read that for the mannerisms and social norms of the times."

"Sure you do." Miriam carried her bowl to the kitchen and Daphne followed with hers. "Do I take it you've given up on the male species altogether?"

"The species is fine, but finding romance is a bunch of hooey."

Miriam turned to study her face. "Is this about the professor?"

Daphne made a rude noise. "Patrick? He wouldn't know romance if it bit him on the ass. Romance implies you care about someone other than yourself."

Miriam stared, then burst out laughing. "Patrick's more a Wickham than a Darcy."

Daphne shrugged. "He's not even that interesting. Wickham has him beat."

"What's gotten into you today? Whatever it is, I want to order more of it. You've never been this catty. Maybe Shadow's rubbing off on you."

Daphne thought of her kitten and grinned. "Shadow *is* naughty."

"So are you today. But we started out talking about romance. What male has earned this much ire?"

Daphne made a face. "I thought for one second that Tyne might kiss me yesterday, but he didn't."

Miriam's blue eyes sparkled with curiosity. "You wanted him to?"

"I could hardly stand not puckering up and planting one on him."

"Oh, my lord!" Miriam went to the refrigerator to pour them each a glass of wine. "This was supposed to go with our pasta, but it pairs great with ice cream, too. And gossip."

Daphne took a sip and gave an appreciative nod. "Tyne looked really good yesterday."

"When doesn't he?" Miriam led them back to the sitting room, and they settled once again in the chairs close to the fireplace.

Daphne frowned and shook her head. "You can't make that man look bad."

"So what happened? Why didn't he follow through?"

"He wanted to finish his hike more than he wanted to make out with me. I have zero sex appeal, Miriam. Nada."

"You have it. You just hide it." Miriam glanced down at her long, thin body. "At least, you're feminine. Men look at me and run."

"Then they're not all that smart, because you'd make them laugh all through life."

"Yeah, what every man wants, to marry a comedienne."

Daphne's gaze went to the flames flickering in the fireplace. "I don't know what men want, but I don't seem to have it."

"To hell with men!" Miriam raised her wine glass in a toast. "To true friendship. You and I will never settle for less."

Daphne toasted to that. Never again. She'd gotten lucky when Patrick ditched her. She wouldn't dodge that particular bullet again. She'd be smarter.

Chapter 22

Tyne cranked up the radio on his way to the inn on Sunday morning. "Old Time Rock 'n Roll" blasted inside the Jeep. The early shifts on Sundays and Mondays were always an adjustment after working nights the rest of the week, but they meant he had two evenings free. He rolled his window down a crack, letting the cool air hit him. *Get yourself in gear, man.* He needed a pep talk. There was something about gray skies that made him want to linger in bed.

Sunday brunch was a big deal. Both he and Paula were there. He always started the huge ham in the morning. Then they worked together on the waffle batter and toppings. Steph took charge of the lemon crepes with blueberry sauce, and Tyne moved on to the potato pancakes with smoked trout while Paula made the fruit salad and fillings for the omelet station.

Guests always left happy. Ian swore the inn offered the best brunch for a hundred-mile radius, and as easygoing as Ian was, he took the inn very seriously. Had to. It was his baby, wasn't it? Best brunch, though? Tyne didn't know about that. How close was Indy? Their small staff couldn't compete with the big hotels and restaurants, couldn't even sneeze at the country clubs. But guests came here for the laid-back atmosphere. They wanted great food, but they didn't expect full menus. The dining room stayed open from eleven to one, and the guests lingered until he and Paula started cleaning up the buffet. A good sign that they'd enjoyed themselves.

After cleanup, Paula took off to spend time with Chase and her kids before she came back for the supper shift. Tyne didn't grump that he and Steph had to stay to start on his part of the supper buffet. As far as he was concerned, working split shifts was the worst. He'd done it before, but it felt like all you did was work with a small break in the middle of your day.

For supper tonight, he and Steph whipped up fifty wine-braised short ribs to serve over mascarpone polenta. Paula was going for an Italian theme, and the short ribs would blend with the veal parmesan she was serving. The kitchen smelled of sautéed onions and garlic, oregano and red wine. Even if you'd just eaten, the aromas would make your mouth water.

Gladys, who came in early on Sundays to work the front desk, stuck her head inside and asked, "What is that? You're killing me out here." She handed Tyne her empty plate from the sample of brunch items he'd dished up for her.

"Short ribs. They won't be tender for another few hours. They're a low-and-slow type food."

She patted her stomach. "I can wait. Everything on that plate was delicious."

Tyne rinsed the plate and added it to the stack to get washed. When their entrée was finished, he and Steph high-fived each other and headed for the door.

"What are you up today?" he asked on their way out.

She wiggled her eyebrows. "Ben's waiting for me at home."

"What? No family get-together?"

Steph gave him a look. "I love Ben's family. You know I do, but his mom's sick right now. Caught the flu from one of the grandkids. No one wants to risk hanging out at their place."

Tyne could understand that. He'd watched whole families tumble down like dominoes when kids' germs struck. He raised an eyebrow at Steph. "Hope you put something in the slow cooker. You're going to be too weak to cook tonight."

She laughed. "I made a big pot of stew yesterday to heat up."

"Smart girl."

"You?"

"I'm hanging out with Harley and Kathy at the winery. Harley and I are going to tinker on his motorcycle together."

She wrinkled her nose. "My afternoon sounds like more fun."

He thought about that on the drive to his apartment. He remembered a small town in South America that completely shut down every Sabbath. He and a female bartender who worked in the same café used to spend most of their Sundays in bed. She was going to marry a man much older than she was in a few months, and she told Tyne that she wanted to enjoy every pleasure she could before she said her vows and became a dutiful wife to Eduardo.

"Does Eduardo know?" Tyne had asked.

"Yes, we have no secrets. He gave me this time for myself before I devote my life to him."

The trade-off had amazed Tyne. He'd balked at first, but then he'd come to terms with it. Eduardo understood the needs of his younger soon-to-be wife, and she respected him for that. Tyne's mind drifted from those pleasant memories to seeing Daphne yesterday. When she'd been so close, almost within reach, he'd wanted to kiss her. *Really* wanted to kiss her, but that wouldn't be fair. She trusted him, and unlike his former lover she was the type who played for keeps. He wasn't. He'd moved on from South America, traveling to Thailand. He preferred monogamy more than meaningless affairs, but only if it was temporary. The last thing Daphne needed was another hit-and-run. The prof had done enough collateral damage.

Her parents were leaving tomorrow. What would she do while they were gone? He'd invited her to the inn for supper a couple nights during the week, but what would she do for supper the rest of the time? Did Miriam cook? Somehow he didn't think so. Maybe they'd go out to eat together. But he'd laid claims on Daphne tomorrow night. He grinned. It was time to push her a little farther, to try something else outside her comfort zone. But he had to be careful. Daphne would be easy to fall for. And he was no good at longevity.

He was almost home when Steph called. "Sorry to bother you, but I checked in with Maxwell, and India's taken a turn for the worse. He's a mess. Could you maybe help me at the bakery today?"

Tyne frowned. "It's closed on Sundays, isn't it?"

"Exactly, but I thought maybe you and I could make some dough ahead, in case Maxwell can't leave India for some reason. I thought we could give him a little breathing space." She sounded disappointed. Why wouldn't she be? Ben and she finally had the chance to find out what "Afternoon Delight" could really be.

Damn. Once he thought the words, the song stuck in his mind. What would it be like to spend an afternoon, alone, with Daphne in his bed? He pushed the thought away. *Don't go there*, he warned himself.

"I'm on my way," he told Steph. The bakery was just down the street from Daphne's stained-glass shop. He pulled to the curb and went to the side door. The minute he stepped inside the shop, Chester started barking.

"The poor dog's been on his own a lot lately," Steph said.

Tyne nodded. Chester was usually either with India or Maxwell. He had to be frantic by now. "I'll go get him and put him in the fenced yard. We can watch him out the back window."

When Tyne opened the door to Maxwell and India's apartment, Chester practically wagged his entire body, he was so glad to see him. "Come on, buddy. Bet you could use some time outside." He scooped up the dog and carried him to the backyard. The dog ran in circles, he was so happy. Once he'd settled, Tyne returned to Steph in the kitchen.

She smiled, watching the Chihuahua run the perimeter of the small yard. "That dog needed to see a friendly face."

They got busy, mixing the doughs that Maxwell made the most. While Tyne's challah and Tuscan doughs rose, he started making the tea breads that Maxwell needed for the week. He could bake those and freeze them. They froze well.

One batch of bread led to another, and by the time they'd made enough to make Steph feel like she could handle the bakery on her own, if she had to, it was later than either of them had expected. Chester had stayed outdoors the entire time, but when evening approached, he started barking. Tyne and Steph finished cleaning up, and Tyne went to retrieve the dog.

Steph gave Tyne a hug on her way out the door. "Thanks. You've saved my ass again."

He waved her away. She'd do the same for him.

Chester stopped barking, and Tyne went to see what was up. He found Chester, tail swishing faster than his Jeep's windshield wipers in a blizzard, sitting on Sadie Deerling's lap. Sadie owned the home-made custard and sorbet shop next to Maxwell's bakery. A bit on the pudgy side, Sadie was a walking advertisement of how good her tempting treats were. As usual, she wore her black-framed reading glasses on top of her head, in case she needed them later. The woman was an eclectic hodgepodge of sartorial influences. She had a thing for ruffles and was wearing a ruffled, polka-dot blouse and pink, ruffled anklet stockings with her sandals. Neither quite went with her jeans.

Tyne bent to pet the top of Chester's head. "Looks like he needed a woman's touch. He misses India."

Sadie nodded. "Tell Maxwell I'd be happy to let him hang out with me when he's at the hospital. I have a sitting room behind part of my shop. I could put a safety gate across the door so that Chester can see me while I'm working, but he can't get in the business area."

A good idea, if Chester didn't bark at every person who walked through the shop's front door. "He's a noisy little thing," Tyne said.

Sadie shrugged. "He'll learn. If I close the door every time he barks, he'll stop in time."

Tyne doubted that. Barking seemed to be in the dog's DNA, but at least when the shop wasn't busy he could spend time with Sadie.

Sadie read his thoughts. "I'm not as busy once the weather turns bad. I'll be able to spend some time with him."

Tyne reached for the dog, but Sadie said, "Why don't you leave him with me until Maxwell gets home tonight? He can fetch him from my place."

"Let me run that past Maxwell first. I don't want to upset him when I'm trying to help out." He called Maxwell's cell, explained the situation, and Maxwell sounded relieved.

"Give Sadie my thanks. Poor Chester doesn't understand why we left him on his own."

When Tyne conveyed the news, Sadie smiled, grabbed Chester, and took off with him. She seemed too happy, too eager. Why didn't she buy a pet of her own? She'd looked lonely. Tyne locked up the bakery and then headed home. He'd had a long day, and he worked the early shift on Monday. He grabbed the book he was reading, took it into his bedroom, but fell asleep before he finished a full chapter. His last thought as he dozed off was that Daphne was his tomorrow night, and he had plans for her.

Chapter 23

Daphne looked up from making change for her last customer when Tyne walked in the shop, glanced at the clock, and turned the sign in the door to CLOSED. The woman—in her late fifties—closed her purse and sighed. She winked at Daphne. "For him, I'd have closed early."

Tyne smirked and gave the woman a small bow. She practically glowed as she walked to her car.

Daphne had to admit that Tyne looked downright yummy in his black leather jacket with his dirty-blond hair tousled and his cheeks pink. Wait a minute. She narrowed her eyes. Pink cheeks. She glanced out the front window and put a hand to her throat. "I don't like motorcycles."

"You haven't tried one. If we don't do it now, we might not be able to. It's getting too cold."

"I'm fine with that."

He grumbled. "Would you never swim in the ocean because there are sharks?"

"There are stingrays, too. And barracuda. That's why we only go in the shallow water."

"We? Meaning your parents and you?"

She scowled. "Big things live in the ocean, things that can *eat* you."

"When I went scuba diving, sharks swam past me. People jump off boats and play in the deep water."

She shook her head. "Too risky. I value my life more than that."

He tried a different approach, but she was already expecting his next argument. "More people get hit by lightning than bitten by sharks."

"They shouldn't be outside in a storm. Why take chances? Why be the highest point when lightning bounces around you?"

Tyne set his shoulders. He looked serious. "You can't live in fear all the time. I'll take you on back roads and won't go full throttle. So grow some balls, pull up your big-girl panties, and get on my damned bike."

She knew he wasn't patient, but she didn't know he could be a bit autocratic. "And if I don't want to?"

"I'll go to the five-and-dime and buy us both tricycles. We can explore the world on those."

"There's no need for sarcasm." She bit her bottom lip. "You promise to go slow and stay on back roads?"

His grin returned. He knew he'd won. "Wear something warm. It's nippy outside."

"I only brought my jacket."

"Then I'll follow you to your place, and you can get your coat."

She liked that idea. Her cabin was on the border of the national forest. The roads wouldn't be busy this time of day, so they wouldn't have to fight traffic. She nodded and hurried to her yellow SUV. Tyne still assumed that she'd bought it because she liked bright colors. He didn't know that her father had advised her that it was a smart safety precaution, and she wasn't going to tell him.

He waited outside while she fed Shadow, changed into a sweater, and topped that with a wool coat. She pulled on a wool cap and gloves, too. Then she went out to climb on the back of his bike. He handed her a helmet.

The minute he pulled out of the driveway, she knew she was going to like this ride. She had to wrap her arms tightly around Tyne's torso to keep her balance. She pressed herself right up against him and held on for dear life. Hanging onto Tyne was a danger in itself, but its joy factor outweighed the risks.

True to his word, he drove at a moderate speed, and soon she felt herself relaxing. The roar of the engine, the fresh air, and gorgeous scenery mesmerized her. Before she knew it, they'd looped around the main road, driven into town and bought two steaks, and returned to her cabin.

When Tyne parked, he pointed toward her flower beds with their mounds of pulled plants dying between them. "Looks like you worked hard this weekend."

"I need to clean the beds before winter."

"Need some help? I love gardening. We have half an hour while the steaks marinate."

Her stomach grumbled, but she ignored it. "Sure, why not?"

They let Shadow outside to play while they worked, and she was amazed how much they got done in thirty minutes. His bed cleared, he carried the steaks outside to cook on the grill and tossed zucchini and onions in a metal basket to cook beside them.

"You know, you should let me build you some raised beds for vegetables and herbs. You have plenty of room for them, a big enough yard."

She darted him a look. "That would imply that I'd pick and cook them."

He laughed. "I'll still be in Mill Pond next year. I'll come over and show you the ropes."

She nodded. Having Tyne goofing off in her backyard was something she could live with.

They had a late supper. The steaks were the best she'd ever had. She had no idea what Tyne had seasoned them with, but they were wonderful. So were the vegetables. The sun was sinking, and the air was growing colder. Tyne went inside and carried the throw blankets she kept on the back of the couches outside. He draped one over her legs, and the other over his. They sat and watched the moon and stars appear until the dropping temperatures chased them inside.

Tyne went to the stove and made popcorn and hot chocolate. Both delicious. She had a feeling everything he made was a wonder. As they sat in her living room, their chairs turned to the back windows for the view, she asked, "What are some of your best memories from your travels?"

He hesitated. It was as if he meant to say something then changed his mind. He settled on: "I met a little girl who stole my heart. We're still pen pals. I send her money once a month."

"And her mother?"

"Had too many children, not enough resources. I send enough to help the entire family, not all that much by our standards."

Daphne frowned. "The dad?"

"Works sixty hours a week to barely survive."

"That stinks."

Tyne shrugged. "Some countries are like that."

Human suffering always overwhelmed her, but Tyne took action, did what he could to change things.

He narrowed his eyes, studying her, and shook his head. "There are some countries that leave us in their dust."

"Really?"

"No children go hungry in Algeria. The government provides free housing, food, and education."

"Even for college?"

"Especially for that. They want their people to progress."

"We should do that."

Another shrug. "We should do more, but we have to find our own path. I like our country. I'm proud of it."

Daphne nodded. She liked it, too. Politics were too complicated for her. So was romance. And men. Was there anything in life that wasn't complex? She couldn't think of it. What she did know is that she'd have to guard her heart. Tyne could prove addictive. She'd be hooked, and he wouldn't be. If Tyne walked away from her, it would hurt far more than Patrick's good-bye. She had to only think of Tyne as a friend. Only that. Nothing more.

Chapter 24

Tyne was expecting Daphne for supper at the inn. He was looking forward to it. Paula had made forty-clove chicken for supper, and the thighs were simmering in white wine and thyme when he walked in the kitchen. Daphne would want to go for that, he was sure, but he intended to tempt her with his cassoulet. He dipped into the empty dining room to see what kind of desserts Tessa had sent for tonight. Each week, he gave Ian's wife a list of the meals he and Paula planned on preparing, and she always came up with the perfect desserts to go with them. The pies on display at the end of the buffet had a little placard that read SPICED PEAR. He hoped there'd be a slice leftover so that he could try it. Next to the pies were GERMAN CHOCOLATE SHEET CAKE and then COCONUT RICE PUDDING. Lord, Tessa had outdone herself.

Returning to the kitchen, he went to the refrigerator for the cubes of lamb shoulder he'd made ahead. He was starting to sear duck breasts and sausages to add to cannellini beans, onions, and tomatoes when Cody stalked into the kitchen. Tyne took one look at his moody expression and frowned. "You're early. There's not much to wash-up yet, hardly any dirty pans to rinse."

Cody grabbed the skillet Paula had used to sear the chicken thighs and filled it with water to soak. His shoulders were stiff, his movements jerky. The kid had enough pent-up frustration that Tyne expected energy to burst from his orifices and fly around the kitchen.

Should he leave it alone or bug Cody about it? He'd throw out a line, and if Cody didn't want to talk about it, he'd let it drop. "So, what's up? Looks like you've had a bad day."

Cody turned too quickly. The words almost burst out of him.

"Lexy said she doesn't want to see me or talk to me for a few days. She said she's in a horrible mood, and I don't help."

"Have you two been arguing? Have you disagreed about something?"

Cody shook his head. "She said it's not me, it's her, that everything looks bad to her right now."

"And this has never happened before?"

Cody's brows crinkled in concentration. "She's gotten a little grouchy before, but I think she's getting worse."

Tyne grinned. "Sounds like PMS."

"PMS?"

"You know about a girl's monthly flow, right?"

Cody nodded.

"Well, it can affect their moods. Usually, it hits before their period starts, but it's different for every woman. The best cure I've found is chocolate and patience. Just hold your tongue."

Cody stared. "You've never been married, right?"

Tyne gave him a look. "I work in kitchens. I've never been in a kitchen that didn't have a woman or two. When a pastry chef looked like she'd like to bite my head off, I brought her a fancy candy bar the next day. What it implied was unspoken, but it made my life easier."

Cody laughed. He let out a deep breath. "I'm taking Lexy a rose and a box of chocolates tomorrow, and I'm telling her I love her no matter what."

"You're learning." Tyne studied him. "You know you two are young, right? You might not hold it together till you graduate."

"If she gets tired of me, it's one thing. But I couldn't understand what I'd done wrong this time, and that ate at me."

"It doesn't take much," Tyne said. "I clanged a pan too loud in a kitchen once."

Cody's shoulders relaxed and he turned back to the skillet he'd been soaking. "Thanks, man."

"No problem." Tyne concentrated on finishing up the cassoulet. He hoped Daphne liked it. Sometimes, he used rabbit, but the Danzas had a special price on duck this week, so he'd gone with that. Besides, rabbit might have freaked Daphne out. Maybe he could tempt her with this version.

He was pulling the roasted potatoes, carrots, and zucchini out of the oven when his cell phone buzzed: Daphne's I.D. He smiled as he answered. "Hey, hope you're hungry. Paula and I made a feast for tonight."

She paused—not a good sign—then hurried to explain. "I won't be able to make it. An old friend of mine from out of town called, and when she heard that my parents were on vacation, she decided to drive to Mill Pond to spend time with me. She should get here in an hour."

"Bummer." He frowned, but after all, he was only offering Daphne supper. The friend was going out of her way to visit her. "How often do you two get together?"

"Only once or twice a year at art events. We met in college. Shelby does stained glass, too. She's getting ready for a big exhibit in her hometown, Nashville, Tennessee."

Another artist. Nice. He knew how much he enjoyed meeting fellow chefs. "How long is she staying?" Daphne's parents were only going to be gone a week. He'd looked forward to having Daphne to himself a few times before they came back.

"She leaves after breakfast on Sunday."

Damn. Her parents returned early on Tuesday. "You're still coming to Harley's Halloween party with me on Sunday night, aren't you?"

"I wouldn't miss it."

He felt himself relax a little. Her news didn't thrill him, but he worked every night this week anyway. She worked during the days. It's not like they'd see that much of each other. It would be nice for her to have company. He tried to be gracious. "Enjoy your friend."

She sounded unsure about that. "I will. Thanks for being so understanding."

He laughed. "Do I have a choice?"

She laughed, too. "Neither of us do. Shelby's on her way."

When she hung up, he glared at the phone before pushing it back in his pocket. Daphne hadn't sounded thrilled to see her friend. He wondered about that. Too bad, really. He'd made up his mind to show Daphne a good time, thought he'd drop by her place when he got off work some night and start getting things ready for an herb bed along her picket fence. He shook his head, laughing at himself. Yeah, that would excite her, for sure. She'd probably do things she liked better with Shelby.

While he helped carry food to the buffet table, he made up his mind to give Daphne plenty of space for a few days. She and Shelby could catch up with each other and yak stained glass until they got it all out of their systems. Besides, he and Daphne were just friends, he reminded himself. The whole point of keeping an eye on her was to keep her mind off the professor. It sounded like he was off the hook on that job, at least, for the rest of this week.

Two days later, though, when he hurried down the shop's inside staircase to slip out the back door, Daphne spotted him and waved him closer. A few customers milled in the aisles, but no one seemed serious about shopping. There were days like that when people browsed more than they bought.

"Can I pick your brain a minute?" she asked Tyne. "I took Shelby to Ralph's diner her first night here, but she doesn't like home cooking. We drove to a restaurant in Columbus the next night and went to Indy last night, but it's late when we get back to Mill Pond. Can you recommend a restaurant that's closer to home?"

"What kind of food does Shelby like?"

He heard footsteps approach and looked up to see a tall blonde, who was striking but not pretty, leave Daphne's workroom. She wore black, tight leggings with a long, hip-hugging, zebra-striped sweater over them. She locked gazes with him.

"Ooh, are you the guy who lives upstairs? Daphne told me you're a chef, but she didn't tell me you're a hunk."

Tyne gave his best self-deprecating grin. "She doesn't seem to notice. My usual ploys don't work on her."

Shelby narrowed black-rimmed eyes. "My friend's a little oblivious most of the time, but I appreciate gorgeous when I see it. I just broke up with my boyfriend—a sculptor. I have a thing for the creative types."

"Nashville's probably full of those." She hadn't been subtle. Why should he? Tyne returned his attention to Daphne. "What kind of food are you interested in?"

Shelby answered in Daphne's place. "I ordered scallops in Columbus. They came with a sun-dried tomato sauce. In Indy, I ordered Steak Diane. I love cream sauces with brandy. I like to be impressed."

Tyne raised his eyebrows, surprised. "You must have brought plenty of money to play. You can only get those at upscale restaurants."

Shelby's gray eyes went wide. "Daphne insisted on paying, since I'm the guest."

Sure she did. He didn't believe her. Maybe if they went to the diner or Chase's bar, but for fine dining every night? Tyne knew Shelby's type. She was going to milk Daphne for everything she could, but that was Daphne's choice. She could tell her friend to scale it down. He thought a minute. "I like the Malibu Grill in Bloomington. Have you been there?"

Daphne shook her head. "Patrick and his wife thought the piano was too loud there."

"Good, so you won't run into them. That might be a good place to try. I'll make reservations for you. I met the chef at the Danzas." Shelby laid a hand on his arm, and Tyne frowned at her. "Yes?"

She cleared her throat. "Tomorrow's my last full day here, so Daphne and I thought we'd go to Chase's bar for supper and stay for the music and dancing. I don't suppose you'd agree to fix us breakfast, would you? Something fancy, so that it doesn't matter if we order hamburgers for supper?"

"I love Chase's hamburgers." Tyne glanced at Daphne. She looked flustered and embarrassed, so he caved. "I can fix you something special if you get up early enough. Say nine? I have to get to the inn earlier than usual. The resort's at full capacity for Ian's Halloween bash."

Shelby's smile was meant to dazzle. It annoyed him. How fake could one woman be?

"What are you going to make me?"

He bit back what he wanted to say. He'd like to make her eat crow. Instead, his smile matched hers. "A chef never tells. It will be a surprise."

She clapped her hands together. It was all he could do not to roll his eyes. She touched his arm again. "You're just everything wonderful wrapped up in one package, aren't you?"

"That's me." Damn, she was full of herself. Tyne looked to the door. "It's always nice to meet a friend of Daphne's, but I have to go. Like I said, the inn's full this weekend. Guests arrive for supper tonight."

On the drive to the resort, he shook his head to rid it of Shelby. How had Daphne ended up with a status seeker like her? But then, he corrected himself. Sometimes in life, you don't choose your friends. They choose you, and for whatever reason, with Daphne and Shelby, it stuck. He started thinking about Saturday morning. If Shelby wanted something fancy, he'd give her fancy. He decided to make duck confit with rösti potatoes and fried eggs. Let her take a bite out of that!

He could do Friday night suppers at the inn almost by rote, so he'd have plenty of time to get things ready for Daphne and Shelby. Ian had decided to serve the usual prime rib and salmon, but since parents brought kids along for the Halloween weekend, they'd added chicken fingers to the menu. Tyne was going in early to help Ian set up a wine and cheese–tasting bar, along with shrimp cocktail, in the foyer when guests arrived. The adults could imbibe while Paula's mom, Maya, and Steph organized a scavenger hunt outside for the kids. Tyne and Paula had made snacks for the back patio—little chocolate coffins filled with cheese slices and pretzel sticks, "eyeball" buckeyes, decorated cookies, and hot chocolate. Supper wouldn't be served until seven, so he had plenty of time to get everything organized. Tessa had made a "dirt" cake and red velvet cake for desserts.

The Halloween extravaganza was going to be a lot of work, but Tyne was as excited about it as Ian was. Tyne had already set up the cooker for the hog, so that he could start the meat on low and slow before he left the inn for the night. Saturday was going to be even busier, especially since he'd added breakfast onto it at Daphne's place. No matter. A little extra effort, sometimes, yielded big results.

Chapter 25

After Tyne left, Daphne meant to join Shelby in the workroom to finish the last panel in her standing, stained-glass screen, but a handful of customers wandered into the shop, and she had to wait on them instead. At five-feet tall, with three panels, Shelby's piece needed larger cuts of glass than Daphne usually used, so they'd gone through most of the workroom's stock, trying to finish it. Behind and almost out of time, Shelby worked on the screen every day while Daphne handled customers, but whenever Daphne had free time, Shelby asked her to help. Even working together, it cost them every spare minute they had. The only saving grace was that Leesa ran the shop on Saturdays, so they'd be able to finish it tomorrow afternoon.

Daphne struggled not to feel used. When Shelby left on Sunday, she was going to have to order more glass to make more inventory for her shop during the slow months. She suspected her friend had come to Mill Pond only because she didn't have the supplies or time to complete her entry for the big exhibit she'd entered. She'd been taken advantage of. She'd never been good at setting boundaries, and Shelby knew it.

In college, as freshmen, they'd been assigned to the same dorm and taken many of the same art classes. Proximity made them acquaintances, not friends. Shelby had been a partier. Daphne preferred meeting people in cafés to discuss books, art, and music. In her sophomore year, Daphne's parents had trusted her enough to pay for an apartment for her—on the condition that she'd drive home to stay with them on weekends—and Shelby had tagged along as a roommate. Daphne had told herself it was better than being alone, but by the time graduation rolled around, Daphne couldn't wait to get away from her.

The apartment was always clean by the time Daphne returned on Sunday evenings, but rumor was a string of men came and went on Friday and Saturday nights. Shelby was smart enough to never push Daphne too far, and when she thought Daphne was miffed with her, she'd bring home a pizza and stick around to talk about their latest art projects. But to say that they were a good fit? Not so much.

Daphne only saw Shelby at major art shows now, and even then, small doses of Shelby were more than enough. Her friend liked being the center of attention. Even when people came to praise Daphne on her work, somehow Shelby always made the conversation about her. The last straw was when she'd had the nerve to throw herself at Tyne. At first, Daphne had been jealous. What would it be like to be that sure of yourself? To go for what you wanted, no matter who got in your way? But then she noticed Tyne's reaction to her, and Daphne could tell he didn't like her. She allowed herself a small smile.

A customer carried a small, stained-glass jewelry box to the counter and chuckled. "That smile looked like the cat that swallowed the canary."

Daphne laughed. "Celebrating a small victory, that's all."

The woman waited for Daphne to process her card. "Every victory counts, as far as I'm concerned. I celebrate every single one of them."

"Good advice." The woman looked the type who'd have lots of wins in life. Daphne decided to heed her advice.

Daphne had three short breaks for the rest of the day. She worked with Shelby during each of them, and they stayed at the shop after Daphne closed up to work a couple hours more. After seven, though, Daphne pressed a hand to her stomach and said, "I'm starving."

They'd made a lot of progress. Another three hours of work, and the screen would be done. Shelby nodded. "Let's go to your place and change before we go to Bloomington."

Daphne was fine with that. She'd be able to feed Shadow and spend a little time with him. It was eight before they left Mill Pond to drive to Bloomington, though. Shelby had changed into a long, navy skirt that flipped at the hem and black, dressy boots. Her cream-colored top draped over one shoulder. She'd pulled her long, blonde hair up in a chignon and added dangling earrings. Daphne felt frumpy beside her, but not enough to motivate her to glam up.

When they walked inside the restaurant, Daphne could see why

Tyne had recommended it. It was classy, but low key, and it boasted a stone oven for fire-roasted entries. A pianist was playing in a room on the far right, and a woman was singing along to his music. When the hostess took Daphne's name, she smiled. "You're a friend of Tyne's. The chef is expecting you." They were led immediately to a table.

Shelby preened as she glanced over the menu. When the waiter came, she ordered a Cosmopolitan and one of their specialty appetizers, the smoked salmon and trout plate. The most expensive item on the menu was their pound-and-a-half, bone-in Delmonico steak, and she ordered that, too. Daphne had no idea how anyone could eat that much, so she ordered the filet medallions with peppercorn-cognac sauce, along with a glass of wine.

When their drinks came, Shelby reached for the bread basket. "I like it here."

Daphne had to agree. The ambience was friendly and upscale. When their food came, Tyne would have approved of it. At the end of their meal, the chef himself came to greet them. "Tell Tyne he was right about the quality of David Danza's quail. We served it as a special, and we got lots of compliments on it."

Daphne assured him she'd pass on the information, and then they took their leave. It had been a long day. She was glad they had a shorter drive to reach home. Shadow pounced on her foot when she stepped inside the house. She smiled and picked the kitten up to cuddle him.

Shelby made a face. "Pets take too much time and attention."

"Cats are pretty independent." Daphne went to the kitchen to find Shadow a treat. He was partial to shredded cheese.

Shelby followed her and glanced out the kitchen windows. "It's so dark out here. There's nothing close by. Don't you get bored with nothing to do?"

"No, I bought this place because of the views. I love looking out to see the forest and park."

Shelby grimaced, then covered a yawn. "I've gotta get some sleep. Tyne's coming early in the morning to make us breakfast."

Food didn't even sound good to Daphne right now. "How do you stay so thin? I couldn't believe you finished that whole steak tonight."

"I work out when I'm home. I usually spend two hours a day at the gym."

"Two hours? How do you find the time?"

Shelby shrugged. "That's why I put my stuff in exhibits and shows and work on commission instead of owning a shop. Shops tie you down. I'd rather work at home and have more free time."

Daphne wondered about that. She *did* spend a lot of time working with customers. She'd worked and saved to put a down payment on the shop, felt a huge sense of accomplishment when she opened it. Would she have been better off freelancing? No, the shop was right for her. She wasn't great at networking or selling herself. Shelby didn't like anything that tied her down, but Daphne liked stability, security.

They headed to their separate rooms, and Shadow came to cuddle with Daphne during the night. Daphne blew out a breath when she set her alarm for eight a.m. She usually slept another hour on Saturdays, but she wasn't going to meet Tyne in her pjs and bathrobe. The idea of a big breakfast brought a sigh. By the time Shelby left on Sunday, Daphne would be lucky if she didn't waddle. She fell asleep, thinking of a week of salads, day after day, until she had an appetite again.

In the morning, she heard Shelby moving around before her alarm went off. She groaned and rolled over, but couldn't block the noise. Finally, she got up and went to see what her friend was doing. She shook her head. Shelby was blow-drying her long, blond hair, carefully rolling each section on a round brush for volume. It was Saturday. Who cared?

Shelby noticed her in the doorway and smiled. "What's Tyne's favorite color? Do you know?"

Daphne blinked. "Not a clue."

"Oh, well, I thought I'd wear something he'd like. I'll just have to go for snug so that he notices I have great boobs."

Did Shelby have great boobs? She'd never noticed. Daphne left her and padded into the kitchen to start coffee. Shadow went to his food bowl, expecting his breakfast. Daphne dutifully served it up, then looked out the kitchen windows. Sunshine. After so many gray days, it lifted her mood. The trees had lost some of their leaves. They looked patchy now, but they were still beautiful. A few of the big, old oaks stood out in the background, their leaves rust-colored and bronze.

A half hour later, Shelby came into the kitchen and frowned at her. "You're going to get dressed for when Tyne comes, aren't you?"

Daphne glanced at the clock. "I still have twenty minutes."

Shelby frowned. "You're going to go to more bother when we go to Chase's bar tonight, aren't you?"

"I'll wash my hair."

Shelby shook her head. "Pitiful."

But by the time Tyne walked to the kitchen door, laden down with grocery bags, Daphne had washed her face, brushed her teeth, and pulled on old jeans and a V-necked tee. She held the door open for him, and he stopped to study her. "You even look good with no makeup. You have beautiful skin."

Daphne could feel heat flood her cheeks when Shelby hissed with displeasure.

Tyne's gaze didn't leave Daphne. "Your friend said she wanted fancy, so fancy I brought."

Daphne helped him unpack his supplies, but Shelby wedged herself between them to hover close while he started cooking. "I'll learn from the best if I watch you."

"The duck's the secret ingredient." He took out a small Mason jar filled with what Daphne assumed must be duck fat. He held up a Ziploc bag filled with shredded meat. "Duck." Another baggie held grated potatoes. "Do you have a bowl?"

She handed him one, then pressed herself into the corner, out of the way. He mixed the shredded meat with the potatoes. He took a few pieces of meat that stuck to the sides of the bag and bent to give them to Shadow.

Shelby rolled her eyes. "You're as bad as her. Pets should eat dry pet food."

Tyne grinned and winked at Daphne. "I'm a chef. I don't feed anyone or anything something ordinary."

He scrounged in a deep, bottom drawer where he knew Daphne kept her skillets. He added the duck fat to one and when it was hot, added the potato mixture. "That takes a while to crisp up and set."

While the potatoes cooked, he added chives and lemon juice to sour cream. "For a topping." Then he started on a quick, spinach salad with walnuts and strawberries.

Shelby tried for conversation while he worked. "How has your week been?"

"Busy. The inn geared up for Ian's Halloween weekend special. You?"

"Daphne's been helping me finish my stained-glass screen. It's kept us busy all week. We can do the last pieces this afternoon."

Tyne glanced up from his work. "Helping you how?"

"It takes a lot of time to cut the individual pieces of glass and solder them in place."

He frowned. "You didn't bring the glass pieces already cut?"

Shelby bit her bottom lip. "No, Daphne always has lots of different colors at her shop. We used those."

Tyne quit working and turned to look at Daphne. "That was all right with you? I thought you needed those to make new inventory for your shop."

Shelby sighed. "I sort of ran out of money for supplies, and Daphne's always helped me out."

He didn't say anything, but he didn't have to. Daphne thought his expression said it all. He went back to working on the salad.

Shelby tried again. "I'm so happy you recommended the Malibu Grill last night. The food was wonderful."

That brought a smile. "What did you get? I love the Steak Neptune. Filet with crab meat and hollandaise is a great match."

She told him her picks, and he looked unimpressed. "You go for big ticket items. I like finesse."

Daphne studied him. Was he purposely trying to bait her friend?

Shelby crossed her arms over her chest. Her eyes sparkled with temper. "Nothing I do seems to please you."

He glanced at her, surprised. "Why would you need to please me? I don't care what you choose."

That pissed her off even more. "I suppose you like Ralph's diner?"

"Sure do. Everyday food cooked the way it should be. Top quality."

Her lips thinned into a grim line. "You don't like me much, do you?"

Daphne squirmed. Tyne made a habit of saying what he thought. She opened her lips to intercept the conversation, but he shrugged. "If Daphne likes you, I like you. That simple."

Daphne didn't know what to say. She stared at him, surprised. Did he mean that?

He laughed at her expression. "Friends are there for each other, right? I get it."

He flipped the potatoes onto a cutting board and added eggs to the nonstick skillet. When the eggs were ready, he sliced the potatoes into wedges, then topped each with an egg and some of the flavored sour cream. He added some spinach salad on the side and carried the plates to the small kitchen table.

Shelby had a sour look on her face, and Daphne doubted she'd like his food, no matter how good it was. But then she bit into it, and a low moan escaped her. A smug smile tugged at Tyne's lips. Damn, the man was good! He could make you like him when you were determined not to.

Chapter 26

It surprised Tyne when he learned that Daphne was taking Shelby to Chase's bar tonight. On a Saturday. With music and dancing. He grinned to himself. The cats went away, and the mice meant to play. It had to be Shelby's idea. Daphne would never brave the bar on her own.

The hog roast at the inn started at five, earlier than the usual dinner schedule, but that didn't mean he'd get off work sooner. Today was an event, a marathon of fun. He'd be dragging by the time it was over. Luckily, the rain and winds had stopped. At five, it would still be light out, and Ian had bought fire pits and placed them at intervals for people to sit around and keep warm. Guests could roast marshmallows if they wanted to. Wagons offered hayrides and took people back and forth between the Kruses' corn maze and the resort. Luke, who oversaw the yard and outbuildings, had piled haystacks near the play area for kids to climb and sit on. Picnic tables were set up with pumpkin-carving stations, and there were low barrels for bobbing for apples. Kids' movies—like *Scooby Doo* and *Hocus Pocus*—ran on the big screen TV that Luke had moved to the lobby, and at seven, each grownup was going to line up and distribute candy so that the kids could trick-or-treat.

Tessa had thought of a truly inspired idea. She'd gone to vintage shops and costume stores and bought lots of different outfits for kids to try on. There were old wedding gowns, flapper dresses, and cowboy vests, along with pirate eye patches and "hooks" for hands, orange prison suits, and farmer overalls. And lots and lots of hats, high heels, and boots. Ian had hired three teenage girls, who were in art classes, to paint kids' faces.

At dinner time, Paula brought Aiden and Bailey to join the fun, and the kids ran to hug Tyne when they saw him carving pork at the long fire pit Ian had rented.

"I bet you want the tail to eat," Tyne teased Aiden.

Aiden went to check the end of the pig and gave Tyne a dirty look. "You took it off."

"Why? Did you want it? It's sort of like eating a curly fry, but greasier."

"Mom says you like to pick on me."

Tyne bent to kiss Bailey's hand. "I can't pick on a sweet, little girl, so that leaves you."

Aiden laughed. Tyne handed him a plate with some of the pork, and when he tried it, he nodded. "It's good."

Tyne piled more on for him and then offered some to Bailey. She took a piece and said, "*Mmm*," then saw a friend at one of the fire pits and cried, "Gotta go."

Tyne shook his head. That girl was going to grow up to be a socialite.

Guests came and went for the next two hours, and by the time serving ended, Tyne was surprised by how few leftovers remained. Ian came to check on him while he was bagging up the end of the pork and said, "What do you think? How did it go?"

"Looked like a success to me." Tyne glanced over to where the parents were passing out miniature candy bars while kids made their way down their line. "I'd have been happy with this when I was a kid." Not that his parents had ever taken him to Halloween events, but the expensive schools Holden and he attended had always done something for each holiday.

Ian nodded. "I didn't think about including kids when I first thought of offering specials for holidays, but I guess parents aren't going to leave them for Thanksgiving or Christmas either."

"We should plan farther ahead for those, come up with something really unique."

Ian reached for a napkin and the pen he always carried. "Do you have something in mind?"

Tyne shrugged. "A friend of mine asked me to go with her when she took her kid to a Harry Potter event. A bookstore put it on, went all out. Had lots of different booths for kids to visit—magnets they could paint for their refrigerators at home, a petting zoo, games, Kool-Aid flavors they could mix into magical brews."

Ian looked excited and would have asked more, but people ran out of marshmallows at one of the fire pits, and he had to go find more. Tyne got back to cleaning the food stations outside and then pitched in to help clean the kitchen. It was after nine before the inn was back to normal, and then he remembered that Daphne and Shelby would be sitting at Chase's bar. Nine's when the band started up.

Should he, or shouldn't he? Oh, hell, why not? He drove home, took a quick shower, and changed into his jeans and a long-sleeved T-shirt. He couldn't stay late. He had to be back to work early to-morrow morning. He and Paula were making more goodies than usual for the brunch buffet before the guests left to return home—pumpkin pancakes and poached eggs in tomato sauce, and serving Bloody Marys as well as Champagne—but he could let loose for a while tonight. Relax.

The bar's parking lot was full. This was where the adults of Mill Pond were celebrating their Halloween night. When he walked inside, Chase waved a hello, and heads turned to see where Tyne would land. He spotted Daphne and Shelby at a booth and went to slide in beside Daphne.

She looked at him in surprise. "I didn't think I'd see you here tonight."

"I've dealt with kids and one roasted marshmallow too many, and I need a drink."

Louise, Chase's waitress, came to take his order. She offered him a big smile. "I didn't think you'd get brave enough to come back."

Daphne frowned, not sure what that meant, but Tyne shrugged. "All of the scratches were shallow. None of the women got their claws into me that deep."

And then Daphne understood, he could tell. "They groped you, right?"

Louise poised her pen over her pad. "He was lucky he escaped in one piece."

Shelby's lips curled in a smile. "So you're fair game on the dance floor?"

"Nope, I came to nab a few dances with Daphne and serve as her protector. She could get mobbed here, too."

Daphne shook her head. "I don't think . . ."

"Really? Since guys know you've broken up with the professor? You're up for grabs again."

Louise tapped her notepad. "Your usual?"

He nodded, and she left. A few minutes later, Chase came to deliver his beer. He slid in the booth next to Shelby. "Hey, didn't expect to see you tonight. How'd the weekend special go at the inn?"

"Paula hasn't come home yet?"

Chase shrugged. "She and the kids stayed to visit with her mom. I'm always busy on Saturday nights."

"I'd give us four-and-a-half stars out of five," Tyne said.

"That good? That's awesome. Paula was nervous about the weather, but the rain stopped in time, right?"

They talked a few minutes before Chase had to go back behind the bar. Shelby looked at Daphne. "He's married, right?"

"Very." Daphne smiled. "Just like Harley. Both taken."

"What is it with men around here?" Shelby asked. "Is there something about lake water the rest of us haven't heard about?"

Daphne laughed. "Ian and Tyne aren't from around here."

"There's another one?"

"He's married, too," Tyne said.

Shelby looked him up and down. "You owe me a dance."

The band started up again, and Tyne led Daphne and Shelby out onto the floor. Before long, they were surrounded by other people. Chantelle tried to worm her way next to Shelby, but Tyne did a sidestep and cut her off. Their space shrank, and soon, they were dancing closer than he'd intended to. Women twirled and accidentally touched him. One wrapped an arm around his back. He took it all in stride, concentrating on the two women in front of him.

He was feeling pretty good until a tall, dark-haired man with a goatee grabbed Daphne's arm and spun her to dance with him. Damn. Tyne reached for her, but then thought better of it. What if she wanted to dance with this guy? Chantelle slid into the space Daphne had vacated. *Oh, goodie.* Another woman moved into their circle. *Not good.* Shelby locked gazes with Daphne, and they switched it up. Shelby was dancing with Goatee Guy, flirting like crazy, and Daphne was practically on top of Tyne. He grinned and wrapped an arm around her waist. They started moving in sync—dirty dancing. Chantelle looked pissed and left. When the music ended, Daphne's cheeks were pink, and she started back to their booth.

"Is everything okay?" Tyne asked, following her.

"I just got too warm." Her cheeks flooded with more color.

He smiled, amused, but then Shelby stepped between them. "My turn."

That was the end of the fun. After he danced with Shelby, women grabbed and yanked at him, pulling him toward them. He finally threw up his hands in surrender and said, "I need a little more beer," and went to join Daphne.

He slid next to her and had to laugh at himself. Why had he fled the dance floor? What was wrong with him? Before he'd come to Mill Pond, he enjoyed all the attention. There'd been times when he'd danced with a dozen women at a time. But now he wanted to be left alone. He wanted to concentrate on one woman—and she was sitting in this booth.

Daphne looked flustered, and he knew why. She was stepping out of her comfort zone, and she wasn't sure if she should. She'd surprised herself when she'd danced with him. No, shocked herself, and it left her uncertain. Shy women were like that, overthinking each and every thing. He backed off and glanced at the clock. "I have an early day tomorrow, only needed a break after a long day of work. I'd better call it quits for tonight. You two have fun without me."

Shelby looked disappointed. Daphne looked relieved. He knew she would. With a grin, he finished his beer and gave them a wave, then made his way to the door. Hands reached for him, and he let them touch. Then he was outdoors in the cool air, and he couldn't stop smiling. He'd made his sweet, innocent Daphne all hot and bothered. Damn, that felt good! Thank God, her friend left early tomorrow morning. He'd be happy to see the back side of Shelby.

Chapter 27

Tyne and Paula sat at the kitchen worktable and finished off the last of the Bloody Marys before they got started on what she'd serve for supper tonight.

"You know, all you have to do is your entrée," Paula argued. "Supper's my shift on Sundays."

"After this weekend? I can give you a helping hand, and when you come back, everything will be ready to go. You've earned an easy night."

"So have you." But she looked damned happy to have his help. Chase's bar was closed on Sundays—always. If he helped her, and they got done fast enough, she could go home and hang out with her hubby and kids a little more than usual before coming back for the supper shift.

Tyne felt like they'd survived a horde of locusts who'd swept in and ate everything in sight. The coming week would be a piece of cake. He grinned at the cliché, but it fit. In November, people began to button down. Only fifty guests would be staying this week. No kids, all adults. So no kid menus. By the second week of December, guests would be sparse, then the number would pick up for the week that Mill Pond went all out and decorated every store and street for the holiday. Ian's December special was scheduled for the three days leading up to Christmas Eve. Then they'd turn around and offer another special for New Year's Eve. Life would be busy. Part of being a chef. While other people played, they worked.

For tonight, when the new guests arrived, he and Paula had decided to keep it simple. He was making white wine–braised rabbit with Dijon mustard and fresh herbs. Paula was going with pork candy ribs. They'd decided on roasted vegetables for sides, along with roasted

Brussels sprouts. They were going to let the ovens do most of the work. Tyne even stayed to help Paula make the mixed green salad.

"Are you going home to put your feet up?" she asked as they left the restaurant together.

He shook his head. "I'm going to help Steph with a few of the appetizers for tonight."

"And *then* you're going to relax?"

He gave his crooked grin. It had a 90 percent success rate with Paula. Smiles melted her resistance faster than well-thought-out arguments. "*Then* I'm going to pick up Daphne and drink wine and dance."

"No Shelby?"

"She had to leave today." He couldn't keep the lilt out of his voice.

She laughed. "One way or another, you have to pay the piper. You'll go home and die after you work the early shift tomorrow."

He nodded. Daphne would be back at work in her shop, and he could catch up on sleep. Daphne's parents didn't come home until Tuesday morning. He planned on cooking her supper tomorrow night. So far, she hadn't had any time to think about the professor, and he intended on keeping it that way.

On the drive to Maxwell's to meet Steph, he thought about Goatee Guy, who'd danced with Daphne last night. That had to let her know that guys found her attractive. If she wanted to get out there and meet someone, she could. He'd have to mention that to her. Aim her in the right direction. So why had it bothered him? That was easy. It left him stuck with Shelby and easy prey on the dance floor. Besides, *he'd* taken Daphne out to dance, hadn't he? Mr. Goatee hadn't had the nerve to come and ask her.

Steph sighed with relief when Tyne stepped through the bakery door. "Thank the Lord." She pushed a rimmed baking sheet toward him. "I haven't gotten to the buffalo chicken bites on crostini or the shrimp in cashew sauce."

He nodded and got to work. Neither of them made small talk. They just wanted to get the job done. Two and a half hours later, Tyne helped Steph load everything into her minivan and watched her set off. He'd asked about Maxwell and India, but Steph only replied, "Same old, same old," so he let it drop.

When he slid behind the wheel of his Jeep, he slumped with relief. He'd been on his feet all day. Had he overscheduled? Who did he think he was—the Energizer Bunny? But he couldn't miss one of Harley's parties. He always enjoyed himself.

Couples were dressing in costumes. Daphne had told him that she was going as a flapper, so he'd decided to dress as a gangster—a three-piece suit, fedora, and fake tommy gun. Before he got ready, though, he needed a long, steamy shower to relax his shoulders and muscles. The hot water soothed him. Maybe too much. When he flopped on the sofa and turned on the TV to chill for an hour, he fell asleep. Luckily, he'd set the alarm on his cell phone. The forty-minute nap did him a world of good, and by the time he knocked on Daphne's door, he was ready for a good time.

When Daphne flung the door wide, Tyne stared. His throat constricted, and he couldn't take his eyes off her. She wore a short flapper dress with swishy fringe that moved to show more of her legs. Great legs—long and shapely. Her hazel eyes were rimmed in dark makeup and her lips were bright with color. She had a feather tucked in a band that circled her head, pinning her wavy brown hair in place.

Did his heart skip a beat? Did that really happen? It ached and he put a hand to it. It was almost painful. How could the prissy prof dump someone so drop-dead gorgeous? And why hadn't she snagged someone long before now?

He swallowed down lust and crooked his elbow for her. "Ready, doll?"

She laughed. "Lead the way, Bugsy!"

The wine-tasting room was full of people when they made their way to the bar. Harley and Kathy were waiting on customers, so Vicki came to greet them. She had her pure-white hair pulled back in a white, ruffled cap, and she and Kathy both wore barmaids' outfits from old English pub days. "What'll be, mate?" she asked.

Tyne grinned. "You look great."

"So do you two." Vicki motioned toward a table near the dance floor. "Miriam's saving you seats. She's probably ready for another glass of wine."

Tyne paid, and they carried their drinks to Miriam's table. Tyne broke up laughing when he saw her. Tall and thin, Miriam had dressed as a basketball player in a numbered sleeveless top with a thermal shirt under it for warmth and matching long, baggy gym shorts. Knee socks covered her calves, and a sweatband circled her head, scrunching her corkscrew curls up in a hairstyle that rivaled the Bride of Frankenstein's.

She reached for her wine. "You like?"

"It's perfect." Tyne never knew what to expect with Miriam, and he liked that.

Miriam turned to Daphne. "So, how did the visit with the leech go?"

Tyne choked on his drink.

Miriam rolled her eyes. "You met her, didn't you? Have you ever met a bigger Me-First girl?"

"I felt used." Daphne sounded irritated. "I hope she never comes back."

Tyne frowned, confused. "Then why didn't you tell her *no*? Why didn't you tell her to buy her own damn glass?"

Daphne squirmed, and Miriam answered for her. "My friend here is *too* nice. She caves when it comes to any kind of unpleasantness."

Tyne shrugged. "Who cares what Shelby thinks about you? You don't need someone like her."

"We've known each other since college..." Daphne fidgeted with her napkin. She didn't have any good answer, and he knew it.

"I bet she's always been a selfish little bitch." Tyne finished his wine and went to get them more. He watched the two women lean in for intense gossiping. Daphne had a good friend in Miriam. He brought the wine to the table, then went to get them all food. By the time he carried back three full plates, Daphne and Miriam looked as if they'd solved all the world's problems. Or at least, they'd had it out and were finished with Shelby.

"Hungry?" he asked.

Miriam went straight for the mummy dog—a sausage wrapped in cornbread dough. Daphne tasted one of the shrimp in cashew sauce. She looked at him. "This one was your idea, wasn't it?"

"I helped Steph make them today."

"See?" She pointed the half-eaten shrimp at him like a weapon. "You knock yourself out helping people, too."

"Friends," he corrected. "People who'd help me in return."

She didn't argue and ate the rest of the shrimp. "This is delicious."

He laughed and reached for the buffalo chicken on crostini.

They'd finished their food by the time the band started playing.

Harley usually hired jazz players, but for Halloween he'd gone with classic rock, mixed with funk. Tyne loved funk. The beat and rhythm called to him. "Ladies?" He held out both hands and led both of them onto the floor. "If anyone tries to cut in, forget about it. The two of you are mine for the next two hours."

Daphne listened. Miriam didn't. She pulled Buck Krieger on the floor to be her partner. Poor Buck ran the local landscape business and knew perennials and annuals more than he knew dancing. Miriam towered over him by a good three inches, but he did his best to keep up with her.

When Tyne did a backward dip for the third song, Miriam stared. Grams jumped to her feet and clapped for him. Before he knew it, Grams and Miguel had joined their group. A few minutes later, so had Chase and Paula. Chase had moves of his own, and Paula was one hot little mama. A half hour later, people stood on the side of the floor, sipping their wine, to watch them. By the time the music ended at eleven, Tyne was wiped out.

Paula grinned at him. "I feel sorry for you tomorrow morning."

He groaned. "When my shift ends, I'm hitting the mattress."

Daphne sagged against the back of her seat for the ride home. "It's been a long week."

He glanced sideways at her. "Are you ready for your parents to come home and for life to get back to normal?"

"No."

He glanced again. Her answer surprised him.

She pulled off the headband and toyed with the feather. "I love my parents. It's not that. And I'm grateful for all they've given me. But once I met Patrick, I realized I wanted more. I love seeing them, but not every night. It was nice going out to restaurants, seeing someone else . . ." She trailed off. "You wouldn't understand. You were never close to your mom and dad."

"I used to resent that, regret what I didn't have. Now, I think maybe they did me a favor. I have total freedom."

She shook her head. "That's no good either, but there's something in between. If I ever have a kid . . ." She shrugged. "It'll probably never happen, but Miriam sees her parents a couple of times a month, and they enjoy each other. And she lives her own life."

He nodded. "I get it."

She turned to look at him. "You always do. That's one of the things I like about you."

Her compliment made him happy, and it made him ache. She saw things in him that some people missed. He felt so connected with her sometimes, it worried him. Maybe she was the sister he'd never had. No, he corrected himself. He had no brotherly thoughts about her at all. If she weren't so innocent, so unworldly, he'd . . . He pushed the thoughts away.

He dropped her at her door, and she gave him a weary wave good-night. On the drive to town, he rolled down his Jeep's window to let the cool air keep him alert. He locked the shop's back door behind him when he got home and sighed at the steps that led to his apartment. Too many of them. Once he reached his bedroom, he dropped, face down, on the bed. That's all he remembered until his alarm woke him for the early shift on Monday.

Chapter 28

Daphne swung her legs over the side of the bed and groaned. They felt like lead. She and Shelby had helped close down Chase's bar on Saturday. When Shelby and Mr. Goatee had disappeared for an hour, Daphne had danced with one man after another until her friend returned, her hair mussed, her shirt buttoned wrong. Embarrassing. And then Daphne had danced till closing time at Harley's party last night.

She stood under the shower and let the warm water revive her. What would her mother say if she heard about how she'd spent the weekend? She toweled her hair dry, then flipped her head down and blasted the hair dryer on high. She wasn't going to look good today, no matter what, so why bother?

In the kitchen, she poured herself a bowl of cereal and went to the refrigerator for the milk. One inch remained in the bottom of the carton. Daphne added water to it and gave it a shake, poured it over her wheat flakes. It tasted like crap, but she was hungry. When she finished, Shadow jumped on the counter to steal a few licks of milk. He sniffed and gave her a dirty look.

"Hey, what can I say? I forgot." She dished wet cat food into his bowl. He acted offended, but chowed down. The damn cat loved Tyne's table scraps. He was getting a little spoiled.

She poured herself a second cup of coffee and glanced at the calendar. Her parents would be home tomorrow. If any of their friends tattled on her, she'd get a long lecture. Oh, well, that worry could wait another day. It was time to get ready for the shop. She threw on her stretchy, black slacks and a long, black tee. Paula would be proud of her. She looked Goth. She slapped on some mascara and lipstick, then took off.

No tourists jostled up and down the sidewalks. The first day of November, the day after Halloween, people were recuperating. She spent most of the day in her workroom, cleaning up the mess Shelby had left. She doubted Shelby would ever come back for another visit. She smiled. That was probably a good thing. They'd still see each other at art shows, and that was enough. By the time she turned the sign in the window to CLOSED at the end of the day, her shop and her life seemed to be back in order. Then she looked up, and Tyne had his nose pressed against the front window.

She braced herself. Tyne could be a serious deterrent to normal.

He hurried through the door before she turned the lock. "Hey, I made a big pot of food, thought you might want to come up and eat with me before you headed home."

She hesitated. She'd eaten so much last night, all she wanted was something simple, easy.

As usual, he read her expression and grinned. "Nothing fancy, just beans and hamburger."

She blinked. "Soup beans?" Did anyone flavor those with hamburger?

"No, baked beans with a little brown sugar, some onion, and ketchup. I like it with garlic bread on the side."

She was so surprised, she climbed the stairs with him. "I didn't think you'd make anything an ordinary cook could make."

He filled her plate and then his own. "Holden and I both make this when we're feeling a little homesick or ready for something cozy. Our grandma made it for us. It'll be one of our favorites forever."

She shook her head. He always did the unexpected. "Does your grandma still make it for you?"

"She's gone now, but she's the one who got Holden and me so excited about food." He smiled, remembering. "She didn't know how to cook for one or two people, always made enough to feed the neighborhood."

Daphne watched his expression soften. "You loved her."

"She was the best. Our parents sent us to camps every summer—sports camps, adventure camps, educational camps, anything to get rid of us. When we finally survived all of them, we got to go to Grandma's until it was time for school to start. She made us feel like the most loved, special people on earth."

Daphne felt sad, listening to him. "Your parents never wanted to spend time with you?"

He shrugged. "They believed in quality time. If they took us to a fancy restaurant once a week, they thought they were champions."

Daphne sighed. "My parents spent every minute they could with me."

Tyne grimaced. "That would suck, too."

She stared at him, irritated. "They didn't smother me."

"Really? Who's afraid of her own shadow?"

She straightened her shoulders. "They weren't in favor of my opening a stained-glass shop, but they supported me."

He raised his eyebrows, unimpressed. "What did they think you should do?"

"Become a librarian like Mom or an accountant like Dad."

"Go figure."

They bickered back and forth, but Tyne stuck to ideas. Not once did he call her a name or take a cheap shot. No sarcasm, like the professor. How do you defend yourself against sarcasm? It's a no win. Tyne knew how to fight fair. Despite herself, she was impressed.

Finally, he raised his glass and waved his white paper napkin in the air. "Truce?"

She smiled. "Thanks for the supper. Let me help you clean up."

"Did you like the beans?"

"Loved them. I want the recipe."

"Really? Would you make this?"

"Hey, I think I can handle browning hamburger and onions, then adding a can of beans."

"I'll copy it for you, but it is our secret recipe, you know. Holden and I don't let it go for cheap."

"What will I owe you?" Her blood pumped faster. Her nipples perked up.

"You'll have to drink another glass of wine with me and be good company."

Oh, damn. The story of her life.

They moved to the living room and he stretched his legs on the oversized couch. She sat in the recliner next to it. He frowned and swiveled to see her better. "I feel like I'm visiting a shrink, but this is comfortable. What do you want to talk about?"

She couldn't fight a yawn. "Sorry, I think I'm talked out."

He put his wine glass on the coffee table they shared. "Me, too. Do you want to watch something on TV?"

"It's too early. There's nothing good on."

"We could rent a movie."

"That would go too late."

He glanced at the book lying on the side table. "Want to read?"

She scanned his bookshelves. Lots of cookbooks. No thanks. Nonfiction. Too serious. Spy novels. She'd have to think. She dragged her purse close and took out Ilona Andrews' *Burn for Me*.

He stared. "Really? Urban fantasy? I pictured you as a literary girl."

"Not when my brain's tired. This is a new series. Lots of magic and battles, and plenty of romance."

"All stuff you love." *Okay, so he did use sarcasm sometimes.*

Her chin shot up. "I like a good, kickass heroine and a sexy hero. There are sparks. A girl needs a little fun once in a while."

"I'll keep that in mind." He reached for a book on his side table. *Prince of Thorns*. "Guys need a little fun once in a while, too."

She didn't think she could concentrate with him so near, but soon, she was absorbed in the story, and every time she shuffled a little impatiently, he brought her another glass of wine or a cup of tea. After a couple of hours, he carried a chocolate pavlova to the coffee table. He topped it with a layer of whipped cream and sliced strawberries.

It tasted like she was eating something too airy to contain calories. She used a finger to swipe up the last bit on her plate and looked at him. "You know how to treat a woman."

"I try." He reached for her tea cup to refill it at the same time she did. Their fingers touched, and electricity shot through Daphne's body. Their gazes locked, and all she could think about was how much she wanted him.

She slid onto the sofa next to him and slowly bent to kiss him. Sleeping Beauty in reverse. She hoped she woke up something inside him. His kiss started slow, friendly, but when she ran her tongue over his lips, he grew more passionate. Finally, he leaned forward to be more thorough. She scooted closer, pressing her body against his. He pulled back and stared.

"Are you sure you want this? It will change things . . ."

"I want it."

"We're friends. This could make things awkward."

"I'm tired of lukewarm. I want to try spicy." Besides, once her parents returned, her mom would do everything in her power to keep them apart. Daphne had a shot at hot and sizzling, and she didn't mean to regret it.

"I have condoms in the bedroom." He tried to move past her, but she pushed against his chest, pinning him in place.

"I'm on the Pill." She placed her hands on both sides of his face and ground her lips against his.

His hand slid under her tee, and her skin sizzled. Her nerves tingled with desire. He moved slightly, and soon she was beneath him. His hand roamed over her abdomen, cupped her breast, and then moved higher, feeling and touching, making her body come to life. He sprinkled feather kisses over her face, down her throat. She held her breath, waiting in wonder. Then his hand went to the hem of her shirt and scooted it higher. Up, up, up until he gently tugged it over her head. The cool air hit her hot skin, and she shivered. But then his fingers slid behind her and unclasped her bra, tugging it off, and her shivers had nothing to do with temperature. His mouth lowered over her breast. His tongue teased her nipple, and her body stiffened with need. His hand moved to her black slacks and slid beneath them. She raised her hips and he pulled them off. Her panties followed, and then his hand was free to explore.

Every touch brought her pleasure. He bent to trail kisses down her abdomen when she rose to switch off the light, and they bumped heads.

"Ow." He rubbed his forehead. "What were you trying to do?"

"I was going to turn off the light. I only make love in the dark."

He shook his head. "I want to see you. Your body's beautiful."

She wrinkled her nose. "It's too embarrassing."

"Then shut your eyes." He bent to nibble behind her ear. She scrunched her shoulders, blocking him.

"What?"

"It tickles." And it sent spasms of pleasure rocketing through her. She wouldn't be able to keep her hips still.

He ran his teeth over her throat and she jerked.

"What now?"

"It's too much. I can't stand it."

"Did Patrick touch you *anywhere*?"

She bit her bottom lip. "We kissed. He grabbed a boob, and then he was inside me."

Tyne grinned. "We're going to have fun. I'll take it slower. Let me do all the work."

She blinked, unsure of herself. "Am I supposed to do something, too?"

Tyne laughed. "Not this time."

His hands and lips roamed everywhere. By the time he flipped her onto her stomach and kissed his way down her spine, she didn't know which sensation to concentrate on. His whiskers scraped a pathway down her body until he reached the base of her spine. He licked her skin, and a shockwave sped through her. Then his hand slid between her legs, and his fingers touched a pulse she never knew she had. Her breath came in gasps. How could anything feel so good?

He rolled her over again, and his lips claimed her nipple, sucked and teased. His hand returned to between her thighs, and she couldn't think. She threw her arms over her head. She arched her back, and then she opened her eyes and screeched.

"Did I hurt you?"

"Oh, no. Not that." She stared. He was fully erect. "You're too big. You won't fit."

The grin returned. "Let's find out—a little at a time."

She was so slippery, he slid in easily, and then he began to move—back and forth. Holy mother of pleasure, the more he moved, the more she wanted him. All of him. Every inch. She moved her hips to meet his thrusts, and he sank deeper and deeper within her. And then she tensed, her body crying for release. And when he came, so did she. When he lowered himself onto his elbows, his strong body hovering over hers, she didn't want him to pull out.

He smoothed her damp hair back from her face. "It's all right. We can take a break, then do this again. It's not like I'd leave you forever."

He was talking about sex, but the words struck home. He would leave her. Eventually. But she wanted as much of this as she could get before he did. He rolled sideways and took her with him, stared into her eyes, and smiled. "It was good for me, too."

"Oh, sorry, I sort of forgot about that."

He laughed. "No need to worry about me. I enjoyed every inch of you." Tears misted her eyes and she blinked them away. He frowned. "Are you having second thoughts?"

"No." She swiped at her eyes. "It's just that no one's ever made me feel so special before."

He grew serious. "They should have. Everything about you is special. Don't ever forget that."

She blew out a long breath. "Thank you."

He lowered his forehead to touch hers. "Thank *you*." He pulled away from her and swung his legs over the side of the sofa. "Want a drink before we try again?"

Her eyes went wide. "How many times can you do it?"

"How many times do you want?"

She shook her head, dazed. "I can't. It's getting late. I need to go."

He didn't pressure her. "We have to clean up first. First one in the shower has to wash the other one's back."

She didn't win, but it didn't matter. He scrubbed and smoothed every inch of her anyway. Then he bundled her into his robe and pulled on his pajama bottoms. Then he made her another cup of tea.

"Do you want to spend the night here?" he asked.

Oh, yes! She wanted to, but someone would notice that her SUV never left the lot, and someone would tell her parents that she never returned home. And Shadow was waiting for her. Her legs felt like jelly, but she finally made them move and got dressed. She gave him one last kiss and left his apartment. He stood in the window to wave her off, and she thought she'd always remember him, framed like that with the light shining behind him. And she'd always remember tonight. And nothing would ever compare.

Chapter 29

Tyne waved as Daphne drove away. *What the hell had he done?* How had that woman stayed so innocent, so untouched? Pathetic Patrick must not have cared whether she enjoyed sex or not. The prof had kissed, grabbed, and done the deed. Tyne wondered if she'd even had an orgasm before. He got the idea she hadn't.

He ran his fingers through his short hair, spiking it. He never thought to worry about having sex with her, thought she'd be more experienced. Not so much. How weird would it be the next time he saw her? Would she want to be friends with benefits? Or would she retreat back into her shell? Her parents came home tomorrow. Daphne was thirty-six, but they'd influence things. How much?

She'd surprised him when she made the first move. Had he done the right thing, taking her up on it? But he'd been wanting to bed her since she'd climbed behind him on his motorcycle. No, not true. He'd wanted to bed her before that, but he didn't think it was a smart idea. He still wasn't sure about it, but he wasn't virtuous enough to push her away when she locked lips with him.

He sank back onto the couch and tried to concentrate on his book. Who was he kidding? Her scent still lingered in the room. He flipped on the TV and zipped through one station after another. Nothing held his interest. Finally, he indulged in what he had as a kid when he wanted distraction. He turned on his Xbox and started the latest fighting game he'd found. He kicked and pounded his virtual opponents. A way to relax or relieve frustration? He wasn't sure, but even at the end of the night, his mind drifted back to Daphne. All he wanted to do was pull her to him and kiss her until she couldn't remember her name. Or her parents.

Finally, he did the one thing that usually worked. He took a cold shower, drank a beer, and went to bed.

Chapter 30

Daphne closed the shop and leaned against the door, trying to screw up her courage. Her parents had texted her that they were home. They expected her for supper tonight. She didn't want to go, but she couldn't hide from them forever.

She walked to the mirror in the workroom and gazed at herself. Same hazel eyes. Same light-brown hair. Was there anything that had changed, that announced that she'd had sex with Tyne last night? Was there some telltale sign that only a mother could see?

She took a deep breath and reached for her purse and jacket. Being late wouldn't make anything better. On the short drive to their house, she noticed that Maxwell's bread shop and the apartment above it were dark. Then she noticed Sadie, from the frozen custard shop next door, walking Chester on what looked like a new leash. Both the woman and the dog had a bounce to their steps—a good pairing. Daphne bit her bottom lip. India must still be in the hospital. Was that a good sign? If no one had moved her to a rehab center, did that mean the doctors could help her?

She considered talking to her parents about India, but the last time she'd brought her up Mom hadn't been one bit sympathetic. She decided to avoid that subject.

She fretted as she passed empty window boxes, cleaned of drooping plants. Autumn's heavy frosts had claimed them. The barrels that overflowed with flowers and vines were prepped for winter, too. November brought sullen skies and colder nights. The bright awnings over windows protected against rain now instead of sun. Once past the stores, she glanced at the big, old homes that bordered Main Street. People were outside, raking leaves, and piling them at the curbs for pick-up.

When she pulled to the curb in front of her parents' house, nothing had changed. The stoic Foursquare looked the same, one season to the next. When she walked in the house, her parents were already in the dining room, waiting for her. Their luggage was put away. The house had been dusted. No one would know they'd been to Carolina for fun and sun.

Daphne's mom waited for her to take a seat, then placed a plate of spaghetti in front of her. Next, she served Dad, and finally herself before she slid onto her straight-backed chair at the head of the table. A bowl of tossed salad waited at each setting. Daphne sat quietly. A distinct coolness had hit her when she walked into the house to greet her parents. They looked tanned, rested, but distant.

She tried a smile. "How was your trip?"

"Very nice." Her mother gave her a sharp look. "But maybe we should have cut it short. I apologize for not having wine for your meal."

Uh-oh. Daphne's defenses readied for artillery fire. "Neither of you drink. I never expect wine here."

"I guess we're lucky you don't expect dance music either. We heard you made quite the spectacle of yourself over the weekend."

Daphne blinked. "I had a wonderful time."

Her mother's lips pinched into a tight line. "I'm sure you did. Beatrice said you practically glued yourself to that unkempt chef who works at the resort."

Daphne didn't like Beatrice, never had. The woman loved to tattle behind people's backs. "Tyne was nice enough to invite me to Harley's Halloween party. We met Miriam there."

Dad shook his head. "I'm sure Miriam encouraged you."

"I'm thirty-six, Dad. I'm past people encouraging me. I'm way past the peer-pressure years."

Mom's eyes narrowed. "Are you interested in the chef?"

"He's a great friend. I have fun when I'm with him."

"He looks loose to me."

"Loose?" Daphne reached for her water, and her hand shook.

"His moral standards, I'm sure, are lower than ours."

"If you consider kindness *loose*, then I'd have to agree. I've never met anyone who helps more people." Her voice sounded sharp, even to her own ears. She hated conflict, confrontation. Her mother knew that. Mom meant to make her uncomfortable, but for the first time Daphne resented it. Why couldn't they respect her choices? It's not like she was wanton and carefree. Would they consider her *loose* because she had sex with him? She didn't need to answer that. She already knew. But they'd never once drilled her about the professor, who was not quite divorced. Suddenly, that struck her as hypocritical.

Mom wouldn't let it drop. "He's traveled all around the world, hasn't he? Lord knows what he's seen or done. He's on the wild side, isn't he?"

"Because he drives a motorcycle?"

Her mom stared. Daphne took a deep breath. "I wouldn't call him wild. He's adventurous and unafraid, but he's considerate of other people. Gladys likes him."

"Gladys is easy to sway. She comes to church every week, but flattery goes a long way with her. She works with him, and he knows how to work the ladies, doesn't he?"

"Betty likes him, too, and she's *not* easy to sway."

"He reminds her of her sons, close to the same age. She has a soft spot for young men."

Daphne tried to think of a way to change the topic, but when her mom got on a subject, she didn't let go. "Most people who know him like him." It was a weak defense, but it was the best she could do.

"Does he attend church on Sundays?"

"For heaven's sake!" Daphne pushed her plate away. "No, and neither do I."

Her father squared his shoulders. "Don't brag about that. We don't approve, and you know it."

"I don't want to be judged. And you don't know Tyne well enough to judge him either."

"You're young." Her mother passed a knowing glance to Dad. "Lots of children go through rebellions. You'll return to the fold eventually."

Daphne curled her nails into her palms. "I'm not a child, and I enjoy spending time with Tyne."

"I don't like your tone." Her dad scowled. "We heard that he took you on a motorcycle ride."

Her mom nodded. "You know how dangerous those are. We've told you over and over again."

Dad reached to lay a hand over Daphne's. "We only want what's best for you, dear."

"What's best for me is Tyne. He makes me happy, but he only thinks of me as a friend. He's been completely honest with me about that."

Her mother's hand went to her throat. "Have you slept with him?"

Really! She was thirty-six, and Mom was going to pry into her sex life? She had to bite her tongue to keep from saying *Yes, I did, and he was ten times better than the professor.* Instead, she said, "You both do realize that I'm a grown woman now, don't you?"

Her mother took that as an affirmative. She rose and pointed a finger. "We forbid you to see him anymore."

Daphne rose, too. She shook with anger this time, not indignation. "I don't live at home, Mom. I have a house, a cat, and a life. And if I want to see Tyne, I will."

Her dad went to stand beside his wife. He rarely raised his voice, and he didn't now, but his words were final. "It's time you leave."

"Gladly." Daphne grabbed her purse and jacket and stormed out of the house. As she walked to her SUV, she was sure her parents would come after her. They didn't. She'd disobeyed them, and they wouldn't brook that. They'd ostracize her until she came around to their way of thinking. Well, that wasn't going to happen. They'd pushed her too far.

Chapter 31

Daphne paced between the living room and the kitchen when she got home. She was upset and hungry. She hadn't eaten anything at her parents'. She couldn't swallow with both of them drilling her. Shadow pounced on her foot the third time she passed him, and she scooped him up and held him close. When she stroked his smooth fur, purrs rumbled from his chest. She couldn't settle and finally grabbed her cell and called Miriam.

"I argued with my parents."

Miriam's voice rose an octave. "You? Good Lord, what happened? No, don't tell me. I'm on my way to your house. See you in fifteen minutes."

"If you stop for food, I'll pay for it."

"Oh, this has got to be good. I'll buy us a feast, my treat."

Daphne went into her bedroom to change into old jeans and a ratty sweater. In the two front rooms of her cabin, the logs had been drywalled over and painted, but the builder had left them exposed in here. They gave the room a homey feel. She glanced at the garden-club quilt she'd made for her queen-sized bed—patches of flowered material all sewn together like connecting diamonds—and she thought of Tyne. He'd seen it and complimented it. He loved her quilting. A knot lodged in her throat, and she slid her feet into her old slippers.

She heard Miriam's car pull into the drive and went to greet her friend.

Miriam took a bottle of wine and a large bag, filled with takeout, to the coffee table and plopped them down. Then she turned to look at Daphne. She narrowed her eyes. "You look different. There's something . . ." Her jaw dropped. "You did the nasty, didn't you?"

Daphne could feel the heat rush to her face. "It wasn't nasty."

"You never looked like that after Patrick spent the night."

"Patrick only made it to mundane."

Miriam hooted. "Oh, girl! You've made my night. I was grading essay papers, and you saved me from dangling participles and screwed-up verb tenses. Pour us some wine, then spill the goods."

Daphne uncorked the bottle and poured two glasses while Miriam dug Styrofoam boxes filled with pork tenderloin sandwiches, onion rings, and French fries from the bag. "Decadent food for decadent gossip." She wiggled her eyebrows. "Was it good?"

"Oh my god, yes!"

Miriam slapped her hands on her knees. "Glory be! It had to be Tyne."

"He's as good at sex as he is at cooking. I never knew so much pleasure."

"Damn it to hell, would he do me if I paid him?"

Daphne smiled. "I think there are limits to what he'll do for a friend."

"But I'm a special friend. You'd think I should get special consideration."

Daphne took a bite of her sandwich. Jeez, it was good. Her mom's spaghetti was good, too, but it couldn't compare to crispy, fried heaven. "My parents asked me to leave their house tonight."

Miriam stared, her humor gone. "They found out?"

"I confessed. They weren't happy with me. Beatrice told them about me dancing at Chase's and at Harley's party. They said I was unseemly."

"Holy shit, they should be happy you're finally cutting loose a little."

"Loose." She cringed at the word. "That's how they described Tyne."

"Do they know what a stand-up guy he is?"

"They don't care." Daphne sipped her wine. "Mom came right out and asked me if I'd slept with him. I wasn't going to lie. I mean, I'm thirty-six. If I want to sleep with *one* guy, I don't think that makes me a slut."

Miriam got that glint in her eye that Daphne knew so well. "Did they ask you about the professor?"

"Not once."

"Hypocrites."

Daphne shrugged. "They thought the professor was going to ask me to marry him eventually. They think I'm just a notch on Tyne's bedpost, nothing more."

Miriam sighed. "God, I'd love to be a notch. At least, I'd be counted that way."

Daphne shook her head. "Some guy is going to fall for you, and when he does, he won't let go. You're special. He'll want to marry you."

Miriam snorted. "Me? A wifey? Don't think so. I'd settle for an affair if the guy isn't married. I can't do adultery." Daphne winced, and Miriam shook her head. "You don't do adultery either. You thought Patrick and the Ice Queen were kaput."

Okay, that was true. Both Patrick and his wife seemed ready to call their marriage a day until they looked at their finances.

Daphne drained her wine glass. "What am I going to do, Miriam? I thought Mom or Dad would call me back when I left the house, but they didn't. And I'm not about to apologize for sleeping with Tyne. If he wants to, I'll do it again."

Miriam hesitated, choosing her words carefully. *Uh-oh*, her friend was going to drop a bomb. Daphne held her breath. "You've bent over backward trying to please your parents. It's time you stopped. It's time you make your own decisions and do what makes you happy. I hate to say this, but it's time your parents start to respect you."

"Your parents do that with you, don't they?"

"Hell yes, we get together and have the most fun. They want me to be happy. Your parents have a control issue. It's time they got over it."

Daphne raised her chin. "I'm not calling them first this time. They either love me as is, or I'll love them but we won't see each other anymore."

Miriam nodded. "Hang tough, girlfriend."

Daphne grimaced. Hanging tough wasn't her strong point. She had trouble staying angry with anyone. "I'll try."

Miriam sighed. "Don't cave on me, not this time."

She couldn't make any promises.

Miriam shook her head. "Let's finish this food before it goes cold. And tell me the important stuff. Is Tyne a good kisser?"

Daphne laughed and reached for another onion ring. Miriam was letting her off the hook, purposely changing the subject. She needed a little levity right now. "He can curl your toes."

"The type of guy who can suck your soul right past your lips?"

"Yeah, and you hope he comes back for seconds."

Shadow jumped on the arm of Daphne's chair, and she tore off small pieces of her breaded tenderloin for him. Miriam tossed French fry bits across the wooden floor for him to chase.

It wasn't until Miriam left that Daphne thought about her parents again. And Tyne. If she took a hard stand with Mom and Dad, if she chose Tyne over them, what happened when Tyne cast her aside? When he found someone prettier, wittier, more adventurous, and moved on like he always did? Then where would she be? Alone. She'd only have Miriam, and even Miriam would get tired of her.

Chapter 32

Tyne knew he wasn't in the best mood when he walked into the kitchen for the supper shift. He'd meant to pop into Daphne's shop to see her for a few minutes this afternoon. It was a chilly, blustery day, and tourists had chosen to stay home. The last of the leaves were blowing off tree branches, so the national forest wouldn't draw them to town. He should be able to spend a little time with her.

Daphne was talking on the phone when he wandered between two aisles. Damn, she was pretty with her hair pulled up in a ponytail, showing off her long, slender neck, her high cheekbones. Lust had curled inside him, and he wanted to take her into the workroom, unbutton her blouse, and fondle her perfect breasts, but when she saw him, her expression closed and she shook her head. Just that. A silent *no*. And then she'd turned her back to him.

What the hell had happened? They'd had great sex Monday night. He'd worried about seeing her on Tuesday, but she'd actually stretched up on tiptoe to kiss him when he'd stopped in her shop before work. He expected the same today, but she'd given him the cold shoulder. Literally. He'd turned and walked away. She might not want to sleep with him again, but he thought they were friends. He deserved something. Maybe a "Hey, I think we moved too fast Monday night" or "I think we made a mistake." Something.

He'd taken off for a long walk. The wind bit his cheeks, stung his ears. Every time his thoughts turned to Daphne, he pushed them away. Damn it! He hadn't come on to her. She'd made the first move on him. He deserved some credit, didn't he?

Finally, he'd had to return to his apartment to change into his chef's gear. He hurried up the inside stairs without a glance at the shop. If Daphne wanted to be left alone, he'd be happy to oblige her.

He didn't give her a backward glance when he left the shop either. Screw her. But boy, had she ruined his day.

Paula took one look at him when he tied on his apron and raised her eyebrows at Cody. Cody shrugged, but when Tyne walked straight to the refrigerator to take out the veal chops he was matching with golden-raisin sauce tonight, Cody cleared his throat.

"If you don't want to tinker with my air intake valve after work, I get it."

Tyne skewered him with a look. "I told you I'd work on it, and I will."

Paula hitched her thumb at Steph, and the two women scooted out of the kitchen. Tyne glowered. *Cowards.* He started cooking with a vengeance. Usually, the kitchen was filled with laughter and gabbing. Not tonight. Everyone kept their distance from him, and he knew it. He tried to work himself into a better mood, but it didn't happen.

Finally, when the last pot was clean and put away, everyone gave a sigh of relief, including Tyne, and they scurried away. All but Cody. He fidgeted, nervous.

"Just spit it out," Tyne told him.

"Lexy called and got off work early tonight. She asked if we could get together."

Tyne waved him off. "We can work on the valve any time."

"Sorry, Tyne." The kid sounded contrite, as though he'd let him down.

Tyne tried for a smile. It didn't feel right, but he made the effort. "Hey, women come first." If you had one. Which he didn't. Maybe he should remedy that. There had to be some girl in Mill Pond who didn't want to bond forever, someone he could hang out with to have a good time.

Cody didn't linger. He took off. Tyne heard his truck engine sputter to life, and then glanced around the empty kitchen. They'd worked so fast, so hard, everything was done. He decided to drive to Harley's, but when he got there, Harley and Kathy had gone on a "date night." Only Harley's dad, Gino, was home.

Gino invited him in and shook his head. "Looks like life's given you a hard knock today, boy."

Tyne made a habit of not talking about the women he was involved with, but Gino wasn't the type to gossip. Tyne liked him, and whatever he told him would stay in this room. "Daphne Ferris is a close friend. At least, I thought we were close. Monday night, she came on to me, and we . . . well, you know. Tuesday, I saw her for a few minutes. She had a decent amount of customers, but when she had a chance, she kissed me. I had to work the supper shift, but when I left, we seemed okay. Today, I stopped in her shop and she wouldn't even talk to me. It's not like we're teenagers. I don't get it." Her snub bothered him more than he wanted to admit.

Gino went to the kitchen and returned with two beers. He handed one to Tyne. "Her parents came home yesterday. She had dinner with them last night. They gave her hell. Beatrice is telling everyone they gave her an ultimatum. You or them."

Tyne stared. "You're kidding. She's a grown woman."

". . . who sees her parents almost every single day."

Tyne shrugged. "Harley sees you every day. Hell, he lives with you."

"It's different for us. We're more friends and business partners now than father and son. Daphne's still Arnold and Sophia's daughter. Their relationship has hardly changed."

Tyne took a long sip of his beer. He rested his elbows on his knees, deep in thought. "What about the professor? Did they approve of him?"

"He's exactly what they want for Daphne. He enjoyed going on double dates with them, especially when they paid for the concert tickets."

"So I'm doomed."

"You're everything they hate." Gino finished his beer and stood to get another one. "You?"

"Why not?" Tyne drained his, too, and handed him the empty bottle. This whole situation was new to him. Most parents took one look at him and pushed their daughters into his path. He was successful, considered a "catch." He avoided those girls. They were looking for marriage.

Gino returned and pointed his bottle at Tyne to make his point. "In all fairness to Daphne's parents, they don't see you as long-term happiness for their daughter. They see you as the love 'em-and-leave-'em type."

He couldn't argue with that. "They're right."

"But Daphne's not like that. She's not a player."

"Neither am I. I don't just blow through girls for the fun of it."

"Harley didn't either, but not every girl wants to hang in there just because you're monogamous. Ask him about Marissa someday. She got tired of waiting and moved on. Some girls want a commitment, and it doesn't sound like you're ready to give one."

Tyne played with the label on his beer bottle, picking off the edges. "You're telling me I'm not right for Daphne."

"Her parents don't think so, but they'd have her stuck with some stick-in-the-mud who pleased *them* more than he pleased *her*." Gino shook his head. "Romance is complicated. It never gets easier. When you're older, you find someone you'd like to commit to, but you can't."

Tyne heard the angst in his voice. He frowned. "Why can't you?"

"Harley and I own the winery together. We share this house. He's invested time and energy into both. What would happen if I remarried? How could I tell Harley that a new wife would get half of everything I own? That he'd have to find a new place to stay?"

"Did you ever think that Harley would be happy for you?"

Gino ran a hand over his face. "He's a good kid. He would be, but that doesn't mean that it's fair to him."

"Let him decide what he wants or doesn't. Talk to him about it. Man up."

Gino looked at him. "You don't back away from anything, do you?"

"Sure I do. It's a lot easier giving other people advice than finding your own."

Gino smiled. "Why not just follow your heart? Daphne's important to you, isn't she?"

Tyne finished his beer and stood. "I have goals. A woman isn't part of them, at least, not yet."

Gino laughed. "Son, life doesn't work that way. It's not that neat, but you'll find that out on your own. If you love this girl, though, I wouldn't let her go."

Love? He didn't love Daphne. Did he? "I love lots of things."

"Which one of them makes you the happiest?"

Tyne blinked. He didn't know.

Chapter 33

Tyne didn't want things to end between Daphne and him in such a mess. He went to Art's grocery the next day and bought all the things to make Parisian tuna sandwiches—boiled eggs, tomatoes, red onion, artichoke hearts, and a bag of arugula. Good tuna. Good bread. Made one for him, one for her. He wrapped them in waxed paper. At lunch time, he took them down to her shop and waited for a customer to leave before handing her one. "As a peace offering."

She stared. She had dark circles under eyes, and he wanted to touch them and make them better. But he stopped himself. He was part of what was causing her stress.

He smiled. "I've heard about the ultimatum. Make it easy on yourself. Let's go back to being friends."

"My parents forbade me to see you again."

"At all? Not even coffee on Saturdays when I hike?"

She shook her head. She looked tired, defeated.

"Won't Shadow miss me?"

She smiled. "So will I."

"I get it. I'm not good for you. We're too different." It hurt, but she wasn't going to change, and neither was he. She'd be in Mill Pond for the rest of her life. He might move on. And then where would she be? It wasn't fair to make her choose. "Let's call this our Last Supper."

She motioned him into the workroom. They sat on stools close to each other, and she fiddled with the waxed paper on her sandwich. "It's my fault. I didn't control myself around you. Beatrice told my parents about how we danced dirty and drank too much."

He'd like to track down Beatrice and make her life miserable. He might. "Hey, we had fun together. I don't regret it."

She grimaced. "Neither do I. It's going to be hard, though, knowing what I could have had, at least for a while, that's now been taken away from me."

He wanted to put his hand over hers. To tell her she could have that and much, much more, but wouldn't that just hurt her in the long run? He tried to lift her spirits. "All you have to do now is find a happy medium. Patrick was too dreary. I'm too spontaneous. There's a guy out there who's just right."

She nodded, and tears misted her eyes. She blinked them away. She didn't touch her sandwich. Neither did he.

He finally couldn't stand being so miserable, so stood with a grin. "Take care, Daphne. I think you're wonderful." Another nod. He had to get out of there. He almost ran for the door.

Once outside, he decided to return to Art's to buy plenty of beer for the nights ahead. He was walking down an aisle when Chantelle turned the corner, walked straight to him, and pressed herself against him.

"Rumor is Miss Prude ditched you. I can make you feel good again." She kissed him so hard, his lips parted, and she jammed her tongue down his throat.

Anger flooded him, and he grabbed both of her arms to push her away when a flash caught him by surprise. He looked up, and Daphne's mother stood there with a smirk and took another picture with her cell phone.

Bitch. So she thought she could intimidate him, did she? Well, he wasn't her daughter, and she couldn't slam him with ultimatums.

Her lips curled in disapproval. "I don't see what my daughter sees in you."

Tyne raised an eyebrow. "I could say the same. How did Daphne get to be so nice?" But then it struck him that Daphne must have defended him to her parents. He pulled Chantelle close and kissed her back. "Thank you. Now go away."

She licked her lips, stunned.

"Shoo! Leave!" He gave her a gentle push, and she walked away, bleary eyed.

Daphne's mother shook her head. "Look at you. Women just fall at your feet, don't they? We didn't raise our daughter like that.

You're not worth her time." She swiveled on her heel to stalk out of the store.

Tyne followed her. When she parked at the curb in front of Daphne's shop, he drove around the block to park behind it. By the time he walked through the back door, her mom was showing the pictures to Daphne.

Tyne came to glance at them, too. "I think she got my best side. I kind of like my profile."

Daphne's jaw dropped. "Tyne ..."

He nodded at the pictures. "You've met Chantelle. She'd hump a corpse if he was attractive. She was having fun with me. Lots of women touch without permission."

She turned to her mother. "They do. Women touch him all the time."

"He wasn't beating her off."

Tyne pointed. "Look at my hands. I was getting ready to push her away, but I doubt you'll believe that. I don't care what you think. I do care about Daphne. We're friends, but you won't believe that either."

Her mother sneered. "*Friends with benefits*. I know that term."

"Good. Did you look it up?" He turned back to Daphne. "From what your mother said, though, I think you defended me, and I appreciate that. You're starting to grow some balls. Quit letting them push you around, or you're never going to be happy." He lifted her off her feet and kissed her properly. "I want you to be happy, Daphne, even if that means I need to stay away from you."

She gasped for air when he set her down.

"Are you leaving now?" her mother asked.

He'd meant to, but now he came to stand in front of her. "Are you trying to make sure your daughter never marries? That you never let go of her? Is that your plan? Because you're doing a good job of it."

"I don't want her to get hurt."

Tyne studied her. Was the woman that naïve? "But she got hurt, didn't she? By the professor. And she survived. Anything worth anything comes with a risk. Are you glad you met your husband?"

Her eyes flashed with temper. "Are you implying that I'm not? That that's why I don't want Daphne to marry? Because you're wrong. We've had a wonderful marriage."

"Could you guarantee that?"

Her mother's chin shot up. "There are no guarantees. You know that."

"Yes, I do. My point exactly. You have a wonderful daughter. Don't be stupid and lose her." He'd said enough. Too much. He stalked out of the shop and drove to the resort.

Chapter 34

Tyne's brain felt jumbled with chaos. Did he just make things better for Daphne or worse? In the long term versus the short? Or would it never unscramble? He'd tried to open her eyes to what life had to offer. Had he made her hungry for more? Or did he just alienate her from her parents and make her options shrink?

He parked close to the kitchen door but didn't leave his Jeep. He needed to sort things out. Daphne had gotten to him. How had that happened? It was his own fault. He'd always connected with women who didn't expect him to stick around, women who wouldn't get hurt when he picked up and left. Daphne was different. He knew that, and that's why he liked her. Too much.

He'd made a mistake. Fallen for the wrong woman. That made him feel bad. He didn't garb himself in guilt very often. He tried to push it away, but it only burrowed deeper. Finally, he walked into the restaurant to work. He needed a distraction.

Paula looked up and smiled. "Hey, I had to change my dinner option for tonight, couldn't get enough Cornish hens. I went with crispy chicken paillards instead. They'll go fine with your ricotta gnudi with mushroom-garlic butter."

He frowned. "What?"

She came to stand in front of him, put her hands on each side of his face. "You beautiful, wonderful hottie, you didn't hear a word I said, did you?"

He blinked at her, lost. "This is Friday. We do prime rib and salmon."

"Not tonight. We switched it up. A group of guests are coming in late to rent the cabins tomorrow, remember? They're only staying one night, so Ian asked us to flip meals around."

"Right." He rubbed his forehead, trying to focus.

She grinned. "What are you fighting it for? Daphne's a keeper. Marriage is wonderful. Ask me. I've never been happier."

He felt his brows draw together in a scowl, what his mom used to call his Stubborn Face. "Her parents don't like me. I know what it's like to be cut off from your mom and dad. Daphne and her parents are close. She'd regret losing them after a while."

"She'll regret losing you, too."

Tyne shook his head. "Once she starts looking for love, she'll find it. She's too special. Someone will snatch her up."

"But not you?"

"I challenge her, but that doesn't mean I'm right for her. And once I don't see her for a week or two, I'll be okay."

Paula patted his arm. "I don't believe you, but you'll have to find out for yourself. Just remember, you were always there for me. I'll always be here for you."

The kitchen door opened, and her kids flew in to see them. Aiden grinned ear to ear, fake punching Tyne. Bailey wanted him to pick her up, and pretty soon, he could feel himself relax. Life went on. He had lots of friends to fill his time. And his heart. When Paula, Aiden, and Bailey left, he was ready to get down to the business of cooking.

He lost himself in the feel of the gnudi he was making for dinner. Mixing the ricotta with the eggs, Parmigiano, and flour. The aromas and textures. Cooking always helped center him.

More guests than usual came to compliment him on the food that night. The foodies who came to the resort were willing to try new things. He could stretch his wings here.

He stayed after work to help Cody work on his pickup. By the time he turned off the lights in the kitchen and locked up behind him, he felt like he was finding his balance again. He was going to miss Daphne, but he'd keep himself busy. He'd experiment on new recipes at home, maybe drive to Indy on Monday and buy new cookbooks and cooking equipment. He'd wanted a tagine for a long time. Maybe he'd buy a few of them, and if he liked them, he'd take more to the restaurant.

He felt tired when he climbed the stairs to his apartment. It was only ten, but the drama of the last few days had wiped him out. He took a quick shower to rinse off the kitchen smells, then sagged onto his bed.

His phone buzzed at three a.m. He frowned, confused. This wasn't Monday. He didn't work an early shift. And then he glanced at the clock. Not his alarm. Early hour phone calls never bade well. "Yes?" He waited.

Steph's voice sounded on the other end. "India died. Maxwell's a mess. I can't stay with him."

"I'm on my way." Tyne dressed and drove to the bakery. This was going to be a long night.

Chapter 35

Daphne didn't answer the phone. She hadn't even dressed today. Come to think of it, she hadn't gotten dressed yesterday either. The phone started again. She glanced at it. Her mom. She switched it off. She and Shadow shared a bowl of cereal while Daphne watched old movies on TV. Marilyn Monroe was swinging her hips as she walked down a train aisle. Jack Lemmon was dressed like a girl. Daphne had never seen anything so sad and started crying.

A voice came from the door. "It's a comedy."

Daphne glanced up as Miriam came to sit on the chair across from her. "Sorry, I meant to return your call, but I've been busy."

"I can tell." Miriam looked at the empty food cartons that littered the floor. "What happened? Did Tyne kick you to the curb?"

"No, I decided to stop seeing him."

Miriam took a deep breath. "Your parents."

"If I choose Tyne over them, and then he dumps me, what do I have left?"

"A life."

"But Tyne's only temporary, brief. We both know that."

"Who cares?"

Daphne wiped her eyes and flipped off the TV. Her teeth felt gummy. When had she brushed them? On Friday morning?

Miriam went to open the drapes. "There's sunshine today. It won't last. We're getting into Indiana's gray months."

"I hibernate during bad weather and get a lot of work done."

"Aren't you the good, little worker bee?"

Daphne blinked. "You never use sarcasm."

"I've never wanted to grab your shoulders and shake you before either."

Tears threatened again. "I'm not that strong, Miriam. My parents would never forgive me."

"Even priests offer penance." But Miriam's shoulders slumped. "So what are you going to do?"

"Hide for a while. Get myself together."

"Do you want some company?"

"Not this time. I'm going to wallow and get it out of my system."

"Good luck with that." Miriam started for the door. "I'll buy you some groceries. It looks like you're out of all your frozen entrees."

"I'm not hungry."

"You say that now. Wait till you're sucking on ice cubes, hoping for nourishment."

Daphne laid her head back on the arm of the sofa. "Thanks, Miriam."

"Don't thank me. I'm your friend, but I'm disappointed in you right now."

The tears started again. They slid off her nose and down her cheeks. Daphne sighed. "I'm sorry."

"I know, and I'll get over it, but it's going to take me a minute." And then she left.

She returned an hour later with bags full of food items and quickly put them in the refrigerator and freezer. "I'll let myself out. When you're ready to venture outside again, let me know."

Daphne heard Miriam's car pull away and buried her face against the couch cushions. She'd live through this. People did.

Chapter 36

Tyne woke early every morning and walked to Maxwell's to meet Steph. The temperatures were cold enough to jerk him awake. Frost covered the shop awnings and wooden kegs that held flowers in the spring and summer. He always glanced in Daphne's window and admired what she hung there. She'd obviously spent a lot of time working lately. Just like him. There were a lot of new pieces, and they stood out from her older style. The colors were moodier, edgier. He liked them.

Between Steph and him, they had the baking routine down to an art. They hadn't had a choice. After India's funeral, Maxwell wouldn't get out of bed. He hardly ate, wasn't hungry. He didn't take showers or step foot in the bakery. The only thing that made him happy was Chester. Even then, Tyne fed and watered the dog. Sadie took him for walks.

In the evenings, Tyne worked the supper shift at the resort. He never saw Daphne. He was up and gone before she opened her shop. He was at the resort when she locked up. In any free time, he perfected new recipes. He was thinking about writing a cookbook. He tested ingredients and timing over and over again.

Paula finally looked at him one day and said, "Do you ever have fun anymore?"

He scratched his chin. "Cooking's fun."

"Outside of that."

"No time or energy."

She put her hands on her hips. She might be short, but she bristled with energy. "It's time to tell Maxwell to get his ass out of bed and get his act together."

"He just lost his wife."

Paula raised a dark eyebrow. "I've been there. Done that. When Alex died, I couldn't see how I'd go on, but I had two kids, and I couldn't suck my thumb and feel sorry for myself. Maxwell's had that luxury, but it's not doing him any favors. He's going to hurt for a year and feel crappy for the next one. But life goes on. Either he runs the bakery or he sells it."

Steph nodded agreement. "I like Maxwell, but he's letting us carry his load. So far, I've been happy to, but I'm not sure we're helping him."

Paula lifted her wooden spoon to shake at him. "Ian's filled the resort for Thanksgiving weekend. We're going to be swamped. You can't do it all. Face it."

Tyne raked his hand through his short, spiky hair. "My brother wants me to fly to California the second week of December for sort of a Thanksgiving-Christmas dinner combined. We're both chefs. We're both busy over the holidays."

Paula nodded. "See? You need to have a life, too. If Maxwell wants to grieve longer, he needs to hire another helper. You need to back off."

He knew she was right. He'd been wondering how long he could keep up this schedule. He nodded. "I'll talk to him."

Paula relaxed. "Good, you need to get out and about again. You've turned into a little, old lady—all you do is work and cook."

He laughed. "I'm sort of tall for an old lady."

"And she'd look horrible with a chin strap. I'm just saying you act like one."

He threw up his hands in defeat. "Okay, I get it. You're tired of me moping around."

She wiped her hands on her apron and went to hang it on its hook. "My job's done now. I can go home. Get a life."

That's what he'd told Daphne, and look how well that had turned out. He was made of tougher stuff, though. When he left the restaurant that night, he went to Chase's for the first time in a long time and took a seat at the bar.

Chase served him with a grin. "The beer's on me. My wife said she gave you a tongue lashing today."

"It's a good thing I have healthy self-esteem."

"Don't I know it." Chase rested his elbows on the bar. "That's why I married her. She doesn't mind giving me a hard time."

"I had plenty of people happy to do that. I don't need any more of it." He thought of his mother, going on and on about what he didn't do right.

"Yeah, you've already earned your stripes. When Holden came to the bar for the burger contest, he told me about your parents."

"I spent the first twenty years of my life listening to them harangue me. I plan to spend the rest of it with people who make me feel good."

"Then you've come to the right place. Mill Pond loves you."

Tyne snorted. "That's because I'm surrounded by foodies. We all stick together."

Chase poured him a second beer. "I'm taking the boat out for one last run on Sunday. Paula has to work, and her mom's stealing the kids for the weekend. Want to come along?"

"Sounds good." He pushed his mug away at the halfway mark and rubbed his eyes. "Gotta go. The beer's making me tired. I've been short of sleep lately."

"Yeah, I've heard."

"Paula." Tyne chuckled. "Tell her I'm on the mend. I'm going to play this weekend."

"Will do."

When Tyne fell into bed that night, he was exhausted. He didn't look forward to talking to Maxwell tomorrow, but he'd rather get it done. He hoped it went better than his talk with Daphne.

Chapter 37

Thursday's gray skies brooded over Mill Pond. Customers came and went in intervals, so Daphne had plenty of time to spend in her workroom. A good thing. She'd had fewer customers lately, but she'd sold more pieces than usual. She was constantly trying to make new pieces to restock partially empty spaces.

She frowned at the wall hanging she was working on. Shades of smoky grays mingled with moody purples. Who knew so many people would want such dramatic colors? On the far side of the table, she'd finished a piece with Christmas reds and greens. Cheerier. Those were selling fast, too. She heard footsteps rush down the side stairs and hurry out the back door. There was a time when Tyne would poke his head around the corner to say hi to her, but not anymore. Why would he? She'd pushed him away.

By the end of the day, she'd sold as many pieces as she'd made. She wouldn't get caught up until the weather turned miserable. She glanced at the sky. Gloomy. Go figure.

She turned the sign to CLOSED and was locking the door when her parents parked at the front curb. Her mom saw her and hurried out of the car. Daphne flipped the lock and walked to the back door to do the same. Mom pounded on the glass, but Daphne went to her workroom and closed the door. Her cell phone buzzed.

"Yes?"

"We're going to Chase's tonight and thought you might want to come along."

"I'm not hungry."

"You're too thin. You've lost weight. Are you all right?"

"No, I'm not. But I'll live. I'm busy, Mom. Have to go." She switched off her phone.

She cracked the door and watched her parents pull away. She didn't want to see them, didn't want to talk to them. Someday, she'd forgive them. Maybe.

Later that night, she ordered pizza and took it home to eat, but after a few bites, she didn't want anymore. She sank onto the couch, her new haven, and cuddled with Shadow.

On Friday, she went through the same routines she used to love. They felt empty to her now. And on Friday night, she dragged herself to bed, too tired to rent a movie.

Saturday brought sunshine, and Shadow meowed at the door. The cat didn't deserve to suffer with her. She pulled on jeans and a heavy sweater, then went outside to sit on the back stoop to keep an eye on him. He still couldn't quite jump high enough to escape the fence, so she watched him chase dead leaves around the yard.

She was sitting there when her parents came to sit beside her.

"What are you staring at?" her mom asked.

"Tyne used to hike that trail every Saturday morning and then stop in to have coffee with me. He hikes a different trail now."

Dad's voice was gruff. "You miss him, don't you?"

"He was trying to help me get over the professor. The thing is, I didn't miss Patrick for more than a few days, didn't fall apart when he dumped me. I miss Tyne."

"Let's go get some lunch and go shopping," Mom said.

"We have tickets to a concert in Bloomington tonight," Dad added.

Daphne shrugged. "Thanks anyway. I'm not in the mood."

"You can't just sit here and mope every day." Mom's voice rose. "You look horrible. How much weight have you lost?"

Daphne didn't answer. She went to pick up Shadow to carry him inside. "Thanks for stopping by."

"Daphne, you have to get over this!" Her mom stood, too.

Daphne gazed at her without seeing. "Why? I don't want what I had before, and I don't have a future, do I?" She went inside and shut the door.

Chapter 38

Harley called Tyne on Friday. "I've got news! Come share it with us." On the drive to the vineyard, Tyne passed the bakery. It closed at two, so the shop was dark. So were the upstairs windows. Maxwell would be back in bed, sleeping off his misery. Sadie had volunteered to keep Chester with her in the afternoons, but the Chihuahua curled on India's pillow, mourning her, too.

Tyne had hassled Maxwell enough to get him out of bed every morning. Not that he was good company. But Tyne worked with him for two hours every day, and between the three of them, Steph said they were doing all right. It wasn't a perfect situation, but it was a start. He knew Maxwell was doing better, because his friend was getting annoyed with him.

"If you call me *Eeyore* one more time, I'm going to stuff you in a pie," Maxwell threatened this morning.

Tyne grinned. "What did you say, Mr. Morose?"

Maxwell's shoulders squared. "I'm getting there, damn it. And you don't have to be such a pain in the ass."

"But that's what I'm good at," Tyne told him. "And I improve with practice."

Maxwell sighed. "If anyone else treated me the way you do . . ."

"You'd hug them and do a waltz around the bakery, because only someone who loved you could put up with your cranky moods."

Maxwell grimaced. "You've got me there. Thanks to you and Steph for hanging around."

"We're both masochists. We like it." Tyne had left when Sadie came to take Chester on one of his daily walks. The Chihuahua and the frozen-custard lady had bonded as buddies.

As he approached the winery, Tyne's thoughts turned back to

Harley. Was Kathy pregnant? Was Harley going to be a father in the near future? He'd watched the change in Chase when he'd taken on Paula's kids. The man adored being a dad. But who wouldn't fall in love with Aiden and Bailey? They were the coolest kids in town, not that he was prejudiced or anything.

He parked near the wine-tasting room and found it empty of customers. Harley, Kathy, Gino, and Vicki all sat at a round table, and they all looked happy.

"Guess what?" Harley called. "Dad asked Vicki to marry him, and she said yes."

Good news indeed! Gino deserved to find happiness again. How had his worries sorted out?

"And?" Tyne wanted the details.

Harley laughed. "Come to find out the old man was fretting that I'd be upset because he'd mess up my inheritance."

"Were you?" Tyne had seen families lock horns over money.

"Why would I be? We're successful enough, and I want Dad to be happy."

"So everything worked out okay?"

"No, now I'm going to have to hire a financial consultant, because Vicki's richer than sin."

Tyne blinked. "Run that by me again."

Gino slapped him on the back. "Vicki here's a widow, who was married to a very rich man. They couldn't have children, so after he died, she was lonely. She only came to work at the winery to have something to do."

"And I've always loved wine." Vicki gave a resigned smile.

Tyne shook his head. "Then you met the Italian stallion."

Gino sputtered, but Vicki laughed. "Something like that. I thought I was going to fill time, to meet new people, but who could resist Gino?" She locked gazes with him. "Some things are priceless."

Gino carried a bottle of champagne to the table. "To true love!"

They all toasted the new couple. Tyne sighed. He was glad someone had a happy-ever-after. That might not be in his future.

"So when's the wedding?" he asked.

"In a month." Vicki passed him a travel brochure. "We're going to the justice of the peace, and then we're taking a river cruise in Europe."

Perfect. Tyne was happy for them.

Chapter 39

Daphne stopped at the grocery store after she closed the shop on Friday. Shadow needed more cat food. On the spur of the moment, she loaded her cart with boneless, skinless chicken breasts, too, and lots of produce for fresh salads.

At home, after she fed Shadow, she changed into old clothes and put a chicken breast in a skillet to sauté. What had Tyne used as flavoring? She didn't have any fish sauce or rice wine vinegar, no coconut milk or curry paste either. She settled on salt and pepper and a dash of basil. Then she chopped the chicken and sprinkled it on top of the salad she made. The dish needed a generous dose of honey-mustard dressing, but it was edible. She rinsed all of the dirty dishes she'd left in the sink during the week, loaded them in the dishwasher, and then went to her sewing room.

She was going to make a grief quilt. It would be one of the most elaborate quilts she'd ever made, one that would remind her of all the good times she'd had with Tyne. She started with a huge, navy square for the center, and then cut out fabric pieces to resemble a chef. She'd stitch that on the square as the quilt's focal point. She cut out a gold rectangle for one side and a motorcycle pattern to sew on it. A black rectangle would hold fall leaves. A small cream-colored one displayed his favorite book; a wider, rust-colored one, a world map. She cut out pieces of a couple dancing. And on and on until her eyes blurred and she was too tired to cut with accuracy.

Time to quit. She drank a glass of wine, turned down her bed, and for the first night in a long time, crawled under her covers and slept well.

On Saturday, she was back in her sewing room when her parents dropped in again. Her mom frowned when she saw that Daphne was still in her pajamas and robe.

"It's two o'clock."

"Really?" Daphne shrugged. "I lost track of time."

"You've lost more weight."

Daphne glanced down at herself. "That's good. Thin is in."

Her dad looked worried. "You've always been thin. You need to eat more."

Daphne picked up Shadow and scratched under his chin. When she was a little girl, she always reached for her teddy bear when she was stressed. She wasn't sure when she'd started to use the kitten for comfort, but he helped, and she was grateful.

Her mom saw the light on in her sewing room and went to see what she was working on. She let out a long breath and stared. "This is for him, isn't it?"

Daphne wanted to hide the fabric patches. They were private, personal memories, but it was too late. "No, it's for me, to remember what we did together."

Her mother frowned. "What's the book for?"

"He likes to read as much as I do. He fixed me supper one time, and then we spent the night reading." They did more than that, but her mom didn't need to know that.

"And this?" Her mom pointed to a clay pot filled with herbs.

Daphne motioned out the window to the raised beds in her back yard. "Tyne said I have the perfect yard for gardens."

Mom pressed her lips together. "He made you happy."

"He's like that. He's helping Maxwell now, baking breads with him in the morning. Maxwell's having a hard time."

Mom put a hand to her throat. "We misjudged him, didn't we?"

"No, you wouldn't like him. He'd rub you wrong on lots of things."

Dad came to lace his arm around Daphne's waist. "Honey, if you like this boy so much . . ."

Daphne moved out of his embrace. She looked out the window. All of her flower beds were clean. Tyne's doing. Her raised beds stood ready for herbs in the spring. Behind her yard, the trees were bare. A couple walked on the trail that Tyne used to love. "Tyne took me on as a fixer upper. He's moved on now. He's not the type to settle down."

"That's our fault." Mom stumbled over the words. Daphne stared. She never thought she'd hear her mother say them. "If we'd . . ."

Daphne waved the rest away. "What's done is done. I can't talk about it anymore."

Dad straightened his shoulders. "We're driving to Indy tonight to go somewhere nice to eat. Why don't you come with us?"

Daphne reached out to touch a fabric piece. "Thanks, really, but I'm going to be busy for a while."

"Hon . . ."

But Daphne cut Mom off. "I can't. It's too soon."

"It's been a few weeks."

Daphne picked up the fabric and touched it to her cheek. "I know exactly how long it's been."

Mom and Dad left, and she returned to her work.

Chapter 40

Tyne glared at his reflection in the mirror. He already looked tired, and he hadn't made it to work yet. Saturday nights were usually busy, and then he and Paula had to gear up for Sunday brunch. Maybe he'd take a nap when he left the kitchen tomorrow.

He heard someone climbing the stairs that led to his apartment and frowned. He finished drying his face. He didn't have time for a visit unless . . . He glanced out the small window of his bathroom to the parking space behind the shop. Not Daphne's yellow SUV. Then he recognized the car—her parents. *Shit.*

They knocked on his door, and he stood perfectly still. The old floorboards creaked, and he didn't want them to know he was home. Of course, since they'd parked in back, they'd seen his orange Jeep. You couldn't miss it, but he often ducked out for a quick walk. Besides, it was none of their business. He had nothing to say to them.

He stayed still, waiting, until he heard their steps go back down the stairs and saw their car drive off. A close one. Then he shook his head. What did he care if he ran into them? He'd been fairly polite to them before. That wouldn't happen now. He sighed to his reflection. He thought Daphne might climb the steps eventually to see him, but after her parents warned her off him, she either stayed in her shop or in her cabin. Well, if her parents could scare her away from him, he hadn't meant all that much to her, had he?

"I'm better off on my own." The words sounded hollow. Damn it. He missed her, but that would fade with time. He'd meant to stay single until he was forty . . . at least. Maybe forever. But he'd never had less energy. Nothing much interested him lately. A phase. It would pass. He'd make it pass. It was a good thing he was flying to see his brother in a few weeks. The break would do him good.

He didn't like the look of his chin strap, so shaved off the sides so that he only had a goatee. He narrowed his eyes, studying himself. Did he look older, more sophisticated? *To hell with it!* He grabbed his jacket on his way out of the apartment and went to his Jeep.

It was only mid-afternoon, but the sky was already growing dark. He sighed. Another storm brewing. The lake water was choppy as he followed its shoreline to the resort. The beaches sat empty, the piers already taken in. No cattle grazed in the pastures. Barn doors were closed against inclement weather.

When he passed the Danzas' house and property, lights blazed in the front windows. David and Darinda would be inside, spending time with their two boys. When he pulled into the inn's parking lot, he was surprised to see it sprinkled with cars. Guests came until bad roads kept them away. January and February were the only super-slow months for business, and Ian had scheduled a Valentine's special to offset that. He'd already told them he wanted romance to pour from the kitchen for a four-day extravaganza. He'd hired masseuses to set up tables, and manicures and pedicures were scheduled, too.

Tyne groaned. He hoped romance didn't make him nauseous by then. He parked behind the kitchen and stalked through its back door. *Romance.* Who needed it? Paula and Steph glanced up at him, all smiles.

"You're early. Good, we can get out of here." Paula showed him the fixings for spaghetti carbonara with fresh duck eggs. He could mix them at the last minute. It would go perfectly with his entrée: seafood fideuà. Both were pasta dishes, but entirely different.

"What are you doing tonight?" he asked the two women.

Paula reached for her lightweight coat. "Mom and I are taking the kids to a movie. We're doing the whole splurge—drinks, popcorn, and candy."

He laughed. "Is Chase happy he's missing that?"

"Not according to him." Paula rolled her eyes. "He swears he loves Disney, but he avoids it whenever he can."

"And you?" Tyne looked at Steph.

"Ben put a big pot of stew on, and we're going to get in our pajamas and be bums tonight."

Tyne thought of sitting in his apartment next to Daphne, reading. It had been one of the most blissful nights of his life.

Steph cocked a brow at him. "What about you?"

"I'm going to Chase's bar to dance with every woman I can."

"Lord, half the female population of Mill Pond will be overheated tomorrow." Paula started out the door. "If you need to be rescued, call for Chase. He'll wade in to find you."

Paula was amused. He wasn't. But he'd be damned if he'd go home and look at four walls tonight.

Everyone must have felt the same. After he finished the supper shift and scooted to the bar, the place was so busy, Chase didn't have time to sit with him. Instead, Chantelle and two of her girlfriends came to join him at his booth. He tried to be friendly. He really did, but their conversation hit on so many things he considered tedious or silly, he thought of shooting himself.

When the band started up, women came to drag him onto the dance floor. He went through the moves, but his heart wasn't in it. He made it through one set of songs with hands wandering over him everywhere they shouldn't, then finally made his escape.

He drove home, dropped into a chair, and put his head in his hands. What was the matter with him? And how long would it take to heal? Just a few weeks more, he told himself, and then he'd be off to California, and Daphne would become a thing of the past.

Chapter 41

Daphne buried herself in work in her sewing room. Her parents knocked on her door after church, but she didn't answer it. She didn't want to see anyone. Tyne's quilt was coming together nicely. She figured it would take a month to finish it, and by then, she meant to get herself together, to square her shoulders and resign herself to a boring life.

Shadow had no such intentions. He attacked the fabric as she moved it through the feeder of her sewing machine. He knocked spools of thread off her sewing table and chased them under the table. He jumped on the back of her chair and threaded his body around her shoulders.

The sky grew darker and darker as she worked until she was forced to turn on every light in the room. The rest of the house was dark, but that didn't stop someone from pounding on her front door. She shut her workroom door. She heard the side gate for her yard open and close. Someone pounded on her sewing room's window. She peeked behind the shade, and Miriam stared in at her.

Crap. Daphne motioned to the kitchen door and went to let her in. Miriam stormed inside, blue eyes flashing.

"Do you know how many times I called you today? I thought we could go to brunch."

Daphne bit her bottom lip. "I turned off my cell phone. I've been busy."

"Busy, my ass!" Miriam stared at her friend. "Damn, you're wasting away. You're thinner than you were before I bought you groceries." She went to the cupboards and flung them open. The same food sat in the same places. She went to the refrigerator and freezer. "What have you been living on—cereal?" She looked at the trash. Three empty boxes.

She crossed her arms over her flat chest. "Come on. Get dressed. We're going to Ralph's."

"I don't want to go out."

"I didn't ask you, did I? I told you, and if you don't come with me, I'll move in here, and I'll share my opinions with you twenty-four hours a day."

Daphne shook her head. "You wouldn't."

"I'll be back in an hour. I have to pack."

"No." Daphne put up her hands in a pleading gesture. "Okay, give me a minute to change."

"Take longer than that." Miriam's tone was dry. "You look like shit."

When Daphne looked in the mirror, she was discouraged to find that Miriam was right. She washed her face and brushed her teeth, but there was no miracle fix for sunken cheeks and flat hair. She pulled her hair back in a bun and applied more blush than usual, but hoped no one would look too closely at her.

A half hour later, Miriam was driving her to town. "Your parents called me. You know that means they're desperate. They'd rather pretend I don't exist."

"What did they want?"

"They're worried about you. So am I."

"Good, let them worry. I don't care."

"Like hell you don't." Miriam glanced at her. "But if you're willing to rock the boat, why not go to Tyne, throw yourself at him, and let them worry about that?"

"I blew it, Miriam. He'd show me the door."

"You don't know that, do you? If you're going to lose him anyway, why not give it a shot?"

Daphne picked at a fingernail, avoiding eye contact. "I can barely survive this. I couldn't stand straight-out rejection. My ego's not that strong."

Miriam sighed. "I couldn't either, but if you're really throwing in the towel, then you've got to get over it. I don't enjoy having a wraith for a friend."

"I know, and I'm sorry. I'm giving myself one month. In the long scheme of things, that's not that much. And then I'll move on. I won't like it, but I'll accept it."

Miriam nodded. "One month. I'm writing it on my calendar. And then, by God, you're going out with me. We'll hit all the restaurants in town."

Like that would take long. Daphne didn't argue, though. She was touched by how fierce her friend was. "Every single one of them."

Miriam pressed her lips together. "This whole thing sucks."

"I can't argue with you about that."

Ralph's diner was crowded, as usual, on a weekend. Miriam surveyed the room full of people and said, "Want to settle on takeout?"

They placed their orders, waited for their food, then drove home.

Miriam handed Daphne her Styrofoam container and said, "I won't come in. I respect your timetable. You have one month. Get your act together."

"I will." By the end of the month, her Tyne quilt would be finished. Tyne would be nothing but memories. Good memories that she could cherish for years to come.

Chapter 42

It was three before Tyne walked out of the kitchen. Sunday brunch always took longer than other meals. Then he had to stay to make his entrée for supper. He'd decided on vitello tonnato, since he was boating with Chase today. *If* he was boating with Chase. According to Paula, the storm clouds were supposed to clear out this afternoon, but it was still plenty blustery.

He'd roasted his veal last night to let it cool, so all he had to do today was make the sauce, but he took longer at that than usual. Not concentrating like he should. When he climbed in his Jeep, a single shaft of sunlight escaped from the gloomy canopy overhead. It was like a sign—a sign that life would get better. He drove to Chase's bar and rang the doorbell at the back of the building. He heard footsteps pounding down the stairs and Paula yanked the door open. Her black hair spilled around her shoulders, rumpled and messy.

"Chase will be here in a minute."

Tyne grinned. "The kids are gone. Your mom took them for the weekend. If you guys would rather . . ."

She laughed. "We already have, and I work late shift tonight. Gotta get to the resort soon."

Heavier footsteps came down the stairs, and Chase came to stand behind his wife. "Good thing you weren't half an hour earlier." He wiggled his eyebrows.

Paula blushed and shook her head. "You two have fun. I'll see you later tonight."

"She wants to get rid of me. Needs a shower." Paula smacked him, and Chase led Tyne to his SUV, heavy enough to pull a boat behind it. "I hope you don't have a queasy stomach. It's going to be rocky today."

"Nah, I'm fine." Tyne loved boats, loved being on the water. If he stayed in Mill Pond, he meant to buy a boat of his own. He stopped to consider that. Would he stay here? He might. Ian gave him so much freedom in the kitchen, he could cook anything he wanted. And the area farmers provided so much variety, he had a lot of options. He'd always thought he'd like to open his own restaurant, because Holden did. But didn't he have the best of all worlds here? Career-wise, anyway?

When they reached Chase's boat, the sun had peeked from behind more gray clouds. Chase shook his head. "How about that? I actually see a little blue sky."

Tyne looked up and down the shore. No boats anywhere. "You waited 'til the last minute to store your boat."

They walked out the pier and hopped on board. "I pushed my luck," Chase admitted. "But Aiden loves fishing so much, I wanted to get in as much of it as I could."

Tyne shook his head. "Those kids have you whipped."

"Don't I know it?" Chase grinned. "Best thing that ever happened to me. I'm still up for one last boat ride. You?"

"Let's do it."

They circled the shoreline and Chase pointed out one person's cottage after another. When they passed Ben's parents' place, Steph was sitting on the front patio and waved at them. Same thing happened at Betty's.

"That old woman adores you," Chase teased.

Tyne shrugged. "It's mutual. She gives me grief at work, but she's the one who gave me the nickname Hot Stuff. How can you complain about that?"

When they reached the reedy part of the lake with no cottages, Chase swiveled in his chair and locked gazes with Tyne.

Uh-oh, here came the serious stuff. Tyne braced himself.

"Look, I know you think your work with Daphne is done, but Paula ran into her at the grocery store a few nights ago, and she's a mess. She's lost too much weight. She didn't have on any makeup, and she had dark circles under her eyes."

Tyne's gaze slid to the lake. He didn't like hearing that. "I haven't seen her for a while. Her parents don't want her around me. When I tried to talk to her, she shut down."

"Grams told me Daphne hasn't visited her parents since the day they gave her hell about you."

Tyne blinked. "That's been a few weeks ago."

"It's unheard of around here. Daphne used to eat suppers with them almost every night."

Tyne's hands balled into fists. "They still haven't forgiven her for dancing with me?"

Chase quirked a brow. "There was more to it than that, wasn't there?"

"Damn, does everyone know *everything* around here?"

"We're not stupid. There has to be more to this than a dance."

Tyne scowled. "Have you met her parents?"

Chase steered the boat past the cottages on the south side of the lake. "They come into the bar most Thursday nights. Burgers, no buns. Water, no beer. Veggies, no fries."

Tyne shook his head. "Then you get it."

"What I don't get," Chase said, "is why a guy like you lets two people like them get in his way."

"I don't give a shit about them." Tyne modified that. "If it's important to Daphne, then it's important to me, but I didn't get that far. Her parents said 'Dump him,' and she did."

"And you tucked your tail between your legs and left."

Tyne glared. "I didn't see you making any headway with her."

Chase reached for a cooler he'd stored onboard. He opened it and handed Tyne a beer, then opened one for himself. "You're right. I wasn't even brave enough to give her a shot, but you were. And you were good for her." He took a deep breath. "Do you want her?"

Tyne was about to say *no*, then realized that would be a lie. "Yes, I do."

"Then don't take *no* for an answer."

Tyne took a swig from his beer and thought about that. Finally, he shook his head. "That's not the issue. I tried. I put myself out there, and she shut me down. Now it's up to her." If she wouldn't take the initiative, he hadn't taught her anything.

Chase shook his head. "You'd rather lose her than go to her cabin and sweep her off her feet?"

Would he? Was he willing to give up and walk away if he could have her? When had his balls shriveled up and died? He took a deep breath. "I usually get what I want. And I want Daphne."

Chase smiled. "Good, now we can enjoy the lake." The clouds scattered, and sun glinted off the gray, restless water. Trees stood in yards, tall and bare, stripped of their leaves. A breeze whipped at their windbreakers. After they'd driven the boat to the marina for it to be stored, Chase said, "You've got to be hungry. Want to come to my place for a burger?"

"Why don't I feed you this time?" It wasn't often Chase was left to his own devices these days. No wife. No kids. Why not enjoy it?

Chase grinned. "As long as it's not a burger. I'm tired of my own food."

"Deal. I wasn't thinking of anything fancy, though."

"It could be scrambled eggs, as long as it's not a sandwich."

Chase had never been to Tyne's apartment before. While Tyne busied himself in the kitchen, Chase wandered from one thing to the next. "Where did the scarves come from?"

"South America."

"The fishing baskets?"

"Thailand." It was the same drill Daphne had given him. He hurt, remembering.

Chase frowned at him. "You didn't like Thailand?"

"Loved it. It's just that Daphne asked me the same questions."

Chase grinned. "You've got it bad, boy. Make it happen."

Damn it, he would. A half hour later, Tyne carried a heavy skillet to the table to put on the trivet. He added a salad on the side. "Dig in."

"Jambalaya?" Chase asked after a few bites. "This is good. I went to New Orleans a few times. Lots of fun."

"What's not to like about Creole and Cajun?" Tyne finished his salad and pushed it away.

Chase laughed. "Does every place you go revolve around food?"

"It's a big part of it. When I think of a city, I think of what I ate there."

Chase finished his meal and glanced at the clock. "Paula and the kids will be home soon. I'd better get moving."

After he left, Tyne realized how nice it had been to have someone underfoot here. What would it be like to wake up to the same woman every morning? To come home to her every night? A few months ago, he'd have run from that. He'd say it was suffocating, claustrophobic. Now, it appealed to him. He thought about what Chase had told him about Daphne.

She wasn't going to her parents' for suppers. She was holing up in her cabin, more of a recluse than she'd been before. That girl needed a good shake-up, and he was just the man to give it to her. He'd like to shake her right into his arms.

Chapter 43

Tyne worked the breakfast shifts on Mondays. By now, it was almost rote. A good thing, then he could just go through the motions. Mondays were like that.

He'd soaked the potato and sausage strata in custard overnight and only had to put it in the oven. He slid the sausage links, bacon, and sausage patties in after them. Then he started on the baked eggs with smoked salmon in ramekins. There weren't as many guests now, so Steph could stay at the bakery to help Maxwell. He could handle Monday's prep by himself. He poured the cooled, homemade granola into a bowl and started on the fruit salad.

Ian came to help him set up the buffet with juices, hot water for tea, and urns of coffee, boxes of cereal, and muffins that Tessa had made. Ian helped out during the slow months when he didn't hire a high-school kid as an extra hand. They filled bowls with ice and nestled different yogurts in there, then set up the toaster with different breads, bagels, and English muffins. When the guests walked into the dining room, Tyne frowned. "You didn't bring Drew in the kitchen with you. What's up?"

Ian walked to the kitchen coffeepot and poured himself a mug of breakfast brew. "I got here a little late, took him straight to Paula's mom. Why? You miss him?"

Tyne was surprised to admit he did. "The little fella's kind of cute."

"He takes after me, but don't tell Tessa I said that."

"I can see both of you in him." That baby had it made. His parents were good-looking, and they both fussed over him. Tyne thought about Daphne. If he and Daphne had a baby, what would it look like?

It couldn't be ugly, right? Not with them as parents. Then he frowned. What if it looked like one of her parents? There went that fantasy.

Once breakfast was done, Betty whizzed into the kitchen. The only day he saw her was Monday. It was the only day their shifts melded. She frowned at him. "You look sort of full of yourself today. What's up?"

"I'm planning a full scale campaign to make Daphne mine."

Her jaw dropped. He couldn't have surprised her more, but she recovered quickly. "It's about damn time. I've been wondering when you were going to flex your hottie muscle."

He laughed. "Chase gave me a pep talk yesterday."

"Good for him. That girl needs to have a man in her life."

"She was seeing the professor," he reminded her.

"I said a man, not a putz." Betty started for the dining room to get it ready for lunch.

Tyne was in charge of that, too, on Mondays. Luckily, Steph showed up to help with the two soups and two types of finger sandwiches for a proper tea.

"How's the bakery?" Tyne asked.

"Maxwell knows you can't help on Mondays, so he kicked into gear. We got everything done. I didn't think he was going to make it, but he pushed himself."

Tyne nodded. "Someday, I'm going to quit coming, and he's going to have to push himself more."

"He's getting there," Steph assured him. "One step at a time."

Tyne knew the feeling; only today, he was going to take a giant step. He could hardly wait.

Betty stayed until two to help with clean up, and she patted him on the shoulder on her way out the door. "Claim what's yours, tiger."

"Tiger?"

"Show your true stripes. Sweep that woman off her feet."

Steph raised an eyebrow. "It's about time."

Tyne shook his head. Women were hard to please, especially coworkers.

With lunch out of the way, he started on his entrée for Monday night's dinner buffet. He'd decided on baked, miso black cod with an Oriental cold-noodle salad. By the time Paula walked into the kitchen, he and Steph had their part of the supper done.

"Tyne's going to make his move on Daphne today," Steph blurted to Paula.

"It's about damn time."

Where had he heard that before? He wiped his hands on his apron. "Give me a break, will you? I thought she didn't want me."

"You thought wrong."

"Lord, I hope so, or my ego's going to be flat as a pancake later tonight."

Paula smiled. "Go see for yourself. I'm declaring a victory."

With those words ringing in his ears, he hopped in his Jeep and drove to his apartment. Instead of rushing up the stairs, though, he wandered into Daphne's shop. She still had a few customers milling around. They always came around Thanksgiving to buy special items for the holiday. Daphne made stained-glass candle holders and cornucopias that were popular. He browsed up and down the aisles and saw Daphne glance at him nervously. The gossip was right. She looked like hell. Too thin. Unwashed hair pulled up in a ponytail. Drab clothing.

The last customer left, and Tyne was about to go to the counter, when a man burst through the door and hurried to Daphne. With a huge grin, he wrapped both arms around her and kissed her soundly on the lips.

Tyne froze. It felt like his blood stopped in his veins.

The man pulled back, leaving Daphne breathless, and said, "I love you, love you, love you! What more can I say?"

Tyne had seen enough. He turned on his heel and stalked out the door. Yes, Daphne had lost weight. A lot of it. But his friends were wrong. She wasn't pining away, thinking of him. She was too caught up in passion to eat. What a fool he'd been! She hadn't been to her parents. Guess what? She was probably with this guy. Somehow, he could claim her every second, every minute. Tyne had never been able to do that.

He jumped in his Jeep and drove. He was in Columbus an hour later, and he had no desire to return home. He booked a room for the night and went to a bar. He was going to eat and drink . . . and be miserable. But at least he knew. Daphne had missed him for about three seconds. It was time for him to move on.

Chapter 44

Daphne shook her head, trying to clear it. Why had Tyne come to the shop? What did that mean? But then she looked at Keavin. They'd known each other since they wore diapers, and she smiled. "I take it that Chelsea liked your present?"

"It's the best anniversary gift I could have given her. You're a hero. You made me look good."

"I'm happy for you." Daphne glanced out the window as Tyne's orange Jeep sped down the street. Tyne had looked upset, no, furious. Was he angry at her?

Keavin gave her one last hug and hurried on his way. She walked to the front window and glanced down the street. Tyne's glare had unnerved her. What could she possibly have done to upset him so much? She was standing there, lost in thought, when her parents pulled to the curb.

Not now. She bit her bottom lip. She'd never thought that before, but she wasn't in the mood to argue with them about Tyne. She was tempted to call him on his cell phone, to ask why the hell he'd stormed out of her shop. When she'd looked up and seen him, her heart felt like it had jumped into her throat. A cliché for a reason. Hope filled her, and then he'd stalked away.

Mom and Dad stepped through the door, and Mom gave her a quizzical look. "You look confused."

Daphne opened her lips to explain, but then thought better of it. She shook her head instead. "It's nothing. Aren't you two out of work early today? Do you have plans?"

Mom looked disappointed. "You were about to share with us, weren't you?"

"It was just a fluke happening, nothing to linger on." Daphne crossed her arms and waited. She wasn't going to discuss Tyne with them.

Dad forced a smile. "An old friend of mine is going to be in Bloomington tonight. His son graduated from there and got a job at a university in Kentucky. Bloomington's halfway between them, so they're meeting there. We thought you might join us."

"So that I can meet your friend's son? Another professor? No thanks."

"He's good-looking," Mom said. "And he's your age."

"I'm sure he's wonderful, but I'm not interested."

"He's very active. He goes white water rafting every summer." Dad gave her an expectant look.

"Is he a gourmet cook?" Daphne knew she sounded snippy and tried to soften her tone.

Her mother grimaced. "You can go to restaurants if you want gourmet."

Daphne shook her head. "Look, I know you're trying to help, but if he's not Tyne, I don't want to meet him."

"You and Tyne are done," Mom said. "You need to move on."

That rubbed Daphne the wrong way. She felt her eyebrow rise. "I'd rather do without, thanks anyway. Have a wonderful time with your friend." Thankfully, a group of customers entered the shop and Daphne smiled. "Sorry. Have to go."

Her mother's expression turned thunderous, but it couldn't compare with Tyne's when he left. Daphne thought about that as she went to stand behind the counter. What had made Tyne so angry? No time to call him now. It probably hadn't been a good idea anyway. Tyne wasn't shy. If he had something to say to her, he'd have said it.

People came in and out for the rest of the day. Once she closed up shop, she drove straight home. The scenery that usually soothed her went unnoticed. Seeing Tyne had made her want him all over again. After a quick supper, she could work on his quilt some more. Had he heard about that? She was scooping food into Shadow's bowl, but hesitated.

That was it. Someone had told Tyne about her quilt. She hadn't thought about how he might react to it. What if he thought she was making a big deal out of nothing? What if he thought she was just plain pitiful for hanging on to memories he considered trivial?

She squared her shoulders and went to the sewing room. Let him think whatever he wanted. This was about her healing, and if she wanted to make and save this quilt, she would. But she'd hide it in a closet so that he'd never glimpse it. She never wanted to see the blistering look he'd squelched her with again.

Chapter 45

When Tyne drove home from work on Tuesday night, he saw Miriam's car parked next to his usual spot. *No, no, no.* He wasn't in the mood. He'd wallowed in pity in Columbus last night and he'd worked Daphne out of his system. To hell with her! He'd never been hung up on a girl before, but enough was enough. He was over her.

Steph and Paula had taken one look at his face when he walked into the kitchen and left him alone. He wouldn't get any grief there. They'd better not treat him with pity either. He'd given it his best, and it was pointless. Time to move on.

When he climbed out of his Jeep, Miriam left her car to join him. If she'd come to lecture him about how he'd treated Daphne, he had plenty of come backs to defend himself. Miriam might be witty and brainy, but he was no slouch when it came to banging ideas around. He turned to her with a frown.

She threw up both hands. "Hey, don't bite my head off. Can we talk?"

He grimaced, but unlocked the shop's back door and led her upstairs to his apartment. He didn't want her to stay, didn't try to be welcoming. "What do you want?"

She leaned her bony hip against the wall. "I want to know why you went to see my girl Daphne yesterday."

Like he'd tell her. She'd tell Daphne, and they'd both have a good laugh over it. "I wanted to know if she'd let me out of my lease early. I'm thinking of finding someplace else to stay."

Her thin shoulders slumped. Damn, the woman ate everything in sight and was still stick thin. She looked upset. She obviously hadn't thought of that. Neither had he until now, but it wasn't a bad idea.

There were crappy apartments on the fringe of Mill Pond. There might even be other rentals above shops if he took the time to look. Maybe he could talk Ian into letting him use a cabin or room at the resort until he found something else. If he had to, he could live a town over.

Miriam didn't give up easily. "She said you looked really angry when you left yesterday."

"I'd already waited around to talk to her. It was my turn, but then some guy rushed through the doors and she ignored me."

Miriam put her hands on her hips. She was so tall and thin, her pose reminded him of a scarecrow. Not nice, so he pushed that image away. He liked Miriam. "You couldn't wait another five minutes to see her?"

Tyne shrugged. "How did I know it would only be five minutes? They looked pretty chummy together. He gave her a big kiss."

Miriam narrowed her eyes. "Is that what upset you?"

"Why would that bother me? Daphne can kiss anybody she wants to."

"She and Keavin are old friends. His wife loved the stained-glass piece Keavin special ordered for their anniversary."

Tyne froze. "They're not a couple?"

"Daphne and Keavin? When she can't get over you? Get real. Would I be here if Daphne found a happy-ever-after with somebody else?"

He frowned. "She hasn't?"

"That's what I just said, isn't it? How many women have you bedded since you quit spending time with her?"

"I don't bed women as sport."

She studied him and nodded. "No, you don't, and you could. I'll give you credit for that."

He was beginning to feel better. He grinned. "What else will you give me credit for?"

"Don't push it."

She looked so dejected, he motioned to his kitchen. "Want a beer?"

"What? So I can cry in it? Got any good snacks?"

"You eat a lot for someone so thin, you know that?"

"I burn energy intimidating kids all day. Try it sometime."

He hung his jacket on the coat tree in the small foyer and motioned for her to join him in the kitchen. He reached for the loaf of

French bread on his counter and handed her a serrated knife. "Slice it about an inch thick."

While she sliced, he drizzled olive oil in a skillet to heat. Then he diced two tomatoes with some basil in a bowl. He sautéed the bread, salted it, and rubbed it with a clove of garlic. Next, he spooned the tomatoes over it. "Hope you like bruschetta."

She bit into it. "I sure as hell do."

He'd eaten at the resort, so sat opposite her and nursed a beer. "What's Daphne doing now? Rumor is she's not eating supper with her parents every night."

"She's making a grieving quilt."

He frowned. "Never heard of one."

"No one has; it's all about you. Every square tells something about you. She says when she finishes it, she'll have you out of her system."

"Is that so?" He looked thoughtful, and Miriam tilted her head, gauging his reaction.

"Are you over her?"

She'd been honest with him. He'd return the favor. "No, but I will be. I give myself two more weeks."

Miriam chuckled. "You and Daphne are on the same timeframe."

"She thinks she can get over me in two weeks?"

"Why not? You're special, I'll give you that, but pretty soon, you'll be history. What do you want, for her to light candles at a shrine for the rest of her life?"

"I could give you a framed picture of me for her to use."

She choked swallowing her last bite, then threw back her head and laughed. "God, you're full of yourself."

"So I've been told."

"Probably often." She quirked her lips. "I wouldn't mind having a picture of you next to my bed, though."

He shook his head. "You might do kinky things to it."

"Now there's an idea." She leaned forward, anxious. "Have you thought of giving Daphne another try?"

"I was going to, but then I saw that guy kissing her. It pissed me off. I took off and had a long think. Now, I don't know what I want."

"Don't blow it," Miriam told him. "I've never seen two people more right for each other. I'll never have that. I need to live vicariously through you two."

He focused on her, and she squirmed. Good to know. He could make Miriam uncomfortable. "Some guy is going to see past your mouthy ways and gawkiness."

She pouted. "Now I'm gawky."

"In a good way."

"Yeah, that's probably what you tell all the girls."

He laughed, and she rose.

"Don't give up on her, Tyne. She loves you."

Daphne loved him. If he'd heard those words a week ago, he'd be racing to her cottage, pulling her into his arms. The words warmed him, but confused him. Would she rather grieve for him than *have* him? Why hadn't she called for him to come back when he'd stalked out of her shop?

When the door closed behind Miriam, Tyne moved to the couch to finish his beer. What now? He decided to give himself time. Guests were pouring into the resort tomorrow for Ian's Thanksgiving special. He and Paula would be too busy to think straight. And maybe that was a good thing. Maybe some distance would make things clearer.

He'd told Maxwell that he wouldn't have time to help him at the bakery, but Steph said that Tyne didn't need to worry about that. Maxwell had gone from sleeping most of each day to working every hour he could. He threw himself into experimenting with new breads, staying in the kitchen from early morning until he collapsed into bed at night. Phase two, she called it.

"First, he shut down," she explained. "Now, he's keeping busy every minute he can. It fills the emptiness."

Tyne understood that. He'd kept busy when Daphne left him. And now, did he really have a chance of winning her back? Or would her parents shut him down again? Did he want to go through that pain again? He couldn't decide.

Chapter 46

A hundred people checked into the inn on Wednesday. Tyne and Paula had decided to make a lighter supper, since Thursday's meal would be so heavy. Ian was excited at how well his specials were going over. If they weren't careful, he'd start making up holidays for guests to celebrate over the winter months. After Christmas, New Year's Eve, and Valentine's Day, he'd already added a St. Patrick's Day special to his calendar.

Paula and Tyne were both putting in extra hours. For tonight's supper, they worked together to make pan-fried bass and a fruited pork stew. They kept the sides simple, only a huge green salad, broccoli rabe, basmati rice, and Parker House rolls. That way, they could get an early start on tomorrow's menu.

They'd agreed to help Tessa make some of the desserts. There were too many of them, so while Tessa made the pumpkin and mincemeat pies, they'd make pumpkin rolls with a cream-cheese filling and the apple and pecan pies. They'd decided to make half a dozen turkeys, each a slightly different recipe, regular stuffing, oyster stuffing, and chestnut stuffing, along with hams for slicing. There'd be the usual green-bean casserole, oven-roasted Brussels sprouts, and corn soufflés. Tyne was in charge of the cranberry sauce and maple-roasted parsnips, and Paula was cooking roasted potatoes and sweet potatoes with marshmallows.

Thankfully, Ian had decided the inn would serve brunch on Friday, as well as Sunday this time, thinking no one would be ready to stir early in the morning after Thanksgiving dinner. And Friday's brunch would be lighter fare—crepes and French toast with fruit fillings and toppings, along with scrambled eggs and juices. Ian switched Friday night's usual menu of prime rib and salmon to Saturday night, and they'd served pasta with vodka sauce and mushroom risotto instead.

The rest of the weekend returned to a fairly normal schedule, just with a lot more people. They'd be busy, but not buried. Ian was offering a charcuterie board for lunch on Saturday, featuring specialty cheeses from the area, along with Brie, Fontina, camembert, cheddar, and blue cheese, along with salamis, patés, and smoked kielbasa. They'd serve pickles, olives, and baguettes on the side. Tyne offered to make sugar-and-spice mixed nuts and balsamic fig jam while Paula made flatbreads. Ian ordered extra wines.

The planning turned out to be perfect. The guests enjoyed the big meals as well as the smaller ones. By the time Sunday rolled around, Tyne and Paula had made so many dishes that took extra care that doing their traditional brunch felt like a cinch. Holidays were always labor intensive in restaurants, but Ian had gone all out for this one. Who knew what he'd think of for Christmas.

When the last customer left the dining room on Sunday, Paula sagged onto a stool at the stainless-steel worktable and stretched her aching back. "We did it. If those people don't spread the word about Ian's specials, something's wrong."

Tyne scraped a hand through his hair. "I'm not looking forward to Christmas and New Year's Eve back to back."

"We'll need extra help, more than usual."

Tyne agreed.

"Did you hear that Daphne spent Thanksgiving by herself? When I stopped at the grocery store, Art told me she'd stocked up on frozen turkey dinners for Thursday."

Tyne wrinkled his nose. Frozen dinners appalled him. "What did her parents do?"

"Before you became such an issue for them, they'd invited Beatrice to their house for Thanksgiving. The woman lives alone, and they felt sorry for her. Daphne said she didn't want to be in the same room with her, so Beatrice brought her famous deviled eggs, and she and Daphne's parents celebrated alone."

Tyne stretched his legs under the table, angling them so that he didn't bump Paula's stool. "Serves them right. Beatrice is the nasty little snitch, isn't she? But who wants a frozen dinner for Thanksgiving?"

Paula pulled a spare stool closer to prop her feet on. "Aah, that feels good."

"You were telling me about Daphne."

"Yeah, right. Miriam invited her to her family gathering, but Daphne said that would feel odd. Bless Miriam, she even volunteered to miss her family get-together to stay with her, but Daphne wouldn't hear of it."

"Miriam's the best."

Paula raised an eyebrow. "Glad you think so. She's one of your staunch supporters. She still wants you and Daphne to get back together, Art told me." Art? From the grocery store? Why didn't that surprise him? Everyone knew everyone else's business in Mill Pond.

Tyne untied his apron, grateful Ian had hired extra help for clean-up so it went fast. "She told me, too. The woman has a set of gonads. Gotta admire that." He yawned. "I'm too tired to think right now. I'm going to go home, stretch out on my sofa, and vegetate. I have to be back in here tomorrow morning." He grimaced. "Sorry, you have to be back for the new guests at supper shift tonight. Want some help?"

"I made pot pies ahead of time, and your loin of pork *cinghiale*'s ready to go. There are only thirty guests. Most people need to recuperate after Thanksgiving, so our numbers are low."

"Good, then we'll have an easy week." He said his good-byes and headed for his apartment. He couldn't help but think about Daphne, sitting alone in her cabin, eating thin slices of turkey—Was it really turkey? It never looked quite right to him—for Thanksgiving. He needed to make a decision.

He left for California to see his brother soon. If he left without claiming Daphne as his, it wouldn't happen. He'd talk himself out of it. He knew himself. Absence didn't make his heart grow fonder. It helped him forget.

Chapter 47

Daphne was busy in her workroom Monday morning. Every time she got caught up on inventory, customers wiped her out again. She was making an oval-shaped, stained-glass piece with green glass forming a pine tree and a cardinal sitting on a snow-covered branch. It would work for Christmas and for the winter months, too. She looked up when the shop door opened and Paula walked inside. She felt a smile tug her lips. Paula and Chase must be tweaking his apartment above the bar. They made a great couple, but Daphne was sure Chase's place could use some feminine touches.

Daphne walked out to greet Goth Girl, as Tyne called her. She'd softened her look a lot since she'd married Chase. Her black hair was pulled back in a ponytail instead of clipped high on the back of her head to form a spikey fringe. She still rimmed her eyes, but not with the harsh blacks she once used. She was more attractive than she realized, and Chase had fallen for her—hard.

Daphne motioned to the rows of stained glass. "Hi, can I help you find anything?"

Paula pressed her lips together, looking uncertain. Finally, she blurted, "I don't make a habit of interfering in people's lives, okay? But I care a lot about Tyne. And I had all the words right in my mind when I drove here, but now they sort of disappeared. I can't think of the right thing to say."

Daphne blinked. Where in the world was Paula heading? "Are you trying to find something for Tyne? A present? Something unusual?"

Paula waved that away. "Look, I've never been diplomatic. I don't say the right thing at the right time. I might as well just spit it out:

You and Tyne are both being stupid. You're perfect for each other. Do something about it."

"Me?" Daphne's voice squeaked. She sounded like a frightened mouse. Why did she crack when someone confronted her? "I don't think Tyne wants to see me. The last time he came in the shop, he left, angry."

"Because he was jealous."

"What?" That didn't make any sense. Daphne shook her head. Impossible. Tyne jealous?

"He was waiting around, trying to make a move on you, when Keavin barged in the shop and kissed you right in front of him. Keavin said, 'I love you, love you, love you,' and Tyne instantly hated him."

Daphne almost laughed. That was just silly. "Everyone knows Keavin's married, that we've been friends since . . ."

"I didn't know you were friends. Tyne didn't even know he's married. We're new here, remember? Tyne's seen Keavin around, but he's never spent time with him."

Daphne put out a hand to brace herself. "Tyne thought I'd fallen for Keavin? So fast?"

"He thought you were settling again, but this time, he thought you might have picked a winner."

The shop spun. Words tumbled out. "Tyne was so mad at me. I thought he'd heard about the quilt I'm making, that he thought I'm silly, that he was angry because . . ."

Paula interrupted her. "None of that matters. Do you want Tyne or not?"

Daphne gripped the counter so hard, her knuckles turned white. "I've never wanted anything more."

"He leaves for California next week. He says he's coming back, but if his brother offers him a new opportunity, an interesting restaurant—you know how he loves to travel, how he loves a new challenge, especially if he wants a fresh start."

Fear lodged in her throat. Misery permeated her bones, burrowing into her marrow. What would she do if Tyne left Mill Pond? How would she feel? Even when they didn't see each other, she still caught glimpses of him, could keep track of what he was doing. If that were gone? It would be as if a giant hole had been ripped from her heart.

Paula gave her an encouraging smile. "He works the early shift today. He'll get off about three or three thirty. Today's your best day to see him."

Daphne nodded. Her brain felt overloaded, numb. What would she do if she threw herself at Tyne and he rejected her? How long would it take for her to lick her wounds this time?

Paula patted her on the shoulder. "Good luck."

After she left the shop, Daphne stood frozen in place while she tried to sort through her thoughts and feelings. One thought that kept repeating itself. She couldn't avoid it. What if she *didn't* try? What if she cowered in her shop and Tyne left Mill Pond? Even worse, what if Paula was right, and she could have Tyne, but she wasn't brave enough to let him know she wanted him?

She took a deep breath. How happy had playing it safe made her? *She wanted Tyne.*

She turned the sign in her door to Closed. She pulled on her coat, locked up, and drove to Art's Grocery. Every important moment she'd had with Tyne involved food. This time, the food had better leave a lasting impression.

She passed a few tourists on the sidewalk, who hurried from Lydia's coffee and candy shop to dash into the antique store next door. Mostly, the sidewalks were empty. In another week, Mill Pond would wrap evergreen boughs around every lamp post on Main Street. Christmas lights and balls would adorn them. Wreaths would don every shop door, and tiny, white lights would sparkle around the perimeters of each shop's windows. The town would decorate a huge tree in front of the courthouse. Music would spill over the shops that lined the streets, and tourists would bustle along the sidewalks again. But for now, there was the quiet of anticipation. And she was anticipating more than usual this holiday.

At Art's, she walked down an aisle stocked with baking goods and vinegars to stare at the meat counter at the back of the store. She sighed. Steaks were too ordinary. Chicken wasn't exciting enough. Maybe she should browse in Art's new section, filled with specialty goods. She was chewing her bottom lip when Art came to help her. She'd known the store owner since she was little, and he always had a friendly smile. Medium height with a stocky build, he gave the impression of being dependable. And he was.

"You look puzzled. Are you looking for something special?"

"Special, yes." She scanned the meat behind the glass nervously, then plunged on. "What do people make for Valentine's Day or anniversary dinners? When they want to go all out?"

"Some people make surf and turf—a filet mignon with shrimp on the side."

She nodded. Simple and straightforward. Surely she could find cooking preparations on the internet. "That's what I want."

"For one?"

She shook her head. "For two."

Art's smile widened, a knowing glint in his dark eyes. "If you're trying to win Tyne with food, I'd make steak Oscar."

Daphne grimaced. "Miriam talked to you, didn't she?"

"We both have our fingers crossed for you."

"Do you have any recommendations for pity parties, in case he turns me away?"

"Send Miriam in, and we'll figure something out, and it will be on the house."

He meant it, she knew. "You're a nice person, you know that?"

"I've known you a long time, watched you grow up. Now, let me find you a recipe. Big stores in the cities offer recipes when you buy certain cuts of meat, so we decided to try that, too." He went into the back room and returned in a few minutes with two pages of printed instructions. "We know that not many people around here have made this, so we have detailed instructions."

She'd need those if this meal had a prayer of turning out decent. "What should I make with it?"

He gave a gentle smile. "For you? I'd go with baked potatoes."

She laughed. "Do you have a recipe card for those?"

"Prick the skin and put them in a four-hundred-degree oven for an hour."

She could manage that.

"And I'd add a side salad." Another grin. "We have ready-made bags. All you'll have to concentrate on is the main dish."

She took her groceries to the check-out lane, and Art's daughter, Melissa, looked at the items, impressed. Her eyes—the same deep brown as her dad's—sparkled. "Even a chef should like this."

Daphne, who usually kept her thoughts private, surprised herself again. "It's a go-for-broke meal. Wish me luck."

Melissa winked. "He's a go-for-broke kind of guy. I'll keep my fingers crossed for you."

Daphne drove home and went straight to her kitchen. The interior of the house was as gloomy as the outdoors. She switched on lights as she went. Shadow ran after her and played in the brown-paper bag after she put her groceries away. She reread the directions twice. They couldn't be more step-by-step. She could do this.

First, she called Tyne and left a message on his cell. "I need to see you. Can you stop at my house on your way home from work?"

She was pretty sure he'd come. He might not want to see her, but he had a hard time turning friends down.

Next, she took a long shower, scrubbed her hair, and took her time when she blew it dry. She dressed in jeans—she had the feeling he liked those better than slacks—and a snug, long-sleeved top. She applied her makeup with care. Then she gazed at her reflection. She'd lost a little too much weight, but she was tolerable.

She seasoned the two filets and left them on the counter to reach room temperature, but she didn't start cooking them. It was too early. If Tyne stormed out before she started dinner, she'd call Miriam and ask her to join her.

Tires scrunched in the driveway at a quarter till four. Tyne knocked on the door and she called for him to come in. He'd changed out of his chef's clothes and dressed in jeans and a loose sweater. He looked so sexy—his blond hair mussed, his shoulders tense—she had to clasp her hands behind her back to keep from touching him.

He looked around the cabin. "Is everything okay? Are you all right?"

"No, I'm not." She went to sit on the arm of her favorite chair. She raised her chin and locked gazes with him. "I want you, Tyne Newsome. I don't want to lose you."

His dark eyes went wide. "What about your parents?"

"What about them?" She motioned to the kitchen. "I mean to bribe you with a fancy supper."

Now, a smirk tugged at his lips. "Does it come out of a box?"

She huffed. "I'll have you know I'm going to make steak Oscar for you tonight."

"With Béarnaise sauce?"

"I even bought the tarragon."

He blinked, impressed. "And what do I have to do to earn this expensive meal?"

She turned toward her bedroom. The quilt was already turned down.

He stared. "You don't have to take me to bed to get me to stay."

"This isn't about you. The bed's for me. You can pay for your supper now or later."

He grinned, and Daphne caught her breath. His grin made her stomach do flip-flops. "I hate being in debt. I'd rather pay up front."

She'd rather he did, too. "Just remember that this is an exceptional meal."

He laughed and scooped her into his arms. His biceps bulged. His chest and abs were rock hard. She could stay here a long time. Before he tossed her onto the bed, though, he stopped abruptly to stare. "You have a new quilt."

"My grieving quilt." She shrugged. "It's all about you."

He gently put her down. "Is this how you see me?"

She pointed to the large center square: "You're a chef." Next came the motorcycle: "You love your bike." Then the leaves: "You love to hike in the national forest." She pointed to each piece and explained it.

He twined his arm through hers, listening intently. When she finished, he frowned. "There's something missing."

She looked at him in surprise. "What? I even added a can of coconut milk for your Thai food."

He turned to gently touch her cheek. "There's no you, and that's the most important piece of all."

Tears misted her eyes. She had to swallow, hard. "I thought I'd lost you. I listened to my parents and messed up, and I thought . . ."

"You think too much." He bent down to kiss her.

She stretched to kiss him back. He placed his hand behind her head to ravage her lips. He pressed closer, and the back of her knees hit the bed. Another step forced her to sit down, and then he moved on top of her, pinning her against the mattress. Her hands went to the hem of his sweater and slid underneath it. She ran her fingers over his hard abs, felt how solid he was, how strong. He yanked his sweater over his head, then reached for her tee.

Shadow leapt on the bed beside them, and Tyne shook his head.

"Sorry, fella, you're too young to see this." He cradled the cat in his arms and carried him out of the bedroom, closing the door behind him. Then he bent and lifted Daphne, moving her higher on the bed, so that he could remove the quilt. "It's too new to be broken in."

She reached for him again, and while her hands explored him, his hands explored her. When his nimble fingers unhooked her bra and freed her breasts, she gulped with pleasure. His lips grazed her nipples, and she sucked in air. His fingers teased one breast while his mouth played with the other. Her nerves sizzled. Then he unzipped her jeans and tugged them and her undies off. His followed. Skin, glorious skin. Daphne's hands explored every inch of him— the hollow of his back, his perfect ass, his sinewy muscles. Tyne interlocked arms and legs with her and kissed deeply, their bodies pressed tight. He licked the hollow of her neck. She gasped as pleasure shot through her.

When every inch of her strained for his touch, he shifted away, and his hand dove between her legs. Blood pounded in her ears. His fingers moved inside her, and his thumb found her passion spot. Her body stilled as tension coiled tighter and tighter until she arched her back and screamed. "Now!" She wanted him now!

Tyne growled as he entered her. They moved together, demanding more and more. They exploded in unison, and Tyne sagged onto his elbows, his breath ragged.

She smiled at him, raised her hand to touch his strong jawline. She tugged at his chin strap. He lowered his face and nuzzled it against hers.

"I love you," he said.

Everything in Daphne stilled, holding its breath. Had he really said the words? Did he mean them?

He moved back so that she could see him. "I love you, Daphne. Marry me."

Tears slid down her cheeks, and she didn't care. "Yes!"

He chuckled, and she loved the sound. "I fly to California next week. Let's make it our honeymoon."

"So fast?" What would her parents say? What would people think?

He frowned. "Would you rather wait? Have a traditional wedding?"

"No, I don't care about that. But . . . are you sure?"

"I've never been more sure." It was his turn to worry. "I don't want to rush you, though."

Rush her? Was he kidding? She wanted to lock him in this cabin and never let him leave. "I want you here, with me, in my bed, every night."

He grinned. "We could do that anyway. We could live in sin until we made it legal."

"I want it legal. Let's go to the justice of the peace."

Tyne nodded. He bent to kiss her again, and his kiss lingered, intensified. They took it slow this time, more gently. This time was more about awe than lust and need. They spooned together for another half hour before Daphne's stomach rumbled.

Tyne laughed. "That reminds me. You owe me a supper."

"It might be edible if you help me with it."

They showered. That took more time than usual, then padded into the kitchen together. They made a good team. Tyne told her what to do, and she did it. And the meal turned out perfect.

"Shadow likes filets." Daphne tossed him the last bit of her steak.

"He likes shrimp, too." Tyne gave him a tiny bit of his.

Tyne helped with cleanup, and pretty soon their hands were where they shouldn't be again. When their breaths finally slowed, she clung to him. "Can you stay the night?"

His arms tightened, smashing her to him. He rested his chin on the top of her head. "People will notice. They'll talk."

"Art and his kids are already rooting for us at the grocery store."

"They are?" His chin grazed her hair as he shook his head. "Hell, most of Mill Pond probably knows I stayed here too long. They're all talking by now. Let's make it official."

She lay against him as they watched TV to unwind before they returned to bed. They were tired, replete, so Tyne left the door open and let Shadow jump up with them. When Tyne rolled to his side, Daphne pressed herself against his lean, strong back. He put a hand over hers and instantly fell asleep. Daphne tried to stay awake. She wanted to make this night last, to remember it forever, but with the stress washed out of her life and her body so relaxed, her eyes drifted shut, and she couldn't fight sleep.

Chapter 48

Ian and Tessa, Paula and Chase, and Harley and Kathy came to stand behind Tyne in the office of the justice of the peace. Daphne's parents and Miriam came to see her married. It was a short ceremony, but Daphne had bought a new, white dress for the occasion—knee-length, but classy. The dress made her feel like a princess with its form-fitting top and full, gathered skirt. She'd pulled her thick, wavy hair into a loose chignon and worn the pearl earrings her mother had given her when she turned twenty-one.

"You're beautiful," Tyne told her, gazing at her as she studied herself in the mirror.

"You're not supposed to see me before the ceremony," Daphne protested.

He grinned. "I've seen everything else. Why not this?"

She had to laugh. He had a point.

He'd bought a new sports jacket to wear with his favorite khakis. And, as always, the man looked good. He refused to shave his chin strap, though, even though Paula had bugged him about it. It had finally grown back.

"I like your whiskers," Daphne told him. So they'd stayed.

At the end of the short ceremony, they drove to Harley's winery to celebrate. Paula had helped Steph and Maxwell make fancy, little finger foods and Harley provided plenty of wine. Her parents felt out of place and didn't stay long, but at least they'd come. The party lasted a couple of hours, everyone festive, but it was still early when they returned to Daphne's cabin.

"What now?" she asked.

Tyne grinned. "You'd better hang that pretty dress up if you want to keep it in one piece."

The rest of the night was all about pleasure. They were officially man and wife now, and Tyne seemed more excited about the idea than Daphne. Daphne liked wearing a ring, but mostly, she just wanted Tyne.

Her parents had insisted on throwing a reception in their church's basement on Saturday night, but Daphne didn't attend the church, and she didn't want to celebrate with Beatrice. Besides, she was sure that if Tyne met her, he'd have something choice to say to her.

Chase offered a compromise, and they'd settled on an open reception at his bar. "Just bring yourselves and celebrate with us," Tyne wrote. "Strictly casual. No presents. We have everything we need."

A sign on the door warned that no bar food would be served, that there'd be a cash bar, and the band was still scheduled. Tyne filled three, huge steel pans with brats and sauerkraut, three more pans with Italian roast beef, and three with sloppy-joe mix. He bought mountains of buns and chips and made coleslaw. Mom paid Grams's church ladies to provide potato salad and three-bean salad. Mom couldn't wrap her head around the quantities of food, but she happily paid Tessa to make a three-tiered wedding cake.

People spilled into the bar for the reception and ate and drank. The music started, and Tyne led Daphne onto the dance floor. They dutifully did the wedding waltz first—Mom's idea. Then they busted out to "Footloose."

"That always gets people moving," Tyne assured her.

Friends crowded the floor. Steph and Ben came to wish them congratulations. Even Betty and her husband came. They mingled with most of their guests, then Tyne went to ask Daphne's mother to dance. He held her at a safe distance and behaved like a gentleman. Daphne pulled her dad onto the floor. After that, people started rotating couples, and Tyne danced with Miriam, Kathy, and Tessa. He'd just walked Paula back to her table when Chantelle came to claim him for a dance.

Tyne hesitated, not sure what to do, when Daphne stepped beside him and shook her head. "Not anymore, he's mine."

Chantelle opened her lips to argue, glanced at Daphne's expression, and walked away.

Daphne wrapped her arms around her new husband and Tyne chuckled.

"You're not as shy as you used to be."

"Your fault." She leaned close to him on the dance floor. Damn, he felt good. He could hold her in his arms forever. She closed her eyes and rested her head on his chest.

"I like the new you." His voice rumbled in her ears. "My wife has more sass than I expected."

She grinned up at him. "Good, because you're stuck with me."

"I wouldn't want it any other way." He spun her around the floor. They'd fly to California tomorrow, and she'd meet Tyne's brother.

"Holden will like you, I'm sure. My brother will be happy for me." Tyne frowned, and Daphne cocked her head to one side.

"What is it?"

"My parents will probably want to meet you. Will that scare you? My mom and dad can be intimidating."

"Do you think *they'll* like me?"

He grimaced. "Probably not. They never approve of anything I do. That will include you."

Sometimes, Tyne could be a bit *too* honest, but she decided she'd rather know ahead of time. Trying to win them over sounded futile. She shrugged. "You lived through my parents. I'll survive yours. Even if I don't like them, and they don't like me, they're miles and miles away. How often will I have to see them?"

"Less than I'll have to see yours." He looked at her, surprised. "I'm glad it doesn't matter to you."

"I married you, not them."

"Someday, when I'm old and bent, your parents might approve of me."

"They like you now."

He thought about that. "They *are* being nicer to me than before."

"They want me to be happy," she told him. "And I won't be happy without you."

He laughed and bent to kiss her. "You're wonderful, you know that?"

"I do now. You've made me feel like a winner."

He held her tighter. "You *are* a winner, Daph, always have been."

So was he. She knew his life had taken a detour he hadn't expected, but she'd come to learn that when the heavens offered you a blessing, why pass it up?

If you like the sound of the foods mentioned in this novel, I used the cookbooks *Essential Emeril*, *Nigella Kitchen*, Nancy Fuller's *Farmhouse Rules*, and Geoffrey Zakarian's *My Perfect Pantry* for inspiration.

ABOUT THE AUTHOR

Judi Lynn received a master's degree from Indiana University in elementary education after attending the IPFW campus. She taught for six years before having her two daughters. She loves gardening, cooking, and trying new recipes. Readers can visit her website at www.judithpostswritingmusings.com and her blog writingmusings.com.

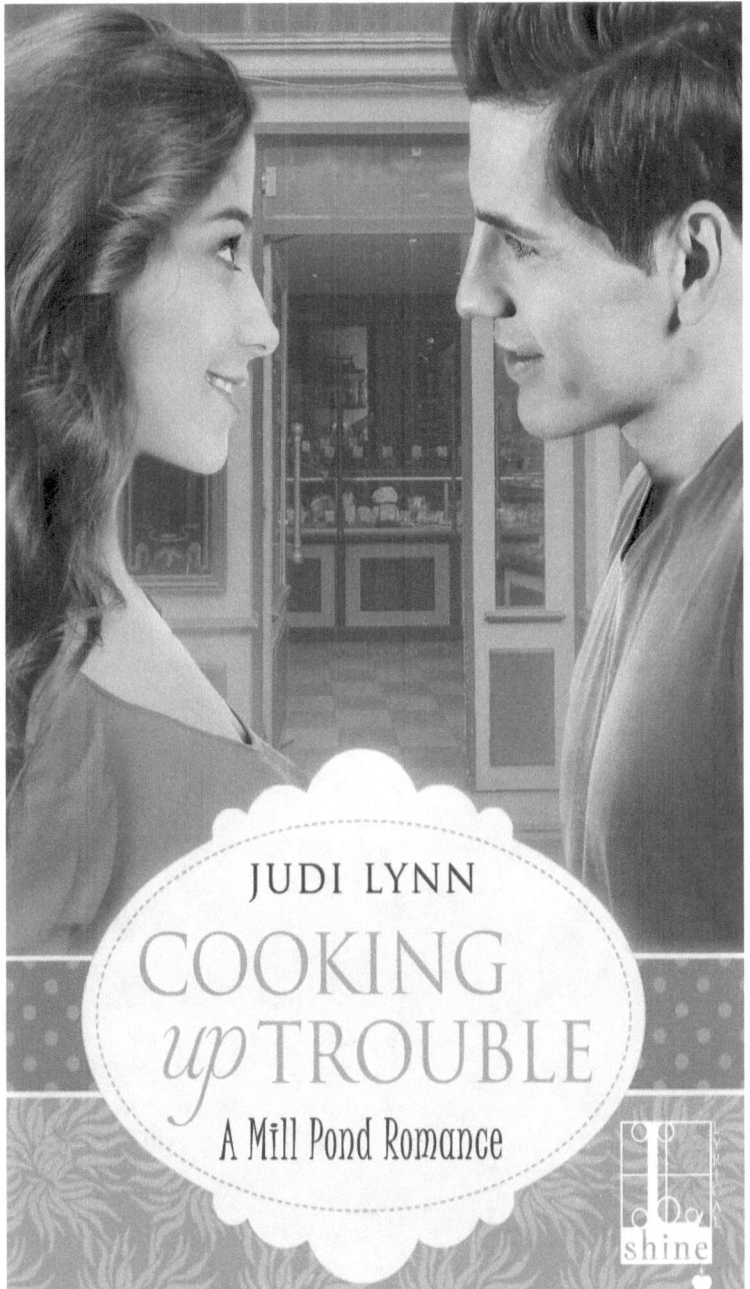

JUDI LYNN

COOKING
up TROUBLE

A Mill Pond Romance

shine

JUDI LYNN

OPPOSITES DISTRACT

A Mill Pond Romance

shine

JUDI LYNN

LOVE ON TAP

A Mill Pond Romance